Paper and Ink

Amanda J. Smith

Published by Amanda J. Smith

© 2021 United States
ISBN: 978-1-7364152-0-7

Paperback edition / January 2021

For Evie and Brian

Our town of Dove Park was small, yet large enough to create a feeling of togetherness, regardless of age. Take Amelia's mother, Shannon. She runs the Monthly Orchid Society at the age of 84, and has done so for decades. She never sits for more than a minute and expertly absorbs herself in the goings-on of every citizen worth knowing. She is the epitome of Dove Park sorority, not a hair out of place, a flower stem untrimmed. She demands only the finest. Amelia seems so unlike her mother in attitude it is hard to witness them together in any space, but her mannerisms speak to her upbringing. Amelia seems to drip kindness, but is careful, too. She takes on her mother's perfectionist mindset, yet deploys it in a natural, kind way that makes one wonder if she is human.

I said, "Stop eyeballing my chocolate, Lu."

"Ha, as if I didn't bring my own." She pulled out a Rolo from her purse and Amelia made a face. Lulu said, "What?"

"That's so unladylike."

Georgia returned from the bathroom, swiftly tying her hair in a high bun. She was always fashionable, regardless of her chosen attire, which currently was a razorback tank and black leggings. At 32, she was the mother of four kids and had even less time for bullshit gossip than Lulu.

Lulu asked, "What minivan did you drive off the lot today?"

"You're only jealous mine has a T.V in the back." Georgia said, "The most ideal distraction to ever be invented for children in the automobile. I can almost hear myself think. Hand me a glass, will ya?"

Parker, the only man in our book club of six, said, "You and those minivans. If my wife owned a dealership, I'd be bringing home a Ferrari."

Hannah, who was sitting to my right, said, "Yes, well suited for children the Ferrari."

"Oh my gosh, you guys are thieves. Testing vans like they're a mall food sampler." He said, pointing.

Georgia replied, "Whatever happened to that tux you bought for your friend's wedding from last weekend?"

"That's different, I returned it because I lost weight."

"Uh-huh, sure. Takes one to know one." Georgia pointed back. "Plus, we're performing quality control." She smiled at him. "And now the hubby is an expert minivan seller, he knows every detail, I might add."

Amelia laughed, "Alright, alright. Now that we're all settled, let's toast." We reached for the remaining glasses and raised them over the scones, the sugar-crusted raspberries hanging tight to the glasses that glistened under Amelia's spotless chandelier. "To Wednesday Night Book Club!"

The clink of glasses colliding lowered my heart rate, the ritual of Wednesday night settling into my bones like a slow dip into a hot sauna. These nights seemed untainted, timeless. After four years, it was like stepping into a time capsule, arriving regardless of current events, weather, a lost job, or recent career change. We found a way to unite, bringing together our shared passion by the way of reading.

Unlike other book clubs, we decided to meet weekly. The six of us loved classics and how relevant and useful to the current times they seemed to be. Our shared fondness for a first edition or rare book find at a garage sale or thrift outlet linked us together. Georgia said she loved holding history in her hands, an artifact that abided by centuries of tacit rules in the world of publishing and the art of storytelling. Usually, Georgia skimmed the last pages at stoplights on the drive over and Parker brought handwritten notes folded neatly in his back pocket. He said old habits die hard, as he used to teach philosophy at the University. He was currently an editor at the local paper, the Dove Daily. He took Wednesday nights more seriously than Lulu and me, but in a charming manner. Amelia always had the book read before any of us could turn the cover, spectacularly memorizing quotes and page numbers. Hannah was quiet and rarely spoke unless called upon or feeling particularly passionate about the topic. She enjoyed the art of observance, yet it was her opinions that usually held the most weight, her thoughts seemingly planned out and careful. Even her speech was quieter, slower, almost raspy. You wouldn't expect the low tone of voice coming from such a petite woman, the long dirty blonde hair and blue-eyed combo a trick to the eye. Hannah and I were an interesting pair when seated next to one another. Our hair matched almost exactly, yet mine fell straight and eyes a dark brown. We were often asked our relation, yet I stood much taller at 5'7".

Lulu said, "There's something about a classic that doesn't follow the rules of the times. Gets my blood racing."

"I love Alice in Wonderland. Tell me you didn't love it," I said.

"I put up with your picks, but I'll admit, this was better than usual. Dare I say *charming*."

"Because the book on Waco was such an upper."

Amelia continued, "What did you guys think? It's hard to find something well-suited for adults and children alike. I actually took this from the boys."

Hannah said, "The more you consider context, you wonder how suited for children it is."

I said, "Do you believe Carroll intended to place hidden symbols within the book, or is it just us looking into something too closely? The caterpillar, the keys, the doors…"

Lulu laughed, "If you look anywhere, you'll find similar little things. Maybe he just liked the way a caterpillar looked? Who is to say, maybe he liked legs and nothing more?"

Georgia said, "Legs can be phallic, can they not?" She stretched hers in front with the pout of her recently glossed lips.

Lulu laughed, "*Your* legs maybe."

Parker said, "You know when you read a line, then stop to re-read it a few times, trying to take in the meaning? I did that when Alice asks, 'How long is forever?' and the White Rabbit says, 'Sometimes, just one second.'"

Lulu popped a Rolo into her mouth as she said, "That's like when I'm waiting on Ellie for carpool."

I said, "Ha! Funny. You're not getting coffee tomorrow."

Hannah said, "It's true, though. One second can feel like forever, but an entire day can feel like a second. Doesn't it seem the opposite of what one wants? I also loved the quote, 'I'm afraid I can't explain myself, sir. Because I am not myself, you see?'"

Georgia said, "I felt that. I'd be sad if that were only a drug reference, you know? I'd like to think of it as something deeper. More contrived."

"Can you truly not be yourself?" Hannah asked, "The words are coming out of your mouth, the mannerisms out of your body. If it's not you, then who exactly is it?"

We continued our discussion as Lulu reached to pick the raspberry off mine and Hannah's wine glasses, sucking up the sugar with one hand and holding her book in the other, legs crossed as her immaculately painted toenails twitched in rhythm to the movement of her foot.

I looked around the room. Everyone had their small quirks on display. I smiled appreciating each one of them. Parker held the pen in his mouth, his habit of chewing the tops his tell of true concentration. Amelia had the most impeccable posture so that whenever I glanced her direction was reminded to right myself, my body falling forward inches more than it should. Hannah was the lounger. She currently had her leg flopped over the side of the chair, foot twitching to the rhythm set by Lulu. I often wondered if they noticed this small connection, but never mentioned it for fear that they would stop, suddenly mindful of their action. Finally, Georgia was the multi-tasker and would often be licking stamps on a handful of envelopes needing to be mailed the next day or crocheting an item for her mother who lived in a group home.

Georgia asked, "Is everyone going to the Orchid Society Gala next month? I just sent in my RSVP."

"Amelia, I cannot wait to see what your mom has cooked up," I said. "Literally and figuratively."

"It's going to be something."

As I lifted the wine to my lips, enjoying these small intricacies, a shattering of glass erupted from the hall which was soon accompanied by a loud thump. We were seated in Amelia's den adjacent to the main living area and had eyes on the front door. The sound hadn't approached from there, but from within the home.

Hannah swung her leg back to a normal sitting position, "What was that? Amelia, did you leave something on in the kitchen?"

Amelia stood, brushing at her skirt, nervous. "Everyone stay here."

Parker stood, "I'll come with you." He eyed me cautiously. Amelia's husband was out of town on business, and her two children were with their aunt in Napa Valley for the beginning of summer break. No one else should have been in the house.

—Marge, her housekeeper, had left hours before. I looked at my watch, it was only 6:45 p.m.

Hannah whispered, "Is everything alright here?" She motioned to the house in general. I began to respond, but a shrill screech echoing from the hall had us jumping to our feet and moving towards the sound.

Lulu, Hannah, and Georgia followed my lead as we stopped at the end of the hall and listened carefully outside of the study. I silently mouthed, 'Really?' to Georgia as she continued to hold her wine glass as if an extension of her person. She shrugged, her messy bun letting a strand fall in response as she downed the rest of the glass.

Upon closer inspection, Amelia and Parker could be heard inside of her study, but their speech was indecipherable.

I said, "Is everyone OK?"

Amelia, voice shaken, responded, "Yeah, come in. Have a look."

We peered around the corner and were shocked to see a gaping hole in the large stained-glass window that sat above the sizable oak writing desk. Glass shards were scattered about the room creating a haphazard mosaic, but Parker and Amelia weren't looking at the hole, or the glass remnants. In her hand, she held a large, thick, glass bottle. When she turned it towards the light, a piece of tan paper could be seen floating in its core, large black ink splattered across the page in a shaky, handwritten font.

She looked up, tears in her eyes. "What does this mean?"

Parker stood beside her. "I think we should call the police. Do you know why anyone would do this?"

She shook her head no, appearing half in a daze, half lost in memories no doubt trying to discern why someone would throw a bottle through her study window.

No one asked what it contained as it seemed intimate, a personal visage of her private life. We had only been in her study once, and that was to unveil the stained-glass window her husband Sunny had purchased directly from Rome for their fifth anniversary. That was six years ago.

Lulu entered the study and embraced Amelia against her side. Under her black stilettos, the glass sounded like the first bite into a spoonful of Fruit Loops as she expertly made her way across the room. The three of us remaining by the door seemed suddenly the voyeurs, but that soon passed as Parker motioned us inside, handing me the bottle.

The glass was cold, heavy. Whoever chose this vessel wanted to impart damage. I turned it over. It read:

"People who don't think shouldn't talk. This is a warning. Stop and we won't resort to further action."

Amelia said, "A warning for what? Stop what?"

I said, "You better call Sunny." She nodded. "Go to the living room, call who you need to, and we'll clean in here, OK? Parker, help Amelia."

Lulu and Parker accompanied her out, his arm looped through hers like an usher at a wedding. This couldn't be less the celebratory moment.

Georgia said, "This is quite the scene." Small rain droplets were throwing themselves through the jagged window remains, the smell of a recent downpour enveloping the space.

I shivered. "Who knew a letter could leave such a mark. Do you think whoever threw this is gone?"

"Let's be quick, I'd rather not find out." Georgia stepped out of the room for a moment, re-entering with extra mops and brooms.

Hannah said, "Seems a little cliché."

"What's that?" I said.

"This a warning? It could be kids messing around."

Georgia took the bottle in her hands, motioning to Hannah. "Think there are fingerprints?"

"This isn't CSI."

"Well if it is, our prints are all over it." After turning the bottle over, Georgia looked surprised, "Wait, isn't that a quote from Alice in Wonderland?"

"Don't pretend you read it now," Hannah said, "our book club is done for the night."

"Ha, ha. No, I'm serious…People who don't think shouldn't talk…I wouldn't have noticed if not for reading it a few minutes before I rang the bell." She glanced at Hannah, "don't look at me like that, you're lucky I finished with four kids."

I said, "I think she's right…"

Hannah took her phone out of her jeans, and typed. "Huh, there it is."

"Who even knows we've been reading it?" I said.

"Anyone's husband or kid, if they were paying attention." Hannah said, "people could have seen us reading it at work, on break, who knows. We only had it a week, though."

Georgia said, "That's insane."

"Is this a threat to all of us?" Hannah peered at the glass with a new look of mixed horror, holding it away from her body as if it were radiating poison.

I said, "We should clean this up and get back to the others. We'll figure this out."

It took a while to clean the shards. Small pieces had lodged themselves into corners and on top of books, a meticulous treasure hunt. When we finally made it back to the kitchen,

Amelia was reciting her story back to the police over the phone.

Lulu whispered, "Sunny didn't answer, we've tried a couple of times with different numbers."

I said, "We cleaned it up best we could, but there's a big draft coming in. Maybe we could help cover the hole. She should probably lock the study door though, just in case."

After some time, everyone excused themselves except me and Parker.

Over the years, Amelia, Lulu, and I had been the closest of the six. We had started the club, and Parker was the first to join. I thought back to that night, the three of us on my deck as we so often did that summer, with fresh lemonade, and Amelia's famous sugar cookies topped with royal icing and sprinkles. Oddly, Amelia and I had both recently read The Metamorphosis and chatted about it throughout the night. We felt like we were going through a personal metamorphosis, soon turning thirty, children and jobs changing shape. Nothing as desolate and dark as the novel that sparked our club, but we enjoyed discussing its many intricacies. When Amelia left for the night, I remember her quoting the book and saying, 'Human beings have to have their sleep', then shutting her car door and thinking it was so clever we had to do it again.

Parker and Amelia had met when she worked at the paper over ten years ago, back when she was a journalist. Those days seemed lifetimes away now that Amelia was staying home with the children full time. We had managed to keep the book club running, regardless, with the same group of six. We were impressed at our longevity given all that life has thrown at us.

Amelia finally hung up the phone. "They're on their way, they want to see the bottle and ask some questions."

I said, "Do you feel safe here tonight? Why don't you come home with me after they leave?"

"It could be a while."

"Come on, you can't stay here alone. You'd go mad."

"Alright." She smiled, even though it was forced she seemed to relax. "Let me go pack some things before the police get here."

I turned to Parker. "Any ideas on what happened?" As soon as Amelia went upstairs my dam broke. "What the hell is going on?"

"I know. My hands are still shaking. It was like watching a character walk through a crime scene, but it was me." He swept back his brown hair. He usually kept it short, but it had started to grow long in recent months. He was shorter but in good shape. Lulu always gave him shit for being taller, then he'd battle her to an arm wrestle ending that argument.

"It *was* a crime scene. And you know what else? The note, part of it was from Alice in Wonderland."

His eyes widened. "You're kidding me."

"Hannah looked it up, swear. People who don't think shouldn't talk."

"What kind of joke is that?"

"Seemed pretty serious to me. Did Amelia say anything?"

"We thought it was directed towards her husband, not like she goes around pissing anyone off. Ever. But now with the quote…could that be total chance?"

"That would be some coincidence. One in a million."

"Do you think they threw the bottle during our book club on purpose?"

"I hadn't thought of that. But it's possible, given the quote."

He said, "I still think it's her husband. He works with international investments, he's probably pissing people off left and right. And it's Sunny." His head tilted to the side, knowing full well what that implied.

"I know he's not the most pleasant man all of the time. But why quote our book if directed at him? That doesn't make sense. I don't think he's ever asked what book we are reading let alone cared to wonder."

"This will freak Amelia out."

"It should freak her out, that's freaky."

Amelia returned and I took her aside. "I think there's something more to the note in the bottle."

"What do you mean?"

"The first part, it's a quote from Alice in Wonderland."

"What?"

"Straight from it, we looked it up. Word for word."

"Are you positive? I assumed it was directed towards Sunny. It certainly wouldn't be the children now that you've told me about the quote, which is a relief. What on earth is going on, then?"

"I'm not sure what it means. But the timing seems well planned, don't you think?" Amelia wouldn't be one to break the law or upset someone enough to result in such vandalism. "Does anything ring a bell? Any person you've seen lately that could be targeting you or Sunny?"

She took another swig of her wine, "No, nothing. Honest."

We continued to wait for the police.

Chapter 2
Black and White

That night, Amelia and I sat on the back deck of my house, the cool night air drifting from the nearby park and small lake visible against the horizon.

"I don't have to go into work tomorrow, you know," I said.

"Don't be silly."

"Still nothing from Sunny? Not even a text?"

She looked down at her phone again, her right hand gripping it hard. The backlight produced no notifications. "He wasn't expecting any calls from me, I'm sure it's just off, or it died. Maybe he forgot his charger. He does that all the time."

I bit my tongue considering the circumstance. It was known that they had been fighting lately. Amelia had never mentioned it, but Parker and I always thought he had a wandering eye, but that would be unfair to broach to her, especially tonight. "I'm sure he'll call soon."

Neither of us thought we could sleep, our adrenaline amped far past what would be required for a normal eight hours of rest. It was now past midnight, and the crickets chirped to the cool beat of the temperature.

Amelia said, "Where's Bill?"

"He's working on the cabin in Red River to sell, he's hoping to have it fixed up for the winter rush."

"You never told me you're selling it, I'll miss that cabin."

"I know, it's been a great place. We just stopped going enough, you know?" I had just turned 29, and we realized we had not visited the cabin since my 27th birthday. Bill was in Real Estate, so thought we'd throw the dice. It was a good year to sell.

Amelia said, "So much has changed in four years."

"Do you ever think back to our first Wednesday night?"

"Ha, no one wanted to argue."

"Except Lu, she always loves a good debate."

As I raised my wine glass, we stopped to take in the moment. It was instants like these, the recovery after a rush of adrenaline or endorphins to the system that the mind seemed most aware, alert. Everything seemed raw and real.

After some time, I asked, "Are you happy, Amelia?"

She paused. "The perfectionist in me wants me to lie through my teeth and say the world is quite alright. A lesson learned from my mother. As long as you appear happy…"

"But?"

"I'm not sure. Things are not often so black and white, are they? Can a person be all happy or all sad?"

"No, I don't think so."

"I think that's what gets me. Who am I to complain? My family immigrated from Ireland when I was five, poor. Now I have an estate, two beautiful children, and food to eat. A beautiful kitchen to bake in. A husband who makes enough to support me staying home and being with the kids. And my parents, they've created a legacy with their food."

"People can be sad in any type of situation. If you are, it's not fair to ignore it. You're worth more than that."

"And if I'm unhappy, then what?"

"Then I think you should alter something, even if it's small. See how it feels. It could empower you for more change."

"I don't think that's possible."

"Anything is possible. Look at your parents, they were able to build a restaurant empire with relatively nothing."

"But see, I don't have any money of my own. I had a savings account and paid my bills long ago, but since then Sunny has been the sole provider. I lean on him for everything financially. It's fine, but if we were ever apart..."

"Is that something you've considered?" I was shocked.

"Not really, no. Divorce would never be an option. Can you imagine my mother? The staunch Irish Catholic with a divorced daughter. She'd keel over."

"What about alimony?"

"He had me sign a prenup when we married. Initially, I never wanted to, it seemed to mark our destiny poorly, but I figured, we're staying together, it doesn't matter. Finances aren't why I'm in this, so sure, I'd sign my name on the dotted line."

"I'm sorry, Mel. I didn't know things were that bad."

"That's what's strange, I can't put my finger on it. During the last year, there has been a shift. He is rarely home, but it's not like he is disrespectful to me, you know? It's not that bad. I feel silly even bringing it up. We have a good marriage in some respects, you know? I should let it lie."

"A lack of interest is a kind of disrespect. Have you guys had a conversation about it? Maybe going to a counselor would help."

"I've mentioned wanting him home more often, but how can I make that suggestion when he's the sole provider? There's not much to argue there."

"You know you have five close friends that would take you in or lend you money in a heartbeat, right? If anything did happen?"

"I'd never ask that of you, you're sweet to say so, though. And I'd never even think of leaving with Aiden and Ryan. They're only 7 and 10, you know what that would do to them? They're at such a developmentally sensitive time for such drastic change."

"I'm sorry Amelia. I don't want to come across as someone who thinks that would be an easy decision to make, especially with the boys."

"And that is why I don't let myself think it through, not now. And I still love him, you know? It's not real, divorce."

She seemed to be shutting down, the weight of the conversation flooding her with shame. It would be a difficult realization to hear your thoughts on separation out loud.

I said, "Even though your parents made something from nothing, their circumstances were very different than yours."

"They always knew it though, you know?"

"Knew that they wanted to come to America?"

"Had goals. Ever since I was little, they wanted to start a restaurant. Everything they did was to make that accomplishment and make sure we were safe. I don't know if I have a goal, other than raising my kids. Living."

"The fact that your husband doesn't meet that equation tells me something, Amelia. And raising your kids is a wonderful goal if that feels right to you."

We sat on the deck for another hour, no more to say, our lips tired from talking, our brain trailing from the task of added problem-solving. It was going to be a long night.

~∞~

The morning was bright, not a cloud to cover the harsh Southwestern sun. I awoke to a headache, the feeling of too much wine and not enough sleep. Unlike Lulu who has one son, Amelia who has the two boys, and Georgia with her four,

Bill and I have not had children, though we discussed it. Now at 29, the subtle hangover from little alcohol was starting to lose its enjoyment, the reality of aging ever-present. Hannah continued happily single at 30, never wanting kids and joyfully uninterested in marriage. Parker was the oldest at 35. He always wanted a family, but his wife of 9 years left him last year. We suspect that he told Amelia the details, but no one wanted to pry. We were a solid group of six, even with our stark differences we had a known respect for privacy.

I turned off my alarm and walked to the kitchen. I was a researcher at the Museum of Natural Science, and the last few months were stressful as our grant would expire if we couldn't plead our case for an additional three years of funding. I started the coffee as Amelia ambled in.

"How did you sleep?"

"Oh, you know." She shrugged.

"I'm sorry. Did you hear from Sunny?"

"He finally texted at 3:00 a.m. and said that he didn't want to wake me, and he'd be home later today to see about the window. I guess he is cutting his trip early. He was due back Sunday. He didn't seem happy about it."

"Well, that's good, you won't have to face the house alone, waiting." I poured my coffee and slid her a mug.

Her phone rang and she jumped to answer, face falling. She ignored it. "It's just my mom."

"Does she know what happened?"

"Goodness no. You know she would send in the FBI or a SWAT team of men." It vibrated again. "It's honestly the last thing I need…" She looked down at her phone and sighed.

"Sunny?"

"A text from my mom, she knows about the window. Parker told her."

"I didn't know they spoke."

"He's been helping her with the Orchid Society Gala. I guess they have these large pieces they needed help lifting. She is preparing early, you know her."

"An Irish woman planning a Greek festivity, I'm glad I already put in my RSVP. Is she mad you didn't tell her?"

"She says she's coming over to look at the damage herself and asked if everyone was at Book Club when it happened. What is she, Nancy Drew?"

"She's a lot of things," I said as I headed to the fridge.

"Tell me you still don't drink a Coke after your morning coffee for breakfast."

"Keeps me fresh," I said as I popped the lid.

"Looks like Lu is pulling up."

Through our window, Lulu's red Miata hummed silently in the drive as I waved her inside. Lulu was the head archivist in the same department at the museum, so we often carpooled.

Lulu burst through the door with bagels and coffees. "How are my two loveliest ladies?" She set down the food. "I see you've already had your coke, so no more coffee for you, El. Beautiful, more for me."

Amelia said, "Seeing you on two cups of coffee this early in the morning scares me."

"Ha, you should be scared. I'm going to catalog and preserve at a speed seen by no other. Which honestly, needs to happen."

Amelia said, "What are you guys working on these days? I know your grant is almost up, right?"

"Well, you know how our research is based on the excavation site I told you about in New Mexico?"

"I remember."

"It's possible they had a breakthrough at the dig site. The archeologists uncovered something a few days ago but it needs to be verified. We're hoping it comes in soon for our grant proposal, but you never know with these things. It's classified enough that they wouldn't tell me what it is, which is odd."

"How exciting!"

"Hey, what are you up to today Mel?" Lulu asked.

"Sunny is coming back at some point to see about the window."

"Screw that, come to work with us. I want to show you something."

"I better not, I don't want to miss him when he comes home."

I said, "Maybe it would be better if you weren't home. Plus, you can't wait around for him like an anxious puppy. Come on. You've got life left to live." I handed her a soda.

Amelia smiled, popping the lid. "Only if I get the poppyseed bagel."

After working at the museum for five years, I still loved the initial feeling of walking in. The large domed ceiling, the smell of discovery. Everyone appeared happy, working on something they loved. We took Amelia the long way through the main entrance and past the large, hanging stegosaurus. We entered before opening hours, and it felt fresh, colossal. Lulu and I lead Amelia to the back of the large 3 building campus, our offices next door to one another. Lulu and I finally decided to have lunch, all those years ago, after running into each other every day for weeks. The memory brought a smile to my face. We rarely missed a lunch date since.

I said, "I have to check in with the team and see when the new find will be dropped. Meet you guys for lunch?"

Lulu pulled out her badge to enter her office, "You know it, sis."

As I dropped my belongings on my desk, I noticed a note taped to my computer monitor. It read,

Call me ASAP. Paul.

Paul was one of my co-workers, a researcher specializing in genetics. He worked in another building, and we often collaborated when interacting with the public. I sighed as I waved to Gaby, my assistant. I dialed his number.

"This is Paul."

"It's Ellie, I saw your note. What's up?"

"I have somewhat of a personal question, a face-to-face kind of situation. Are you free for lunch?"

"I'm not today. Sorry. Can you meet tomorrow?"

"That'll have to do." He hung up. That was strange. He was the introvert type, not one to seek social engagement. I don't think I've ever seen him eating lunch at the museum or nearby restaurants. He must have a burning question.

At lunch, the three of us opted for the small café, Floyd's, on the corner of 1st and Main near the museum. The smell of hot coffee and fresh pastries hit our senses as we found a small table in the corner, sun shining through the large windows, pink flowers blooming in hanging pots on the patio. A man and woman duo were playing acoustic guitar and piano on a small wooden stage, the music radiating a warm, friendly feeling. A coffee grinder vibrated in the background, adding to the sound.

I said, "So how did you like accompanying Lulu this morning?"

"Honestly, it was a breath of fresh air. Makes me miss working, if not for the kids. For once I didn't think about the bottle, the note, or Sunny."

Lulu said, "I showed her the prototype belonging to Alexander Graham Bell."

"One of my favorites. Isn't it quite the find? Are you done appraising it?"

"I should be done today, but the museum might be getting in some new documents that are considered high importance, so they might take precedence."

Amelia said, "You guys have such exciting jobs."

"Catch me on a paperwork day and you'd think quite the opposite." Lulu chugged her coffee and asked for a refill.

I asked, "How's Gabe?"

Lulu smiled, "He's somehow managed to get himself into a gifted program at school. Can you believe he turns 10 next month?"

"Ryan is so excited about Gabe's birthday party. Before they went to California, he was shooting Sunny with his new nerf gun every chance he got. It was quite a pleasant treat." Amelia laughed.

As we were eating lunch, I noticed my coworker Paul drinking tea at an adjacent table. He seemed out of place, uncomfortable.

"Can you guys give me a second?" I walked over. "Hey Paul, sorry I missed you today."

He said, "Don't take this the wrong way because I'm sure this seems odd. But I couldn't wait until tomorrow."

"To ask me your question?"

"I'll just be a moment if you don't mind. I saw you walking here, from my office. Thought I could steal a second."

I motioned to the ladies that I'd be a minute. "Ok, I'm all ears."

"Do you know a man by the name of Parker Fowler?"

"Parker?" My eyes widened. "Sure, he's a close friend. What's going on?"

"Small world. I've known him for some time, I don't think he's made the connection that we work at the same place. He knows I work genetics for the State, but I don't know if I've said specifically where." Paul was tall, thin. He wore round glasses and sneakers and always came to work with dark jeans and a button-up shirt, usually of the blue variety. He was kind yet reserved and lived and breathed science to an impressive degree. Our peers knew to approach him with any question regarding microbiology or genetics and he'd always supply an answer.

"That is quite the small world."

"I feel uncomfortable even saying this."

"Paul, what is it?"

"I'm trying to word this appropriately. But our mutual friend has started something I'm not sure he can maintain."

"I'm sorry, but you're going to have to be more specific. And how did you find that we knew each other?"

He sighed. "That is beside the point, but I saw you walking in with Amelia. He has a picture of them in his living room- and has mentioned a book club in prior conversations. A convenient thing that I saw you go in through the main lobby together."

"Alright. What does this have to do with me?"

"I wish it didn't, trust me. This is much too uncomfortable." He took a deep breath, stirred his tea, then squeezed out the residual liquid from the bag with his fingers, letting the dripping sound fill the void in conversation. I gave him time to think, granting him a warranted stillness.

"I won't judge you if that's your concern. Parker is a good man, I trust his acquaintances."

"He is a good man, far better than me. I'm sorry this is taking me longer than I thought." He shifted. "I'll start here. I used to be a private eye, before I earned my second doctorate, and before I worked for the museum."

"I never knew."

"Yes, well." He deposited the bag carefully in his napkin, placing it on the side of his plate. "I graduated with honors, you see."

"I'm sure your parents were proud."

"Hardly the point. What I'm getting at is that I've learned some tricks."

"And Parker knew this."

"He started asking some questions. I was soft to his cause if you will. So, I helped him. But now it seems he's in over his head."

"Why are you telling me this? It seems a private matter between you and him."

"It certainly is, but I care for him as a person. I don't have many that I would call close. My mother would say I don't care for a soul, but here we are." He shrugged.

"What can I do to help?"

"He's acquired information on someone, a person you both know."

"Illegally?"

"In a manner of speaking."

"On whom?"

"That I'll keep vague."

"Alright, why is he in over his head? I'm gonna need more information if I'm to piece this together."

"I see you are also friends with Amelia?"

"For years, yes."

"Again, I'm keeping this short. His original goal was to help her leave her husband. This information was going to help him achieve that goal."

"What?"

"I'm not in the position to discuss his motives or feelings. But rather the arena of his actions. Objectivity."

"Why would he do that? She's not even sure she wants to leave…why would he assume something like that?"

"Again, not my field of expertise. I don't know Amelia, all I know is what he's discovered. He may be uncovering more than he can handle, from a person he knows little about. I know enough that I'm concerned enough coming to you, and I'm not sure he's going to stop."

"You can't be serious. This so unlike the Parker I know."

"I wish it were nothing but a fable."

"And you're sure of this? Who he's investigating?"

He sighed, "Yes, I helped him enough that I'm certain. I hate breaking his confidences, you know, coming here like this. I'm quite beside myself." His facial features expressed nothing but apathy, but I took his word for it. "I am hoping you can talk with him, get him to stop."

I noticed that Amelia and Lulu were starting to pack up. "Hold that thought, I'll be right back." I rose and went back to my table. "I have somewhat of a work emergency. Are you alright sticking with Lulu?"

Amelia said, "Of course! I hope everything is alright?"

"It's fine, no worries. Just time-sensitive." I noticed that Lulu was looking between Paul and myself. She knew that we didn't have many work-related items in common. She would be asking about this later. "See you guys, I'll catch up before 5." As Lulu and Amelia left the coffee shop, I turned back towards Paul, and he was gone.

Chapter 3
The Wretched

The weather proceeded like the weekend itself, lazy, lingering. A hazy fog began dripping off the tree branches and hanging tight to the windowpanes. I wasn't sure about my newfound knowledge and I was dodging questions from Lulu. I tried to concoct a story that was surely half-assed, something about a joint presentation to the Museum board. She didn't buy it, but let it slide.

I hadn't mustered the courage to speak to Parker. Part of me wondered if my encounter with Paul happened, it was so bizarre that I continuously replayed his explanation, the way he spoke. Why was Parker worried about getting Amelia out of her relationship? They had issues, but nothing drastic. I hoped. And who could he be investigating that was so dangerous? I thought about going to Paul's office to finish our conversation, but that would be unfair. He told me more than his guilt allowed, regardless of the disturbing situation. What else was left to say?

As I made my way up to Amelia and Sunny's the following Wednesday, the usual pristine scene of carved shrubbery and clean brick was tainted by a large wood plank covering the hole where the stained glass once lived. It transformed the house into an ominous state, the trees suddenly protruding an eerie glow against the home that seemed too quiet with her kids away. Lulu parked and met me at the bottom of the walk.

She said, "Is Amelia sure she wants to do this again? I know it's Wednesday but..." her voice trailed as she stared at the poor attempt at a band-aid covering the window.

"I don't think she wanted to give the vandal the upper hand. Plus, nothing else happened, maybe it's a one-off kind of thing. Maybe it's over."

"Well, I brought an extra bottle of wine, just in case." Lulu said.

"Now you're talking."

We stopped walking. "Do you think she's ok?"

"Amelia? I think she's figuring things out, you know?"

"Aren't we all."

Georgia ran to meet us at the front door, hair tie in her mouth and a bottle of vodka in each hand. She looked like she had just gone for a run, yet still looked pristine, ready for the runway. She hated compliments about her appearance. When she was younger, her mother placed her in beauty pageants until she was old enough to protest by piercing any flap of skin available and blasting black sabbath through her bedroom speakers. She managed to consistently make Wednesday nights, with four kids and working part-time as an audiologist at the local hospital a few miles down the road. It helped that she lived close to Amelia, only two blocks away.

I said, "How many people are going to be here? Two bottles!"

"It's the only way I know how to cure, well, anything." She shrugged as Amelia opened the door. Georgia hugged her, enveloping her in vodka, voice impeded by the rubber band in her mouth. Lulu ran up in her Louis Vuitton's and snapped the hairband as Georgia howled, trying to kick her with her sneaker and missing by a mile. Lulu taunted her by shaking her hips as they both threw their shoes off at the door.

Amelia looked at me, "It's almost like my children haven't left at all."

"If your children wore $400 stilettos, swore like it was their favorite language and drank like a fish, maybe."

Georgia and Lulu made themselves at home and headed for the kitchen, reaching for our Wednesday night glasses from the top cabinet. In all her glory, Amelia had ordered personalized crystal glasses with our names etched across them, our favorite books listed underneath. It was these consistently perfect details that made the hole in the study window so much starker.

I heard Lulu yell, "Where's Hannah Banana?"

I yelled back, "Gonna be five late, she stopped to get ice cream."

"If it's not mint chocolate so help me."

Amelia led me aside. "They haven't gotten anywhere with the window. The police made it sound like there was nothing more to be done, no one has reported any information, and nothing was witnessed. It's frustrating, you know?"

"Things like this take time, I'm sure. Are you doing ok?"

"Still shaken up, of course. Trying to figure out what to do with the window, not like we can replace it. But that's more of a distraction. Something physical I can attach myself to. The note baffles me. I'm up thinking about it, and when I finally sleep, I wake up with a new theory that makes no sense when morning comes."

"Did Sunny say anything that might be helpful? Any ideas on who did this?"

"He says it was a prank, nothing that he's done, apparently, would warrant such an atrocity. But we both know he couldn't know that for sure, especially with what he does every day. I've heard him on the phone, he deals with huge investments and they don't always go as planned. He's had more arguments than I can count."

"We're here for you, you know?"

"I know." The doorbell rang and she made for the door.

The kitchen looked like a mad scientist had been set loose. I said, "Is this what happens when Amelia relinquishes drinking responsibilities? This is terrifying."

Georgia had two cherry stems sticking out of her mouth and was wiping a wet glass against her leggings. She always seemed to be juggling sixteen things at once. She asked, "How much would you give me if I could tie two stems in a knot in my mouth at once?"

Lulu laughed, "How about we *don't* turn you in for stealing minivans off your husband's lot?"

"We give them back!" She spit the stems in the hidden trash compactor inside the large kitchen island. "Did you see the one I pulled in with today? They call the color, Blizzard Pearl." She wiggled her fingers like a magician.

Lulu said, "I think I just threw up in my mouth."

"You're just jealous. Hand me that lemon squeezer."

I said, "What are you guys making?" The room seemed to percolate happiness that began to seep into my bones. AC/DC was playing in the background and Georgia was moving to the beat, mixing drinks, Lulu pausing to twirl her around the kitchen. Their laughter was infectious.

Hannah burst into the kitchen singing, "Lemon drops!" She handed a bottle of triple sec to Georgia and plopped down three containers of ice cream.

Georgia said, "She's petite, yet handy to have around."

"This looks like a frat party," I said.

Lulu waved her hands, "Please, we are much more put together. I wouldn't touch a solo cup with my lemon drop.

Although, back when I bartended in Dallas, I'd try and get any lemon drop order changed. Too *sticky*."

Hannah said, "Ever the lady."

I asked, "What's with all this anyway?"

"We felt Amelia needed a little lift, you know?"

I smiled. "I'm not complaining."

Amelia entered the room with Parker and her mother. She hugged Shannon as she curtly nodded our direction, exiting the kitchen. I stood back, slowly pouring my drink, taking in Parker's appearance. He seemed unchanged, acting nonchalant next to Amelia. I suddenly felt nauseous, the weight of my discovery barreling down from days of purposefully forgetting its existence. I couldn't mention anything tonight. I'd have to decide soon, though. Do I observe from a distance, or act, like Paul claimed was a necessity? Parker never approached me with this information. Would it be too forward to assume he wanted my help?

We began digging in, taking our concoctions back to the small sitting area that was our Wednesday night home. It was easy to forget what happened the previous Wednesday, the six of us together again, the sun shining in its orange warmth. But when Sunny and Amelia's mother, Shannon, walked past the den, our voices fell.

Trying to ignore the shift in mood, the six of us gathered our drinks together and said, "To Wednesday night!"

Amelia, sitting in front of her bay windows per usual, lifted the book of the week, *Frankenstein*. "What did you guys think?"

Lulu squeezed more lemon in her drink, "I can't believe everyone finished it in time." She eye-balled Georgia.

"Oliver had a sick day last Thursday, what can I say? I got my shit together."

"Hallelujah." Lulu downed her drink.

"This screams a Lulu pick if I've ever read one." Parker adjusted the glasses on his face. "I read it years ago, but it was different the second time around. Can't quite put my finger on it."

Hannah said, "I think it's the more you live, the more that you see smatterings of similarity in our world and theirs, hidden under the folds. Everyone has a monster."

"Some monsters take on different shapes." Lulu puckered her mouth after eating the lemon wedge, rind, and all.

Georgia gave Lulu a disgusted look, "I do think everyone has monsters, but some are more easily caged than others. Some perhaps, invisible. Is that sad?"

I said, "No, I don't think all monsters have to be bad. Do you know what I loved? 'Nothing is so painful to the human mind as a great and sudden change.'"

Lulu said, "It's kind of beautiful."

"Change is hard under most circumstances, even if yearned for," Hannah remarked.

"It's very poignant," I said. "The author has a way of making everything so relatable with only one sentence."

Amelia looked down at her drink. "It always seems the case doesn't it?"

"What's that?"

"The pain of change. It seems we never know if we've fully made it to the place we want to be, always seeking a new type of happiness, always heading towards something, yet there is a fear to do so. Can we ever be happy with the now? Without change?"

Hannah said, "I think we can be both happy with the now and still be working towards something, a different place, or even attitude, perhaps. Humans are always evolving, right?"

"But to be genuinely content?"

"I think so, yes. But you have to work towards it. Not having goals makes one unhappy, I think."

Amelia said, "I think people with sure goals take that drive for granted."

We continued our discussion as the spirits flowed. The sun was setting, lighting the room like amber sap dripping from a tree.

Amelia said, "It suddenly feels so *creepy* in the room after reading this." The room fell silent. There was an eeriness in the knowledge that someone knew when our book club met, who was there, and what we were reading. Then using that to threaten.

Lulu changed the subject. "Who has the kids tonight, Georgia?"

"My mom, God rest her soul. Chase is with Bill in Red River. They're living it up right now."

I said, "*We're* living it up."

"I'll cheers to that."

At the moment our glasses collided, the sound of popping firecrackers erupted from the front of the house. The vodka in Amelia's glass tumbled over its rim as she set it down, trying to right her vision, to stand. It was already 8:30, we looked at one another in wonder as she started towards the door.

Parker stood, "Amelia, don't."

"Don't look outside my window?"

He looked anxious, "It could be them again. Sit down. It might not be safe."

We stood in a circle around the table, unsure of future action as the fireworks seemed to gather towards a high crescendo. Small tendrils of light could be seen popping through the windowpane highlighting our six worried faces. Sunny broke our trance as he glided down the stairs. He stood just over 6 feet and was lean and fit. His eyes were dark, his chin square. His stature seemed to beg performance, like he was ready to act, tell a story that only he knew the secret. He said, "Is that you guys?"

"No, honey, we're just having book club."

"I know you're having your club. What's that noise?"

Parker said, "Sounds like firecrackers, would you know anything about that?"

"Why would I light firecrackers outside my own house while upstairs? Then ask *you* about it?"

The room fell silent as the firecrackers ended their assault. It was notable in recent weeks that Sunny was none too happy about another male presence in Amelia's life, though he never said it directly, or why he had the sudden change in attitude. It was strange timing, given the longevity of their friendship. From the observances of others, Sunny appeared skilled at passive aggression, and Parker was his current target for reasons unknown.

Parker finally replied, "Are you going to check on it? Being *your* house?"

Sunny glared at us then moved to the front door. We were still.

Georgia whispered, "If this is another message in a bottle... on book club night..."

Amelia said, "It couldn't be. I can ignore one coincidence, perhaps, but two?"

Suddenly, Sunny bust back in through the front door, his voice a harsh echo. "Can anyone explain this?"

"Darling, what is it?"

"Come look for yourselves." He slammed the door shut as he exited. The six of us eyed one another and headed for the entrance, suddenly sober.

As we walked to the lawn, past the large stone overhang and cobblestone pebbles under our feet, we saw yet another message. Written on a white sheet and hanging across one of her many garage doors, was a note written in blue:

"All men hate the wretched. Stop now. We're watching."

I looked towards my right to see Amelia, face white as the hanging sheet, waver unsteadily then tumble towards the ground unconscious. She was quickly caught by Parker and Lulu and gently placed on the grass.

"Give her space," Georgia said.

Sunny pushed Lulu and Parker out of the way. "She's my wife, I've got this. If you could please leave for the night, I believe your little *club* is over. I think you've caused enough drama for the night." He looked at Parker and said, *"especially* you."

Amelia stirred and Sunny helped her to her feet, wrapping his arms around her back. We silently followed, entering the home to grab our things and call it a night. Amelia reassured us that she was alright but slightly shaken. Sunny kissed her head and held her close.

As the five of us somberly walked back to our cars, Parker took me aside. I was shocked to be speaking with him after my conversation with Paul, his nature taking on a surreal form.

He said, "You seem quiet this evening."

"It's the vandalism. What if this turns violent?"

He scuffed his hair back, thinking. "Just, keep an eye on Amelia. Ok?"

"Why does it sound like you know more than you're letting on?"

"It's her house. I'm feeling protective, is all."

I nodded an affirmation as we saw Lulu, Hannah, and Georgia hop into her minivan, waving us to join. We'd have to continue this conversation later.

Georgia closed the van door behind us. "What do you think now Lu? If this were a Ferrari…your drunk ass would be hanging out the back."

"I'm ignoring the spacious legroom." She opened a container of ice cream that she pulled out of her purse with one of Amelia's spoons and took a mouthful, wiping the moisture from the container on her pants.

From the driver's seat, Georgia said, "Ok, what the *hell* is going on?"

I said, "I'm afraid to look it up, but I already know the answer. We've all just read the book."

Lulu turned her phone towards us, "All men hate the wretched. Straight from *Frankenstein*."

The van was silent as a siren's squeal began to increase in resonance, approaching its mark. Police cars began to circle close, their lights bouncing off the windows of nearby houses. A red and blue reflection caught like magic in the lenses on Parker's face as he rubbed his eyes, flicking their power away.

"That doesn't answer the question," Georgia was sitting forward, her face in the rearview mirror a subtle shadow, making her seem thin, impressionable.

Lulu said, "I think it's safe to say this isn't about Sunny. I doubt he got his jollies from a trip down the rabbit hole or from Frankenstein's monster."

"Then who does that leave as a target?" I asked. "It seems to be specific in targeting someone here."

Georgia said, "I haven't so much as a speeding ticket in the last five years. I'm an audiologist with four children for crying out loud. When would I have the time to partake in crime? I can hardly pee alone."

Lulu began picking grass off of her pump. "I know I seem like an easy target, what with my dark clothes and impeccable style, but truthfully I haven't a clue. I certainly wouldn't let things get this far if I had."

"I don't think we need to sit here and answer for ourselves." Hannah grabbed the ice cream and took a large bite. "We know each other. We're good people. I trust all of you with my life."

Georgia said, "Have we thought about the fact that this could be Sunny? Not as the target but rather the perpetrator?"

Parker said, "He may be connected. In fact, I'd bet on it."

I said sharply, "Why do you think that?"

"He's not a good guy. Of everyone that was in the home now, who seems the likeliest candidate for disaster? For a threat?"

"Why would he vandalize his own home?" I said. "For what? He holds all the cards. He could kick us out at any time if that was his objective. Why spend time playing games? He doesn't hide his dissension for us as it is."

Hannah said, "He could kick us out, true, but not without pissing Amelia off. And maybe that wasn't his goal. It's hard to imagine how he thinks, maybe he's having fun watching us squirm. Even so, his reaction did seem genuine."

Parker nodded, "I don't think he cares much for her desires."

Georgia asked Parker, "You seem to have specific spite towards Sunny. Care to impart? He is her husband, that has to count for something."

He looked to be holding back a comment that struggled to seep past his lips, but his common sense whisked it away. He

41

turned to Georgia, "You see the way he talks to Amelia, do you feel comfortable with that?"

"That's none of my business. We see a little speck of their relationship. Yes, I think he's an asshole, but he's *her* asshole. I respect that until she tells me otherwise."

I broke the sudden tension. "What does the note mean, then? Sunny or not?"

Lulu said, "I don't think any of us can answer that. I think the solution lies within that house, with Sunny and Amelia."

"It does feel a little like we walked in on a private moment." Georgia said, "Amelia runs book night, I don't want to assume it's pointed at her, but that makes the most logical sense. Nothing else indicates it's anyone else. No one else has been handed a threatening note."

I said, "It's Amelia…she's the most ethical, value-driven person."

"Perhaps," Georgia said, "she doesn't recall something she saw that was important. Sunny is in finance, he deals with people in high places, people with money. Maybe they're trying to quiet her with something she truly knows nothing about."

"I'm exhausted." I placed Amelia's spoon in the ice cream container and passed it to Parker.

Hannah said, "We've done what we can, let them handle it. It's late and the authorities can piece the puzzle together. They have the means."

The van was beginning to feel thick with the smell of melted chocolate and adrenaline, our breaths tainted with alcohol and we were parked directly adjacent to a crime scene. I said, "We should call it a night."

Georgia said, "I can't drive, I'm walking home."

Lulu flicked grass out from under her nail, "Can I crash tonight? Too much. To drink." She made a face and rubbed her eyes, smudging her dark eyeliner in a way that made her look like a Broadway performer.

"Of course, don't be stupid. Anyone else? Got the house to myself tonight."

Hannah opted to stay on Georgia's couch, while Parker and I decided on a Lyft. For the second time tonight, I found myself next to the person I wasn't ready to speak to, in front of a vandalized house with too much vodka and ice cream in my stomach. I sat on the curb with *Frankenstein* sticking out of my purse and a bar of chocolate tucked in the folds. I carefully unwrapped the candy, fiddling with the foil.

"Are you alright?" He asked, following suit, and joining me on the sidewalk.

"Too much to drink is all."

He nodded. "How's Bill?"

I couldn't handle the casual banter. Before I could help myself, I said, "I spoke to Paul."

"Who?"

"Your friend, Paul. The geneticist."

In the darkness of the street, I couldn't see his face, but I could feel the air tense, the chemicals in his body shifting.

"What did he say?"

"What's going on Parker? I've known you for almost a decade. Let's not play this game."

He looked towards Amelia's house, the streetlight catching the dark circles under his eyes. Before he could answer, his Lyft arrived. He sighed. "How about we go to O'Neill's for a nightcap? I don't want to have this conversation here."

I canceled my ride and accompanied him in his.

Chapter 4
All Hat and no Cattle

When we arrived at the bar, it was only 10:00 p.m. but it felt like 2:00 a.m. in the morning. The bar usuals were beginning their nightly escapades, ordering shots and appetizers, shouting at one another, shaking hands. The scene was such a dichotomy to our current state it almost seemed an illusion.

Parker led me to a separate room near the back of the bar and away from the outside area filled with college grads and beer games. He ordered a whiskey on ice. I thought it poor taste to fill my body with a myriad of different liquors, so ordered a vodka tonic, the waitress much happier than our moods portrayed.

We had been silent in the car. I finally broke the tension, "I want to hear it from you."

"It's a long story."

"I didn't want to get into this, but the situation seemed to have found me."

"I didn't know you knew Paul. And I didn't ask for you to be involved in this."

"Well, I certainly didn't know it was *your* Paul. We work together at the Museum."

"Ah."

"Don't make me fight it out of you. I came to the bar, I'm not mad. Just, tell me what happened."

"I'm trying to think of where to start." He opened his mouth as if to explain, then closed it. His jaw appeared the puppet of an unsure master. Finally, he said, "Last year I came into some money after my Aunt Louise passed away."

"I remember her funeral, you had to travel to Texas."

"Right. I wasn't expecting anything at all. I knew we were close, but…that's hardly the point. It wasn't a massive amount, but certainly helpful." He shook his head. "I asked Amelia if Sunny could help me with the financial aspect since he's high in the world of money and I'm an editor for a small-town paper. I couldn't know less about investing money."

"I never knew you and Sunny did business together."

"He specializes on the international side, as you know, but he is well versed in the world of stocks, bonds, investing in general. So, I went to his office a few times. At first, it was fine. He wasn't my favorite person in the world, but I trusted him because Amelia trusted him, you know? He seemed to have a good reputation."

"I get it."

"Remember when my tire blew on the freeway?"

"Sure." The waitress interrupted with our drinks. We politely shooed her away as I wiped the perspiration from the glass, shaking salt on the small napkin before setting it down.

"I was supposed to see Sunny that day, at noon during his lunch break. I called to let him know what happened, that I'd be pretty late, if at all. He understood, said we could reschedule if needed. Well, I ended up getting it fixed a lot quicker than expected so I headed over. I left a message with his secretary, and she said he was in, had a clear schedule, no big deal."

"I'm guessing it was a big deal."

"The timing was like the butterfly effect in action. Little things throughout the day led me to his office at that *exact* moment. From what I was told, his secretary had just walked to the fax machine on the other end of the hall before I arrived because Sunny's fax broke an hour prior. When I didn't see her there, I walked past her desk and knocked. I thought I heard him inside, so I walked in."

He was quiet.

"Parker, what happened?"

"Sunny was on the phone, facing his large window. He didn't notice me there. I started to back away, thinking I'd wait with his secretary, that I was interrupting, but his conversation caught my attention."

"You eavesdropped on Amelia's husband?"

"Once you hear what he was talking about, you may sing a different tune."

"Alright, go ahead."

"I stood by the door. I figured if he saw me, I'd pretend I had just walked in, no harm no foul. But it was intimate. He was speaking with a woman, *that* was certain."

"Are you saying what I think you are saying?" The room had an electric feel, the shared information more than the atmosphere could handle. The feeling that nothing would ever be the same seemed to resonate along the ceiling and walls.

"He was talking about the night before, how it was such pleasure he couldn't wait to see her again. I knew it wasn't Amelia, he would never call from work to say something like that. But I told myself, perhaps it was. Maybe they do this to keep things fresh. Who am I to judge?"

"Did you ever find out who it was?"

"No name, but he said verbatim, 'It's alright, Amelia will never find out. She rarely leaves the house, she trusts me.' I was so shocked, I stood in the doorway, stunned immobile. The scene is burned in my memory. He continued for another minute, then began describing things I felt too young to hear at 35."

"He *cheated* on Amelia? I can't believe you're telling me this. Even with our previous suspicions it never seemed real. I never thought he actually would."

"I should have left after hearing that. That was enough. But my body seemed stuck. Sunny finally swiveled in his chair and glanced up. Our eyes met. I thought he would have been sly or careful in his response as he usually is, but I caught him off guard. He started screaming at me to leave and hung up the phone. I rushed out, of course."

"Parker, this is crazy."

"I couldn't believe it. My mind was racing. I had to get out of there."

"Why didn't you say anything? If not to Amelia, to any of us?"

"I wish I was done with the story, but I'll get to that." He took a large swig of his drink and motioned for another. "I started running out of the office, as fast as possible. Honestly, the look in his eyes terrified me. It was as if he shifted into another creature, dark eyes, sharp tongue. I was completely startled so I headed for the exit. But he caught me at the elevator, disheveled. I had caught him in the most uncomfortable, intimate conversation, and he was not used to being put on display like that. He's the one in control. He didn't even seem to notice that his entire workplace was gawking."

"What did he say?" I was enraptured, drink untouched.

"He said we better talk. No, he said we *need* to talk. He was grinding his teeth as he spit out the words. I swear he wanted to physically grab me, El. He seemed infuriated, as if I didn't catch *him* talking about his nightly escapades, cheating on my best friend. It was completely bizarre. So, I agreed and went back to his office. I wanted to lend him an ear, being Amelia's husband. I imagined he wouldn't say anything that would make a difference, how do you explain something away like that?"

"You don't."

"Exactly. Unless you have leverage."

I was shocked. I replied, "Like blackmail?"

"Something like that."

"What did he use against you, Parker?"

"I was investing a large sum into a company, per Sunny's guidance. They ran a background check as 'due diligence'. I didn't know that it would go so far back. Part of me thinks he may have done extra digging, using this as an excuse, but I don't want to seem so pessimistic."

"You don't have to tell me any more, Parker." This was suddenly more personal than I expected. I felt dirty for prying, telling him to come to the bar like I had a right to his story.

"No, it's good to get out. This has been weighing on my mind for some time." He sat back in his chair. "I'm glad I'm talking with you."

"I won't tell anyone, you know. This is between us."

He nodded, but his eyes seemed far away, his memory dragging him through the tunnels of time. "When I was young, my brother and I weren't exactly star students. I don't think I ever told you, but my dad left our family when I was 15, my brother Mason was 17."

"No, I don't believe you ever mentioned it. That must have been tough."

"We didn't expect it, either. It was shocking, to say the least. Our parents never fought in front of us, there were no signs. It *crushed* us. Anyways, we started to get into trouble."

"Understandable."

"When I finally turned 18, Mason and I got risky. We wanted to be out of the house, on our own. After dad left our only goal was to be away from home, as sad as that sounds for our mother. But she understood, she wanted us to be happy. It reminded us of things, you know, being there. The family photos, the kitchen chair that he always claimed at Sunday dinner. But this isn't a story about my childhood." He waved the memory away.

"I'm sorry."

"It's been years, it's alright. Long story short we were arrested for arson, and I was tried as an adult. I didn't know this at the time, but the others we were with had ties with the local Mafia. I hope you believe me when I say I was not involved in anything more with them, it was a one-off circumstance. I had met them that night. I suspect Mason may have known and wanted more involvement, but I was only following his lead. Getting arrested was a saving grace, though, because it got us on the right track. I got into college with help from the State. And as you know, Mason is a doctor."

"Was he going to use your arrest record against you? You were only 18. That hardly seems relevant twenty years later."

"This is the part I'm anxious to tell you about."

"What do you mean?"

"Amelia and I have been friends for some time, now."

"You've known each other for more than 10 years, right?"

"Just about. I like her, you know?"

"Of course, you have been through a lot of life changes together, like all of us six. It's quite the connection to know people from your teens and twenties forward."

"Absolutely. But it's more than that, for me..." He shifted in his seat as he struggled to make eye contact. His finger toyed with the top of his glass, perspiration sticking to the tip of his finger.

"You're in love with Amelia, aren't you?"

"I think I have been for some time."

"And she's with Sunny."

"And I'm respectful of that. That's why I've never said a word or spoken out of place. It kills me, seeing him speak to her the way he does. Knowing what I now do."

"I'm sorry Parker. So, Sunny said he was going to release the information on your arrest if you told Amelia about the affair?"

"After he led me into the conference room, he made it noticeably clear that I was not to tell a soul about what I had heard. I, of course, told him I would be telling Amelia. How could I not? He started pacing the room, piecing together what he could to demolish me. He's a quick thinker, maniacal. It was all too easy. He said he would tell her I was a criminal working with the mafia, an arsonist. A liar. All he did was have a simple phone conversation, I could have easily taken it the wrong way. Misunderstood."

"You couldn't plead your case to her like you're doing to me right now? I believe you."

"That's what I said to Sunny. His word against mine. He said he'd get others to collaborate the story, people from my past. He has connections like you wouldn't believe. He's a director at his company, he said he could have me fired from the paper and subsequently un-hirable. I think he planned on scaring her with the information, telling her to stop seeing me. Even though I had no ties to the mafia, he wanted to convince her. He could drum up the arrest record, too. Even if we remained friends, she'd never think of me the same. It would always be there, in the back of her mind. And to bring someone with that record near her kids? I would have understood her hesitation."

"Parker, he's insane. That's the work of a mad man."

"I know. So, I went home, started to think. I couldn't be brash."

"When was this?"

"The conversation was about six weeks ago."

"That's a long time to be holding all of this in." I said, "then you went to Paul? That's the part I'm not connecting."

"I decided that I needed to piece together my story, alongside proof of Sunny's actions with the other woman. Carefully. I couldn't go to Amelia without something objective. He's too smart, and the blackmail too real. I'm sure he's been using these weeks to make a strong case against me, too. I figured the only way I could get legitimate information was to hire someone to follow him. After all, it was only a conversation, he could lie it away, say it was a colleague. Then there would be me, fired, a criminal, tainted in her eyes."

"You hired a private detective to follow Sunny?"

"I went to one, yes. But he charged almost $200 an hour."

"That's *a lot* of money."

"I know. I had some money left from my aunt, but I used what wasn't invested for the divorce lawyers. The majority of the money was held up in ways that would be hard to get, and I'd have to go through Sunny. Or he'd find out, one way or another. I kept some cash, sure, but this would require more than I had."

"So, where did you get the money?"

"I didn't. I decided to call Paul instead."

"Who used to be a detective."

"Exactly."

I said, "Paul was concerned with the information you found and thought you should stop. He didn't specify what it was. Now that I know it's Sunny…"

"I went into this expecting to expose an affair, but there was more. Sunny is involved with some bad people."

"What do you mean? Illegal? Who are they?"

"Paul brought up his bank accounts. Took some time, Sunny's not stupid. Everything was more secure than a bank. He's been getting *massive* amounts of money."

"From where?"

"I don't know. It's from an offshore account, according to Paul."

"How do you know this is illegal and not sound investments? It is what he does for a living."

"Finally, he was able to track one transaction, and he recognized the name. A man with strong ties to the drug trade, among other things. He's somewhat infamous among those in Paul's previous profession. The moment he saw the name, he refused to help any longer, said I'd be a fool to continue. He was even afraid his tampering would be discovered and spent the next week beside himself. He's lightened up now that it's been a month, but I told him I wouldn't stop. How could I? It's Amelia."

"And you can't tell her anything for fear of his blackmail."

"Not unless I found undeniable proof. Evidence on who he truly is. The money Paul found and knowledge of a name, it's not enough. An overheard conversation, it's not enough. And both obtained unethically. I can come to terms with being fired in exchange for telling Amelia this information. But she has to see it clearly, have facts. Otherwise, it wouldn't be worth it to either of us."

"This sounds like dangerous territory. They're professionals. You don't know one thing about investigating a person."

"I don't, no. But I used the first three weeks to save money, writing freelance, taking on odd jobs. I even helped Amelia's mother Shannon with items for the upcoming gala."

"What happens now?"

"I'm meeting with the private detective tomorrow. Care to join?"

～

The detective's office was minimalistic, placed in a neighborhood with higher-class strip malls and the occasional dollar store thrown in for good measure. Now we sat, waiting for Shelby to answer our barrage of questions.

He waved us in. "I'm going to tell you straight away," he was not what I was expecting. He donned a cowboy hat and boots, and Texas five-point stars decorated what wall space he decided to adorn. He had his accolades prominently on display- and it looked impressive: former military, two Master's Degrees. "You may be a little disappointed."

We sat down with a mutual glance. Parker said, "Let me guess, clean as a whistle the last few weeks?"

"Near it, although everyone has a tell. Even if you're trying for spick and span, there's gonna be something you give away. And I'll find it, let me tell you." He pointed his finger at us for emphasis.

"What did you learn?"

He pulled out a manilla envelope, opening it to reveal several photographs and notes. "He keeps to a pretty common schedule and isn't home often. Seems to be at the office from

7:00 a.m. or 8:00 a.m. and gets home between 7:00 p.m. and 9:00 p.m. most nights, but not all. A couple of times he's been out of town. If I'm being honest, he's all hat and no cattle. Talks a big game, you know?"

"That's an understatement. Is he working the entire time he's gone from the house?"

"Couldn't tell you what he's up to while in his office at all hours, unfortunately, that place is like a mini Fort Knox. I got my girl in, though, asking finance questions. It was gonna be two birds one stone kinda gig if he started throwin' her the eye, but none too lucky that round." He placed his feet on the desk and threw his hat on an empty chair close to his own. "On Tuesdays, he gets together with two of his guy friends. I'm not sure if there's a pattern since I've only been following him for three weeks, but I'd guess on it. Each Tuesday it was the same three men, but a different location. They went to one of those high-class fake-ass speakeasies the first Tuesday, the second to a bar off-campus called Stan's where they got *stupid* drunk-"

I interrupted, "Stan's? I don't see him going to a college bar like that. Especially to get wasted..."

Shelby said, "You know, I thought the same thing. Read weird to me. It's not their normal digs, that's for sure. They were still in their suits. Stood out like a sore thumb." He threw us a photograph of them walking up to the bar. "Even weirder, he entered through the back."

"Is that VIP or something?"

"Not unless it's a strip club or cigar bar, that I know of. Stan's is one of those feel-good trashy bars that hasn't been mopped in ten years, each beer adding a new layer of stick. You're lucky if your shoes come back with you. It's also a good twenty miles out from his house, but I kind of wondered if he was meeting his friends halfway. That's always an option." Shelby seemed to be enjoying his reveal, enthralled by his tale of events. "They were inside an hour, which doesn't tell me much. I made my way inside to get a closer look, but they never made their appearance near the main bar. They finally left at 11:00 p.m. and got a taxi back to his friend's house. His name I gather is Antonio. Big Hispanic guy, seemed close to Sunny. The other guy is small, pale, doesn't like to talk much. Name's Rick. And just two days ago Tuesday, they met at The Sky Lounge in downtown Newcombe."

Parker said, "Those three locations could not be more different. And Newcombe? That's a far drive…"

"Maybe they like variety. But you know what?"

"What's that?"

"He's not one to get around like that. I know his type. Easy to peg. They find one expensive bar with their overpriced rare whiskeys, and they go back every week. They get to know their favorite waitress, learn about her kids so they can look at her ass a little while longer, get a good laugh to make themselves feel special. I've seen it more times than I can count."

"What do you make of it?"

Shelby grabbed a toothpick out of his top drawer and began sucking on it, taking his time. "There are parts I know, and parts I don't. Lucky for us, my girl Vanessa knows some people. One of the reasons I hired her. That, and she blends. Not something easily taught." He pointed his toothpick in our direction. "As I was sayin', her uncle Terry works The Sky Lounge. She's from Newcombe. Had him over for drinks, turns out the Tuesday in question was locked for a private event. Said the guests spent a *ridiculous* amount of money. She said it seemed like there was a business deal bein' made. With a twist."

"Couldn't it be networking? Like minds in the field of investments?"

"Could be, but my hunch told me otherwise. My intuition is rarely wrong. Turns out they had the room guarded, and a password to enter. I think we can safely assume all other bars were the same. It's gonna be hard to find what's going on inside unless you *are* inside is the gist I got. Even Terry didn't know much more than the meeting time and bar tab. He only assumed it was illegal because his boss gave them a disclaimer not to tell anyone about it. Gave him the creeps, it did. We got lucky he was willing to tell us what he did."

Parker said, "That's pretty huge. I'm not surprised that he's up to something illegal, either. Why did you think we'd be disappointed?"

"Well, it's nothing concrete. No hard proof, which is what you were looking for. I'm in the business of hard facts. It's all hearsay, and the information I got will be hard if not near impossible to prove. They could say they were there for a nightcap, three men out on the town. Nothing wrong with that." He threw another photo our way. Antonio and Rick were on either side of Sunny as they exited the main hotel doorway of The Sky Lounge, Antonio had his hand on Sunny's back as the three of them laughed.

Parker looked closer at the image. "What's that in Antonio's hand?"

"I wondered if you'd pick up on that." Shelby looked towards me, "Good eye he's got." He leaned further back in his chair making us wonder if he'd ever come back up again. "It's a matchbook." He threw us another photograph, enhanced. "From the Mirabelle Hotel."

I said, "I've never heard of it."

"You wouldn't, more than likely. It's down South, quite the ways from any of their homesteads."

"Think it means anything?"

"I took a drive down myself, just yesterday. Couldn't find anything. The owner said he doesn't keep surveillance and they've had quite the turnover. He wasn't very talkative, that one. He was a hard read. On the outside, real middle of the road hotel, large. But it looks like they've recently spiffed it up. Lots of recent improvements, maybe they're on the up and up. It's not necessarily a dead-end, but something to remember. Maybe Antonio goes there to get his Jolly's. Hard to say." He snapped his chair forward. "There's not much else to Sunny. Gets home late. Weekends, when he's not working he's with the wife, kids. They like the same park on Louisiana Street. I don't think what you're looking for will happen from a typical Friday night through Sunday, but people surprise me. On Thursday he met a friend at a pizza joint near their house, seemed pretty run of the mill." He threw another picture our way. He asked, "Any of this mean anything to you two?"

I said, "I don't know much about him now that I'm thinking about it. I've known Sunny since they married, but he tends to divide himself from her life."

Parker said, "They seem to live together yet separate."

Shelby nodded. "I saw that play out."

I said, "Anything redeeming?"

Shelby said, "Nothing particular. He did buy his wife flowers last Friday. Thought that was sweet."

Parker tensed. "Thank you for taking this on, it's been helpful."

"If you ever need me to continue, or dig deeper, let me know. He piqued my interest, that one. Not your usual adulterer or drug dealer. Hell, I'll even throw in an extra day. It's been nice workin' with ya." He placed his feet back on the ground and shook both of our hands as he handed Parker the envelope.

As we sat in the car, neither of us noted the heat radiating off the leather seats or from the plastic interior. Sweat started to gather in droplets at the peak of Parker's nose and he nudged it away. He opened the envelope, scanning.

"He's up to something. This has to be connected with the money Paul found in his account. Did he trade for something? Deal drugs?"

I said, "I think we need to tread carefully, here."

"What do you mean?"

"We'll need to decide how and what we will tell Amelia."

He said, "We will tell her everything. We have to."

"We can't be brash about this, you said it yourself. If he's into money laundering or drugs, we can't approach him without a plan, this could get dangerous. Not just for us, but Amelia. Of course we'll tell her, but we have to be safe."

Parker sighed. "I'm not planning on busting down their front door, please tell me you have more faith in me than that."

"Of course, but love can make even the soundest person make irrational decisions. This is more than an affair. You've uncovered something important here."

"I agree. I don't want to tell Amelia anything until we have something concrete. As Shelby said, this is all based on assumptions. Sunny could twist any of this and make easy sense out of it. And she would believe him. I wouldn't blame her. And-"

"What?"

"I don't want her to think I tore up her marriage for my own gain. I may love her, but I don't want to see her in pain. My mind has been made up long ago that loving her from a distance is enough."

"Parker, you can't live like that forever."

"I know. I suppose I'm just not ready to fully grasp that quite yet. I've seemed to have hit a road block, in a lot of ways."

"I know. We can figure this out, let's think it through."

"You keep saying 'we'. This is my problem, Ellie. I know it's in your heart to help anyone in need, but this might be time for you to walk away. He has information on me, not you. I could be in deep, here. And you know what else?"

"What's that?"

"Amelia's house. The stained-glass, the white hanging sheet."

"You think the messages are targeting you? That someone knows you're investigating Sunny?"

"Potentially. The glove fits. Who else could it be?"

"I still don't see why Sunny would destroy his own home to send a message when he's already blackmailed you."

"Ellie, I don't know."

"Has Paul received any gentle reminders to stop?"

"Nothing that I've been made aware of."

"It doesn't fit. But look, I'm in this now and I want to be. It gives me the shivers to imagine her laying in bed with Sunny after he's been with other women. And there's still a chance that the bottle isn't for you, let's not jump to conclusions."

He rubbed his temple hard. "It's overwhelming."

"We'll figure it out. Let's take this one step at a time."

Chapter 5
Pede Claudo

It was Wednesday once again and the full summer heat barreled down on the neighborhood sidewalks. Illusory waves cascaded upward, forming a blurry cartoon caricature of Amelia's house.

Parker and I eyed each other from our seats at the Wednesday round table, margaritas encircling a hot pile of sopapillas. The honey containers perched around the outer ring looked like guardian angels, watching over the spectacle, and waiting for their cue. I watched as salt slowly slid down Hannah's glass as she casually spoke with Lulu. I envied their position, their ignorance in the events slowly unfolding around them.

Parker and I decided to take the week to see what was discovered with the investigation into Amelia's vandals, and to come up with ideas on how to safely find information on Sunny. We were planning on having drinks after leaving Amelia's tonight to recap.

I shook my head, concentrating on the book club before me. I could feel an anxious air in the room, a static of wonder and question. Were we safe sitting here, in our circle by the window? Sunny had installed a state-of-the-art security system, and even he was remiss at the idea that such petty crime would hamper Amelia's plans in the house. So, we agreed to try again, another Wednesday to add to the list.

Amelia looked immaculate in her yellow sundress and was the first to grab her glass. We clinked our drinks and began to discuss a book I could hardly get through, my mind unfocused throughout the week, my grant renewal gathering dust on my desk as I imagined what horrors Sunny could be up to.

Georgia said, "I love when we throw a dark classic in the mix."

Lulu was wearing a custom-fitted black suit and red pumps and had come directly from a museum auction. She looked impressive and chic as her foot slowly hit the side of my chair, the rhythm bringing my mind back to the present. "This may be a first, but I almost picked this book last year. Who woulda thought being an Amelia pick this week?"

Amelia replied, "I'm trying to decide if that was a compliment." She winked in her direction. "Alright, *Dr. Jekyll and Mr. Hyde*." She flipped through the pages. "I can't stop thinking about the quote, 'good and evil are so close as to be chained together in the soul.'"

Lulu said, "Are you getting dark on us?"

"I'm not sure about *that* Lu. But it does make you think, what makes a person evil or good? Are they closer than we think?"

I said, "I don't think anyone is all evil or good."

"Do you think it can happen to anyone, like in the book?" Hannah said, "Some catalyst flips a switch, whatever it may be, and suddenly you're another version of yourself? Something that has been there the whole time, waiting."

Georgia put down her crochet needles and commented, "I think people could use that as an excuse to do bad. Ya know? Saying it's a part of their being, a reason for madness."

"I think there *can* be bad things in the mind." Lulu's foot taped twice for every one of Hannah's.

"But you always have a choice," Amelia said, "to be a nice person or not."

"I suppose weeding out any disorder of the mind, sure. But people do have different natural tendencies, don't they? What if you were raised poorly, in a harsh environment?"

Parker said, "I think some people tend to lean more towards one side of good or evil, regardless of environment. Maybe they chose to do so. Maybe something in life made that choice easier."

Amelia said, "I hope I never interact with someone who *chooses* to be evil." I almost choked on my ice, thinking of Sunny. I wouldn't call him evil, but he certainly wasn't running in the right circle.

Lulu said, "I do have to say, never has a quote seemed more like myself when he said, 'I'm a creature of fine sensations.'" She tilted her drink back, mocking dramatics.

Georgia laughed as she picked up her needles, "Now *that's* the truth. If that's you, perhaps I'm the quote, 'he's about as emotional as a bagpipe.'"

Amelia said, "Oh Georgia! You're much more beautiful than a bagpipe."

Lulu said, "Can you embroider that on a pillow for me, G?"

"Sure, add it to the pile. How about another round?"

Lulu swiped her finger across the salt on her rim, "Throw me an extra lime, will ya?"

As we continued to talk, enjoying one another, there seemed to be an edge, waiting for something evil to throw another threatening book quote our direction, another shattering of glass or loud bang from the lawn.

Hannah asked, "Where's Sunny tonight?"

"He's here. Said he had business to finish from home. I guess some breakthrough with his partners." She hunched her shoulders, a clear lack of disinterest. I looked at Parker as he left for the bathroom. I said I needed another drink and met Parker in the hall.

He said, "What do you think Sunny is up to?"

"I don't know much about finance, beats me. Sounds like just another night at work."

"I think we should take a peek."

"What, stand outside his office? Everyone is *here*."

"It's the perfect time." Parker said, "maybe we'll catch something. If he sees us, he knows were here for Amelia. We can fake stupid. How else are we going to get information?"

"Unless he knows you're *investigating* him."

"Then I'm screwed either way. He already knows I know about the affair."

"And his office is upstairs, from what I remember. Far away from our den. It's risky."

"Cover for me." He had made his choice.

"Parker-" he was off towards their back staircase as I called unsuccessfully in a harsh whisper. I jumped as Hannah approached.

"Are you talking to yourself in the hall?" She laughed.

"Parker isn't feeling the greatest, he might be a second."

"Ah, I never could trust Lulu's cooking." She rolled her eyes and I followed her to the kitchen

Lulu approached, "You guys aren't doing shots without me, are you?"

"Ha, I haven't done a shot in years." Hannah toppled ice in her glass. "Makes my throat spaz just thinking about it."

Amelia joined. "Where's Parker?"

63

"Not feeling well." Hannah said, "He's in the bathroom. I think Lulu tried to poison him."

"Yeah, I poured all my cyanide in one sopapilla, a lucky shot I guess."

I changed the subject. "When are the kids coming back, Amelia?"

"Next week, can't wait. They've had quite the time in California though."

"Is it weird being alone in the house?"

"Well, Sunny is here, of course."

I said, "Seems like he works a lot."

"Comes with the territory." She shrugged. "I think I'll go check on Parker."

"No! No." I grabbed her shoulder softly. "I told him I'd bring him some water. I'll join you guys back at the table." I filled a water glass and headed down the hall, avoiding Amelia's glance. Their home was 5,000 square feet and new amenities popped up every time I ventured to have a look. The stairway entered in the middle of the second-floor hall, then two wings fanned at the end of each. If I remembered correctly, his office was at the end and to my right. I passed the boys' bedrooms and two additional bathrooms. I startled as I almost ran into Parker, back pressed against the wall like a criminal, flush on the same wall as the office door.

I whispered, "What are you doing?"

"Why are you holding water?"

"That's what you're concerned about? Beverages? Have you heard anything?"

"He hasn't said a word, sounds like he's typing away. Boring. I don't know what I was expecting. To catch him in some kind of act? Not at home with Amelia here. Guess I was wrong."

We started to walk back to the den when we heard footsteps approaching from the hall.

"*Shit.*" The water threatened to tip above the rim as I set it down.

He said, "I have an idea." I watched as he touched the paneling across from our stance, the footsteps close. You could hear the soft padding of the owner's shoes hitting the nearly forty-foot-long rug. Suddenly, a slight click opened a small closet within the wall's folds, hidden amongst the crown molding and ornate wood adornments. We slipped inside, enveloped in black.

I whispered, "How did you know this was here?"

"Amelia showed me on the tour when they bought it. This place has some secrets to tell. It was built in the early 1900s, and when they remodeled, *wowzah.*"

We quieted as someone knocked on the office door. He announced, "It's Antonio." I was relieved it wasn't Amelia, wondering where we escaped to, suspicious. The tendrils on my back stood on end at the mention of Antonio's name. He seemed nothing but a character until this moment.

Sunny opened the door. "Took you long enough, I haven't got all day to wait around for your exploits."

"Are you going to let me in, or not?"

"Where's Rick?

"With Jason, finalizing plans."

"He's down south? Why didn't anyone tell me?" He sighed. "Whatever. Come in." As he shut the door with a snap, we waited a minute than exited, backs against Parker's original wall. Their verbiage was hard to catch, the walls thick. I watched as Parker walked up to the door and placed his ear against it.

I mouthed, "You're insane. What if they open it?" I was jesting with my arms madly, the butterflies in my stomach feeling like they were trying to escape through my belly button in a massive explosion.

He placed a finger to his lips. I shook my head and joined him, if they opened it, I'd be in the same amount of trouble. I wondered what Sunny would think if again he was caught in a private moment by Parker.

A phone rang. Antonio answered. "Yea. I'm with him now. Ok. I'll let him know." A shuffling of feet. "That was Rick. The Mirabelle is still a go, but something came up."

Something slammed on the table. "What in the world now? I feel like all I do is babysit you two. What do I pay you for?"

"Things in this business are rarely so cut and dry, boss. They won't be able to accommodate us tomorrow like expected."

"That changes a lot." He sounded enraged. "When exactly will the space be available? Jason is going to get an *ear* full. She's not going to be happy."

"She'll have to cope. Rick said next Thursday."

"*Thursday?*"

"They have a convention through the weekend that was extended, and they don't want to risk having such a large group together at once. I'm sure the convention is anything but legal. Said they're just thinking about the operation. Said we'll have our time."

"Like it's *their* operation. *They* didn't find the buyers. They're merely a location."

"They're getting a pretty big cut, they're in this. We'd be in trouble without a place to do business. Do you seriously want our merchandise walking through a hotel full of people?"

Sunny ignored his question, "That's in eight days. What are we supposed to do with the haul until then?"

"We have partners. People in town."

"You better hope so." He huffed. "Fine. We'll head down late Wednesday with the haul if the buyers are willing to have the viewing Thursday. We'll make sure the Mirabelle isn't going to stick us. Rick should have what we need by tomorrow, regardless. Everything seems to be going as planned on his end."

"The buyers are antsy to purchase. We've got their attention, it shouldn't be an issue. They'll wait."

"And they'll have the money?" Sunny asked.

Antonio seemed annoyed. "Leave those details to me." A pouring of some liquid into a glass. "Now that we have a location to sell, it will change things. For the future, too. Your investment was wise, I believe."

"If they hold up to their end of the deal, perhaps."

"We can trust Jason. Leave the haul to me until Wednesday."

We realized the conversation was concluding and quickly ran from his office door, down the hall. Arriving at the staircase, we relaxed.

Parker said, "What on *earth* was that about?"

"If I only knew. Do you think he's dealing drugs?"

"He certainly wasn't selling car insurance. It has to be. I don't know. But whatever it is, it's *shady*."

"Looks like you were more than right about Sunny, by the sound of it." Neither of us appeared excited at that thought. Amelia was going to be in for some news. "Let's get back to the group." We crept passed the study, the downstairs bathroom, and the living room, finding ourselves blissfully in the kitchen again.

Parker said, "I'm not sure where to go from here."

Before I could answer, Lulu waltzed in. "What on earth are you guys up to? Hoarding sopapillas for yourselves, I see? How are you feeling Parker?"

"What?" I shot him a look. "Oh, right. I think it'll pass. I'm feeling quite better." His acting skills were not on par.

Lulu looked between us and grabbed the stack of napkins as she left with a bottle of honey.

I said, "She's not stupid."

"She'll have to keep wondering, then. Nothing else we can do about it." We both grabbed another margarita and made our way back to the group, chatting. We startled as Antonio left, crossing paths with our own. His eyes were set forward, no eye contact made. He carried the smugness of a person who got exactly what he wanted.

After leaving Amelia's, Parker and I met at the local bar, Spirits.

Parker said, "We're in over our heads."

"Now you have something on him, though. Think you can use this to block the blackmail?"

"I think that would make him angrier. Plus, it's nothing concrete, once again. We're not even sure it's illegal."

"Sunny's hard to peg down. He's careful."

"We need something objective. Pictures, evidence."

"Don't get too wrapped up in bringing him down, this isn't as much revenge as it is helping Amelia. Helping her see who Sunny truly is."

"I know, you're right. I'm glad you're with me in this."

"On a positive note, nothing happened at book club. No message. That's promising." As I finished the sentence, I glanced at my phone. "Amelia is calling."

He said, "I have a bad feeling about this."

"Hello?"

Amelia said, "Hey, El. I hate to call you like this, but it happened again. There was a letter pinned to the front door, a simple postcard. Something is menacing about the quietness of it, the subtlety. This is week three, El. I'm not sure what to do…I felt strange calling the cops for a postcard. I'm starting to feel paranoid."

"What does it say?"

I could hear Sunny in the background, a door slamming. "Yeah. Hold on, let me go to the study." She began to walk, the swish of her dress a delicate echo through the receiver. "Sorry. Ok, Sunny is mad. He found a glass outside his office, got angry, and said someone was spying. Can you believe he said those words? *Spying.* He's not a Kennedy."

"A glass?"

"Yeah, it was probably the housekeeper. Anyways, here it is. It says, 'it must be that; the ghost of some old sin, the cancer of some concealed disgrace: punishment coming, PEDE CLAUDO.'"

"What does that mean?"

"That's just the first line, but it's straight from *Jekyll and Hyde.* I looked twice, both on the eBook and paperback. Pede Claudo means something similar to, 'punishment comes limping'. I almost couldn't believe it, but I knew what I would find. And under that phrase, it says, 'you have until the Orchid Society Gala to stop.'"

Goosebumps ran up my arm at the mention of a deadline. There was a finality to the message that wasn't there previously. "What does the gala have to do with it?" Parker tried to pry information from me, and I batted him away. He stood, pacing around our table.

"It's what everyone in the town is attending, and anyone who's anyone regarding flowers. Perhaps it's a good marker of time. I don't want to drag my mother into this. I hope they don't cause a scene, she's been working on this for *months*."

My teeth clenched. "I'm sure it'll be fine."

"I still don't know anything about this, El. Seriously. I've been wracking my brain, thinking, maybe I missed something? Maybe I *did* enrage someone and just didn't realize it."

"I know you better than that. Don't go blaming yourself. What does the postcard look like? Any clues?"

"It's plain black, white font. The police checked for prints. Said the fingerprints stay in their database for seven years. *Seven* years, can you believe it? That people sometimes have to wait that long?"

"I know, but this is different. What did Sunny say?"

"He thinks it's us, one of us six. Said we aren't digging deep enough. He says were causing harm to his home. It sounded like he didn't even want us to meet anymore. He made it sound like we were degenerates. We're holding a *book club*."

"He'll cool off, Amelia. I'm sorry. Don't let him get to your head, you've done nothing wrong."

"I know you guys didn't do this, but I don't get it. I didn't sleep last night, worried. I baked almost a hundred cupcakes after you left. The kitchen is a *disaster*. I'm thinking we might need to find another place to have our Wednesday nights."

"You might be right. I don't want to put you in danger. And your boys will be home soon."

"Thanks for understanding, this is a mess." She sighed, "I gotta go, Sunny is yelling something. See you soon to shop for books?"

The moment I hung up Parker said, "What was that? What's going on?"

"Another threatening note, this time a postcard stuck to the door. It said that punishment is coming if someone doesn't stop by the gala."

"The *gala*? That's in a week and a half. Any other clues?"

"Nothing."

"The notes must be targeting me. I came into this wanting to help, and look at what I've accomplished, risking Amelia's safety. The irony."

"Have you done anything this past week in regards to Sunny? Any additional investigating?"

"Nothing since Shelby."

"Why keep sending the note if you stopped looking into him? Something isn't adding-" Before I could finish my thought, I snapped my head towards the door in a double-take. Lulu was walking towards our table. "What in the hell..."

Lulu huffed. "Ok, what's going on."

Silence.

"Guys, don't. Are you having an affair? You're being *weird*. First, you go off with *Paul* who I just found out knows both of you. You're getting drinks after book club out of the blue, then El gets all bent out of shape when Mel asks to go check on Parker, and you grab him a glass of water. Weird timing that Sunny finds a water glass outside his office. Both of you are all whispery. What are you doing wandering their halls? I had to follow you here like a *psycho*." She stopped to catch her breath, tapping her foot like an angry parent.

We were stunned into silence. Little could be said without telling the whole tale. Once we started, it would be hard to stop, a small flake of snow building to its avalanche finale.

Parker said, "We're not having an *affair*, Lu. But I don't know if you should know all of the details..."

"You're suspicious of Sunny." She said.

71

"Isn't everyone?" He snapped.

I piggybacked off of her thought. "Lu, we have reason to believe he cheated on Amelia, but we don't have proof. Parker and I went upstairs today during our book club to-"

"Cheated?" Her eyes were wide. "I did not expect that. Why would you think that?"

"I don't want to tell you more, Lu. But it happened."

"Why haven't you told Amelia?"

I sighed. "There's a lot to this that we can't talk about right now. Can you trust us? Sit down a minute."

She nodded and flagged the waitress. I continued, "We have reason to believe he cheated, but we don't want to tell her in case we are wrong. That would be devastating. We're not taking this lightly."

"Ok, I get that."

"We thought maybe we'd hear him talking to another woman or catch a phone conversation if we went upstairs. It was stupid, a long shot."

"So, I take it you're feeling just fine, Parker?"

He said, "I don't like lying to you, Lu."

She ordered a coffee. "Who else knows?"

"Only us two."

"What are you guys planning to do?"

"We're working on it. Wait, how did you know that Paul knew both of us?"

"You had me curious. I only asked him a couple of innocent questions. He didn't say anything useful."

"Lulu…"

"I know I'm sorry, I shouldn't have pried. But things are so odd right now. I trust you both but everything is off-kilter. Wednesday nights are my getaway. Now it's terrifying, wondering what will happen next should we blink the wrong way twice. Did Amelia call you?"

"Yeah, the postcard on the door. A third message."

"What if someone doesn't stop what they're doing by the gala? Every one of us says it's not them. It has to be *someone*. I'm not in the business of pointing fingers, but we have to figure this out. Any ideas?"

"Not one."

We sat, sipping our drinks, thinking. I wondered if it would be beneficial to tell her more, but that wasn't my story to divulge. I was caught between lying to one friend and exposing the secrets of the other.

Lulu said, "If it is one of us six, that means someone has been lying. Someone is holding back pertinent information, knowing full well they're threatening Amelia and Sunny."

Parker said, "The person must think it's worth it, then. They've weighed their options."

"I can't imagine one of us would risk the other. We're all so close, I can't believe something like this would ever come to fruition. Unless it's that serious. Which is scary."

I said, "Or it isn't one of us. I don't know, Lu."

She finished her coffee. "I need some shut-eye. I will see you bright and early, Ellie. Isn't tomorrow the big artifact reveal?"

"That's what they just texted me, I feel like it's Christmas morning for nerds. The team is on pins and needles."

"I can't wait to see what they found."

Lulu left and Parker said, "Did she just drink a cup of coffee before going to bed?"

"She's an interesting creature."

Chapter 6
Spiderweb

Lulu and I stood dumbstruck in front of my office door the next morning, coffees in hand, the briefcases once slung across our shoulders now dumped on the ground as we gaped.

Lulu whispered, "Don't go in, El. Call security."

"Yeah, alright. I don't know what to do. Where does my team go?"

"Let security do a sweep. I'll call the head director. Don't go in there." She stepped aside as we made the calls. I felt stranded, vulnerable, nowhere to go but the hallway. Lulu ushered me into her office as we watched teams of individuals approach the chaos. "Lu, this is odd. Who are all of these people?"

"Good question. I didn't know the archeologists found something *that* important?"

"I still don't know what it is, how crazy is that? My team was going to open the boxes this morning. Celebrate the last find in the dig. I feel a little pushed to the side." A police trooper approached and finally allowed me inside my office.

He said, "You might want to brace yourself. And when you have a minute, jot down anything that is missing and let Hugh know. He's heading the investigation with the police."

I walked inside. It was in ruins. The middle conference table usually erect with photographs and notes was overturned, one of the legs broken in two, the wood shards leaving a breadcrumb trail to the photograph that usually hung on the wall of me at the dig site with my archeologists last May. It was lodged sideways in the corner of the room, glass shattered, our smiles out of place. I opened the door to my personal office. The desk drawers were open and thrown to the ground unceremoniously. The fax machine was thrown across the room, the heavy piece of machinery blinking red, asking for help. I sighed and wondered where to start.

The police informed me that someone had ransacked the room early this morning, according to the museum tapes. They let my team watch the footage to see if anyone was recognizable. The thieves were wearing the traditional black attire, face masks, holding spray paint for the cameras. The tape was short, useless. They sprayed ink across the lens before the damaging commenced. In the corner of the room, though, I caught the crates of artifacts, sitting and waiting for us to examine and for Lulu to start appraising.

A trooper asked, "What do you know about the shipment?"

"Not a lot. I was informed that it had arrived late last night. They wanted to do the drop outside of regular museum hours. I knew it was supposed to be in our office this morning so we could start getting to work. As far as I know, the director had only informed me and my team that it had officially arrived. If you want more information, it would be wise to speak to him."

As if on cue, Hugh Benson, the Director of Research and Development waltzed in, full suit and a stern look plastered across his face. He was a man of few words, liked business done quickly and efficiently, and hated small talk. He was a closed book when it came to facts about his life but enjoyed making harsh jokes at the expense of his first wife, Wynona, who was well-known and liked around the office.

His voice was particularly gruff today. "What's this about, Ellie?"

"The police know more than me, sir. We only just arrived."

"Humor me." He pushed his small spectacles higher on his face, the bridge of his nose shallow. His face seemed to pulsate in red.

"Lulu and I walked down the hallway this morning and my office door was ajar. All of our equipment and belongings were scattered about, some broken. It's a mess."

"Who do you think did this?"

"You're asking me?"

"I have to cover every base. There were only a few people who knew about this. And you seem to be skirting around my question."

"I'm sorry sir, I don't have any information."

He silently scanned my body. "Who did you tell?"

"Lulu knew about it. Other than that, just my team. You only informed me about it yesterday."

"I explicitly told you to only tell those who work directly in your office. Did you break my confidence in telling your friend?"

"We work together. She was going to begin appraisal soon. As far as I'm concerned, she *is* my team. I meant no harm."

"We'll see about that. Strange behavior during a grant renewal. I'll be talking to you shortly." He approached the police team, patting a larger man on the back. No more to be said. With his large build and booming voice, he took over the entire space. I walked back to join Lulu, needing a minute away from the high energy and irate faces.

She said, "Don't worry about him. He's all talk, you know. I don't know one person he has fired."

I put my face down against her cool desk, looking at her with sad eyes. "I better start looking for another job. Who is going to renew a grant after something like this? They'll think I'm toxic."

"How will they know? It's not like that's going to be in your introduction."

"Funny." I said, "Other than the Orchard Gala, this will be top gossip for the next few weeks."

"Seems interesting predicaments are finding us, no matter how hard we hide."

"I seem to be the common link."

"You didn't steal it for crying out loud. Everyone is acting like you arranged for it to go just as planned. You're the *victim*. Your office is in ruins."

"I feel more empathy for Amelia after this. You feel wrong, knowing people have been in your things, destroying your property. Into your business."

"I'm getting a headache thinking about this along with Amelia's situation."

"I'm right there with you." I lifted my head, rubbing my cheek.

"Have you found anything out about the artifacts? The police must have said something."

"Gaby overheard Hugh talking with the police chief. She said it's worth more than we can imagine. It's what all this hubbub is about. It all comes down to money. I'm sick about it already, I only want to continue our research, write our paper. It seems odd, doesn't it? Of all people, you would think the head researcher and archivist would be made aware of what was inside the boxes, what was stolen."

"It is unlike anything I've seen since working here. We *always* know what's coming in so we can prepare. How much do you think the artifact is worth?"

"Well into the millions, from the sound of it. But no one is forthcoming. I'm certainly not getting any information from Hugh. And I spoke with the head archeologist. She was told not to speak to anyone outside of the museum, which is odd. But I suppose if it was something so large, they have to be safe?"

"We've had big items come through the museum, this isn't the first and won't be the last." She shut her laptop. "We aren't getting much work done today, they've blocked the lab and people are trolling for gossip. Let's go get some coffee."

As we exited the building, the hot summer air hit us like a furnace, the initial feeling soaking us in comfort, a warm blanket to the senses. That quickly changed as our bodies adjusted, faces flush with the dry air and radiating heat from the sidewalk. We were at the stoplight waiting to walk to Floyd's when I heard someone shouting my name. Turning around, I saw Paul running, hand covering the sun as he squinted his eyes towards us.

The light turned green, but we waited. "Paul, what is it?"

"This is why I never leave my office. It's *blistering*. Can we go inside?"

"We were headed to Floyd's…"

"That's fine, anywhere is fine."

There wasn't a wait, and we found ourselves at the same table as before.

He began fanning a small paper menu towards his face, reclaiming his composure. "Forgive me, I'm not one for athletics."

"You're worrying me."

The waitress interrupted and he ordered an iced tea, extra sugar. "I have some information that may be helpful." His voice lowered and he bent closer to the table. "I heard about the artifact."

"You and the whole museum."

"I should be clearer. I knew about it yesterday."

"Do you know what it is?"

"I do."

"How do you have this information and not my team?"

"I'm in close with Hugh. I've handled some situations for him."

"Detective situations?"

"I'll leave that to the imagination." His eyes peered suspiciously around the café.

"Well, what is it?" She eyeballed me at the mention of his prior detective work.

"You cannot tell anyone I'm mentioning this. Especially Hugh. Do you understand? He acts like I already know too much."

I said, "Of course."

"I would not be telling you, if not for helping Parker. This isn't my information to share. I don't involve myself with petty *gossip*."

"Paul, spit it out."

"As you know, the New Mexican excavation site was about 15 miles from the main Chaco Canyon entrance."

"Of course, it's what we've been researching for the last few years. It's what my paper is on. What are you getting at?"

"They recently moved north twenty miles, following a trail using advanced astronomical alignments. None were made aware of the change at the museum, to my knowledge. I'm sure you were under the impression that they found one item, perhaps in the arena of tools or a dress, seed jars or ladles. Those types of things."

"It's what they had been finding thus far. Beautiful finds. Why hadn't I been made aware of the move? This whole situation is rather odd, Paul. Usually, I'd be one of the first contacted with such a drastic change since it impacts the research."

"It's a sensitive matter. And this is different from your regular finds. What do you think when you envision New Mexican artifacts? Jewelry or pottery perhaps?" He lowered his voice, his mouth forming a thin line, lips unreadable. "It appears they found a collection. The largest known in the world of Lander Blue Spiderweb Turquoise. If it's legitimate."

"Turquoise?"

"Extremely rare, typically found in Nevada, which adds to the mystery. Anyways, it's inlaid into pottery, silver, you name it. Some stones are *large*. It's not just the turquoise, but the jewelry, the art. It's unlike anything found in the Southwest to date. What was sent to your office was a haul equaling at least 50 million dollars' worth of pottery and jewelry. *If* it is dated as such, and *if* it is found to be natural."

"I can't believe it."

Lulu said, "This is insane. Why rush over to tell us this? I'm sure someone would have told us today."

"You'd be surprised. The reason I'm here is to tell you that there is a reward for its retrieval. This is not common knowledge and Hugh doesn't know. He absolutely cannot know this."

I leaned back in my chair. "Alright...why can't Hugh know? That doesn't make sense, he is in charge of the campaign to find them."

"I don't like the way he was thinking, his mind started to race with ideas. If he knew about the reward...I'm not sure at what lengths he would go." He shook his head.

I said, "This is starting to sound odd."

"Because you're helping Parker, I'll give you some insight. There have been rumors circulating in the past ten years or so of a massive hoard of Native American valuables, made with what they're coining the Gems of the Southwest."

"I've never heard of such a thing, and this is my livelihood. I live and breathe the Southwest."

"It's because you run within a legitimate group of individuals. This is all underground, illegal art trade chatter. Initially, it seemed the idea of a madman for such a grouping of artifacts to be together. And with this find, suddenly it's not so crazy. But I'm not here about Hugh, I'm here about the reward money. If you did happen to locate said artifacts, I could help you retrieve the money."

"Who is offering the reward?"

"I can't say, but it's legitimate. The source is someone I trust. A friend of the museum. They'd do right by the artifacts."

I said, "A reward. I know what you are getting at."

He said, "May I speak freely?" He was indicating Lulu's presence.

"Yes, go ahead." She remained silent.

"Parker wants to help Amelia leave Sunny but is afraid he will tie up their finances. It sounds like there is a prenup, and according to Parker, she'll want to keep the home for her children. And judging by what I uncovered, she and the children are not safe. The man he's working with...I feel targeted just thinking about his name. Regardless, she needs a safe way out. Am I on the right track here?"

"Something like that."

"Well, then. $200,000 would be a good start for something like that, I'd say."

"$200,000?"

"As I said, this isn't a game for children. Not only could the money help her leave, but it might also help Parker find out more information, and safely. I know he's on the warpath for something objective. And, I know those artifacts mean a lot to your career here at the museum. Just a thought. Money and you save the artifacts from thieves."

"I see your point, but I'm a researcher, Parker works at the local paper. We don't have ties to people who would know about the illegal art trade if that's indeed who stole them. That's not something I can go on Craigslist to discover, and this is appearing more dangerous by the minute. 50 million dollars' worth of goods? That is a large operation."

"Yes, but when you're desperate, things suddenly happen, don't they? People find a way. And you're well versed in the way of archeology, research. It matters to me little, one way or the other. I thought I would pass this on to help a friend digging into dangerous territory. But I've already said too much."

"Are you saying the $200,000 reward is for information on the artifacts or handing them over?"

"From what I understood, it's the physical artifacts. If you retrieve them before anyone else, the money is yours."

"This is insane."

"The choice is yours."

"What about the police at my office? Aren't they using their resources to find out what happened to the best of their abilities?"

He sighed. "I know one of them personally, and he's got ties. That's all I'm going to say."

I sat back for a moment. "Say I did find the artifacts, who am I handing them over to? I'm not gaining $200,000 at the risk of losing the artifacts to someone in the art trade."

"A trusted source. They have similar goals as yourself. I can't verify further, you'll have to trust me. If you did find the artifacts, I could engineer a meeting, calm the nerves. But until then…"

"Paul, you're sounding more wrapped in this by the moment."

"I wish I could say otherwise. This is sensitive. Be careful around Hugh, will you?"

I didn't want to pry further about Hugh, but something wasn't right. I asked, "Why are you so protective of Parker, anyways?"

"Let's say we go back. He's one of the only people I unquestioningly trust." He shrugged it off, poured four sugars in his iced tea, and gulped its entirety before exiting the café. Farewells seem to be lost on him.

Lulu turned to me. "I about lost my shit, El. What is going on?" She took off her blazer and unbuttoned the top of her blouse, fanning herself from the heat.

I sighed. "It's not that I didn't want to tell you. It's Parker's information to share, not mine."

"Well, I think I'm in this now."

"You can't tell anyone."

"You're like Paul, out with it already."

"It's a long story."

"Give me something, El, this doesn't seem right."

"Alright, you wanted to know. Parker caught a conversation between Sunny and another woman. Presumably, he cheated.

The conversation was ugly, and it was pretty clear what had transpired. Parker and Sunny were doing business and Sunny was helping him with investments. Parker walked into his office at the wrong time. Or right time, depending on how you look at it." Lulu looked as if she was going to burst out the side of the café and find Sunny herself. "Let me finish. Sunny has something on Parker. I won't go into the details on that, it's irrelevant."

"You're saying that Sunny blackmailed Parker to block him from telling Amelia about his affair."

"Exactly. Parker is ticked off, wants more information on Sunny so when he does tell Amelia, it's valid, and the blackmail won't have the same relevance."

"Why did Paul say that Sunny was working with dangerous men? Is he a detective?"

"Paul used to be. He helped Parker do some digging. They uncovered a name, a person Paul says is high in the world of drugs. Bad people, Lu. Total coincidence they found it, he was searching for information on the affair. Blindsided him."

"I honestly can't believe what I'm hearing."

"At the end of the day, Parker doesn't want everything resting on one phone conversation if he is to tell Amelia. So, he hired a private eye. They're pricey. He also wanted to pay for Amelia to leave, with the kids. But he's stuck, can't tell Amelia about the affair without his dirty laundry being aired. And this information, if it got out, could sink him."

"This is a lot to take in."

"And a lot of money."

"Amelia and Sunny are living quite expensively at the moment."

"Parker wanted the boys to stay in their school. It would be hard for Amelia to leave with them, we're guessing Sunny would make it difficult. Doable, of course, but she wouldn't want to hurt her sons. Her happiness for theirs, you know. And now it's more than just love and affairs, it's the safety of the kids. He's not running in a good circle. It make me nervous, thinking about the man Sunny is working with. I can only hope, even with the affair, that he is keeping their safety in mind. But can that be guaranteed?"

"So, if Parker had this lump sum he could swoop in, the decision easy. She could leave, no guilt, no harm done, and if Sunny tried tying up her finances, she's in the clear at least for a little while."

"That's the gist of it. It's complicated. I think Parker feels the weight of guilt, knowing about the potential affair for so long and not telling her. I think he feels that he owes her more than just the truth." I left out the part where Parker professed his love. I already said more than I intended.

"What did the private eye say?"

"He gave us good leads, but all hearsay. No pictures or documents worth anything. He believes Sunny met with people on illegal business but we're not sure what. With everything…it sounds like drugs, laundering. Something shady. It's not that we think Amelia is unwise or wouldn't be successful leaving now, we just want to be prepared. It's taking longer than we thought…now we're in deep."

"You're afraid Sunny has connections."

"All I'm saying is Parker and I want to be prepared. Sunny seems to know people. This isn't as cut and dry as it may appear on the surface. We're way past a simple affair."

"I can't believe it."

"It's been a ridiculous couple of weeks."

"You're telling me."

"I'm sorry."

Lulu leaned back. "You have nothing to be sorry about. You're trying to help Parker help Amelia, and now I'm trying to help you help them."

"Paul wants us to find the artifacts and get the reward, pay for Amelia to leave, and possibly have Sunny followed. The issue with all of these plans is that Amelia isn't even aware. She has no say in this, it's awful. And that's assuming we have any way to find stolen artifacts."

"She has a say, of course. Parker will give her the resources once he tells her, and she can take it or not. We're not *kidnapping* her, we're waiting for the best moment to let her know. It's not a bad idea if we knew where to get any information. And we'd be getting our artifacts back in time for your grant. Two-fold. You need those artifacts returned, and Amelia and Parker need the money. But I'm not a criminal, I don't think like that. I wouldn't know the first place to look for stolen goods."

I said, "I think we need to call Parker." We left Floyd's, the heat severe. Suddenly everything seemed suspicious, off. We didn't say another word until we reached our offices, sullen and unsure.

Chapter 7
8 Days

We decided to meet with Parker the next night, on Friday, to discuss the artifact reward. Bill and I had a standing date, and I needed a moment to gather my bearings. That night, I decided to test the waters with Bill. He had been out of town, off and on the past month, and I wasn't one to hide information from him. It had been wearing on me, this battle between keeping Parker's confidences and being forthcoming to my husband.

Bill was straightening his tie and changing his work shoes for a more casual pair. We were planning to eat at our favorite Italian restaurant down the road.

He said, "You look great tonight, honey."

"I don't feel great. But thank you." I kissed his cheek.

"I was robbed once, in college."

"You never told me that."

"Back when James and I lived in the small house on Market. There wasn't a lot to steal, back in those days."

"What did they take?"

"Some textbooks, weed. Our collection of change over the years."

I laughed, "Big-time haul." I finished putting my hair in a high bun. "It still feels violating, though. No matter what they take."

"I remember that. And wondering if they had an old key. We changed the locks, of course. But that night we were wary, we hardly slept."

"I'm wondering about sleep tonight, too." I continued fixing my makeup, curling my hair. I said, "I was going to wait until the restaurant, but I don't think I can. I have a situation. I need your thoughts."

"Is this how you're going to leave me for good..." He joked.

"You wish, so you could run off with Georgia's husband."

"Chase does have more muscle..."

I hit his shoulder. "Parker confronted me with something. It's kind of a long story." He motioned me to sit. I proceeded to tell him about the affair, the blackmail. We were sitting on the corner of our bed.

He said, "You know, I think this story requires some libations. How about we head to Spirits and you finish telling me there. Let's get some crappy bar food and nix Fernando's."

"You read my mind."

I hadn't arrived at the larger portion of the story, and Bill was already processing the blackmailing bit. When we arrived at the bar, he was stunned when I finished.

"This sounds entirely made up, but too insane to be false."

"It's taken me a minute to absorb everything."

"Why didn't you tell me sooner?"

"I've been nervous about spreading Parker's issues, his story. It's all very personal for him. But I realized I couldn't hide it from you, I never wanted to, believe me. And now with the robbery..."

"And I've been away a lot, I get it. I'm not mad or anything, I promise. I don't want you to get into something dangerous."

"What do you think we should do?"

"For starters, *you* don't need the money, that's Parker. And even he doesn't need it. This is his choice."

"I know. It's Amelia though, you know?"

"I get it, I don't want you risking something for a situation that you fell into. You're not the one being blackmailed. But I trust your instincts."

"I'm glad I'm talking to you. You ground me."

"Just don't go so far as to stress yourself into madness. If Amelia finds out, she finds out. Even if she thinks Parker is a nut job fire starter, the world doesn't end."

"It could for her, though. With Sunny. And with the people Sunny is surrounding himself with, her safety is a real issue here."

"It is a complicated situation. If at any point her safety seems acutely in danger, the police can be called. I don't think you two would ever let anything get that far."

"It's hard because we don't know exactly what we are dealing with. You know, it's hard to see them together now. She needs a man who can respect her, and she doesn't even know that's what she is lacking."

"When are you telling Parker about the reward?"

"Tomorrow after work. Honestly, it's crazy. Neither Lulu nor I have connections. Paul is the closest thing and he's spilled all he's willing to. You can't easily hunt down an art thief. And like you said, we don't want to put ourselves in danger. It's probably a moot point."

"I can't believe I'm going to say this."

"What is it?"

"I think I might know someone."

"You have a guy in the *illegal art trade*?"

"You meet a lot of people as a realtor, from *all* walks of life. It's a husband-wife deal. I wouldn't say they're illegal per se, but I know they have made a good amount of money from buying and selling art. With their day jobs, there's no way they could afford the house on Hampden. It sold for over 2 mil."

"Do you know them well?"

"I've helped them sell two condos and buy their house. We've worked quite a bit during the last year."

"Now that this is becoming real, I'm not sure I want to do this."

"I'm not sure this is a good idea, either. But I'd hate to see Sunny get away with cheating and blackmail. He's never set right with me, you know?"

"I never knew that."

"Wasn't worth mentioning, but he's sly. He seemed fine at first, but he seemed to change over time."

"To say the least. I think there's been a transformation over the years. Hard to realize unless you step back."

"If you are going to continue helping Parker and Amelia with hunting down the artifact, I'm in this with you. But I want to be there when you meet Mike and Lucy."

"Of course. Do you think this could burn a bridge for you?"

"I'll make sure that's not the case."

"You don't think we should involve the authorities? I've been thinking that we can bring them in, but I don't know how without it blowing up. We have no hard facts and it's become one large mess."

"Let's see where this leads us, we can always call them in at any time. You've done nothing wrong."

I smiled as we finished our deep-fried basket, finishing the different local beer flights. I hated to admit that Amelia's predicament made me more grateful for Bill, for our life. I realized how supportive he was, not only a listening ear but helping with a situation that wasn't his to delve into. It also made me more determined to help change her situation, if anyone deserved better, it was Amelia.

Work on Friday was strained. Hugh decided to set up shop in my office, then wouldn't leave. He continually shifted his concentration from his laptop and snuck peaks at mine. He was quiet for hours then finally broke the tension.

He asked, "Have any ideas on how to move forward without the archeologic pieces? What are you planning to do now that your grant proposal is almost due?"

"I'm hoping the authorities can track them down. If that's the case, then our project is made, right? Plus, we have the pieces that were found before this collection. All isn't lost."

"You haven't asked what was in the shipment, aren't you curious?"

"I'm sure it's similar to what they've been finding, but I did hear that it was a big haul. I'm excited to see what they unearthed."

He stared at me for an uncomfortable minute, then silently proceeded to work. He was fishing. Why he thought I had any information to give was beyond me.

I asked, "Any leads on the investigation?"

"You'll know when you need to."

The clock finally pronounced it's five o'clock status and I couldn't leave fast enough. I met Lulu in the hall.

She said, "That looked like a *long* day."

"You have no idea. I'm ordering wine in a bucket."

"Add two straws."

"Do you think Parker will go for the reward?"

"Only one way to find out."

Parker entered the bar, sitting heavily on the chair across from us. I found myself nervous, yet again, not for the first time this day, week, or month. The bar stool seemed cold, radiating an impermanency. We wasted no time in explaining the situation and delving into our conversation with Paul.

I said, "I'm curious, why is Paul so keen on helping us? He seems fairly forthcoming with information he would otherwise keep to himself."

"We've known each other for some time."

I waited for more of an explanation, and when none came, continued. "So, what do you think?"

"This sounds like we may be getting ourselves into more trouble."

"Or out of it," Lulu said.

I said, "We'd be vigilantes, not criminals."

Parker said, "Where is the reward money coming from?"

"Paul said he'd help us get it. He said it was legitimate but didn't reveal the source. A friend of the museum."

Parker said, "I do trust Paul...but that's strange. Not knowing where the reward money is originating?"

"Paul hasn't spoken to you recently? He's not a man of many words if you can recall."

"No. I think he's worried I will be mad that he approached you. We often go months without seeing each other, it's not completely out of character. He seems to get lost in his projects." Parker tapped the pen he had been holding in his mouth against the table like a drumstick without a pair. "I don't know if I have a choice at this point, I think we need to meet with Bill's contact."

I thought about Bill's words. "You always have a choice, Parker. You could confront Sunny or Amelia. I know that could end poorly, but you're not without options. Everything would be out in the open."

He said, "I know. I feel like I keep swimming deeper into the abyss. But I don't think it would hurt to meet with Bill's connection first. If we come up short, then we can move to plan B. I have no other way to track art thieves. How does that sound?"

We agreed and swiftly moved on to shots of tequila.

Chapter 8
Reflection

Bill was able to schedule dinner with Mike and Lucy for the next night, Saturday. He approached them with an invite to a small dinner party.

When the couple entered our home, I was surprised at how casual they appeared. Based on Bill's explanation, I anticipated two formidable faces in black suits, harsh faces. Lucy was wearing a white maxi dress and Louis Vuitton sandals. She was dressed expensively, but not ostentatiously. Mike was similar, khakis, and a casual button-down matching Bill in style.

After drinks in our front room, Bill led Mike and Lucy to the kitchen. Parker, Lulu, and her husband, Rex, were in the front parlor. Despite the tension we were trying to conceal from our guests, the room had a light air, and the evening seemed to be spinning in a positive direction. Bill had been gone for some time. I caught myself glancing towards the kitchen, wondering what was unfolding. Finally, Bill re-entered with a smile.

"They said they know people they can contact. They want to speak to you."

"What did you say?"

"I didn't let on to anyone else being involved, I said you were the researcher of the stolen goods and wanted to find the pieces before your grant expired."

I smiled. He got the job done without lying. I took Parker and Lu aside and told them I'd handle everything for now.

Bill led us four into the study that also served as his office. It was tastefully decorated in cream and blue hues, his fishing medals and degrees displayed on the wall to the right, his desk sitting under the pronouncements in an understated manner in front of a large leather chair. The room smelled like cinnamon and cloves, and I loved that it reminded me of him.

Lucy said, "I'm so sorry to hear about the robbery. What an awful thing to be tied up in, and such unfortunate timing." Her black hair was short and curved around her jawline perfectly, her makeup pristine.

"Thank you, it was quite the shock."

Mike commented, "Do you know much about the artifacts and jewelry?"

"It was listed as highly classified, which was odd given the previous objects discovered from our site. They were valuable, no doubt, but nothing worth millions of dollars. The stolen artifacts were made out of Lander Blue Spiderweb Turquoise. I never saw the items myself, though."

"Interesting. Where was the dig site?"

"New Mexico, near Chaco Canyon."

"And the robbery just occurred?" He seemed interested, I began to loosen up.

"Two days ago, Thursday."

"That's recent enough. We may be able to ask around."

"Any insight into how an operation like this works?" I said.

"It depends on what their goal is. Some use art as collateral, with no interest in their origins. It's merely a price tag. I don't want to be a downer here, but art theft largely goes unfound when stolen from museums. But not always. What is interesting is that the thieves cut it off at the pass, before the appraisal. An interesting way to do business. It tells me they may have a larger operation running."

Lucy said, "Makes you wonder not *if* but *who* was involved at the museum."

Mike said, "It is a risk. If the pieces are not legitimate, they have risked a hefty federal sentence for costume jewelry and pots."

I said, "My boss, Hugh, said there were only a few people informed, but I don't particularly trust what he tells me."

Mike said, "An operation of that magnitude will have more people aware than you would think. Security guards, the people at the dig site itself, management. It only takes one small conversation to get someone's mind reeling. And news of that caliber moves fast."

Lucy said, "Has it been uploaded in the art loss register?"

"I don't believe so. But I haven't been informed of much."

She turned to him, "That tells us something, too. Odd business. You said the police were notified?"

"There were officers present after we notified security. And an acquaintance of mine seemed to believe that the officers were friends of the museum. Whatever that may imply."

"I bet Lucas may know something."

"I hadn't thought of that." She said, both of them engrossed. "Or Maggie."

He turned to me and Bill, "We have some people we can contact. We don't want our names being used if anything comes of this, can you agree to that?"

I said, "Absolutely. I just want the art returned."

"What was the original intent of the art once appraised?"

"To study the pieces, gain timelines, more information on their way of life. Then we were to give the pieces back to Chaco Canyon and the tribes involved in the dig site within a pre-arranged amount of time. They agreed that some of the finds could be displayed at our museum as well, but that was to be decided after completion of the dig and appraisal of the pieces."

"When was the research to be completed?"

"We had three years, which was the duration of the grant money. We only have a few weeks left. This last dig happened much later than we intended. The archeologists followed an unexpected lead, and here we are."

"Do you have other artifacts from previous digs at that same site on display yet?"

"No, we're still dating, taking samples and cataloging. My friend Lulu that is here tonight is an appraiser."

Lucy nodded. "I think we have what we need, I'll call you if I have any more questions."

I said, "Is there any way we can reimburse you for your efforts?"

Lucy waived it off. "Making sure that this art is found is reward enough. People trying to steal history…it doesn't sit right in my book."

My stomach did a small flip, thinking that we were also in it for monetary purposes. I wondered how legitimate we were being, after all.

⁓

That night, sleep seemed a dream. The alarm clock was an ominous reminder of my acute insomnia, the red numbers burning my eyes through the darkness. The numbers slowly flipped to 2:00 a.m., a cruel performance.

The ringing of Bill's cell phone snapped me out of the clock hypnotism and we both jumped. He struggled to reach it, the phone falling off the bedside table.

"Hello?" He faked wakefulness quite well. "Yes, great. Sure, hold on." He turned to me, "pen and paper."

I riffled through my drawer and pulled out an old receipt from Bed Bath and Beyond and handed him a pen. The top chewed, it must have been Parker's.

He turned the light on next to his bed after hanging up. "They have a lead. In fact, they gave me a number."

"Who is it?"

"They didn't say. But here it is." He handed me the thin paper, the pen having pressed small holes into the corners of numbers seven and four. I counted the hours until sunrise and readied for another fitful sleep.

～

The next morning Bill found me sitting at the kitchen island staring at the number instead of frying up Sunday breakfast.

"Have you decided to call?"

"I'm nervous. I know, that sounds odd since I've been up most of the night, waiting."

"Not at all. Want me to give it a shot?"

I shook my head and lifted the phone, dialing the number.

"Maggie's Flowers." The woman didn't appear fatigued for such an early morning call.

"Hi, my name is Ellie Monroe, I got your number-"

"Ah, yes. I've been waiting. I can't talk now. Is there somewhere we can meet?"

I hesitated. She sounded kind, but this situation was abnormal.

She continued, "It can be public. Or not, it's your information you'd like to have." She seemed straight to the point.

"Of course, sorry. Do you know Floyd's?"

"Downtown?"

"Yes. Off of Main."

"10:00 am." The line went dead.

Bill said, "Do you want me to go with you? I can reschedule my viewing this morning."

"No, I think it'll be alright. I wouldn't want to scare her off. Her name was Maggie, it sounds like she owns a flower shop."

"Be careful. Looks can be deceiving."

I parked at my office and began the walk to Floyd's. It was a short distance and downtown had limited parking, even for its small size. Before leaving, I researched Maggie's Flowers and found her to have a positive reputation in the flower industry.

The doorway let out its joyous ding as I walked inside, deciding to order coffee while I waited. The smell of fresh beans hit me like a wave, the sensation hard to skew any direction but happy. From behind, someone tapped my shoulder.

"Are you Ellie?" A petite woman with fire-red hair and a smiling demeanor stood directly beside me, wearing a pink shirt that said, 'Maggie's Flowers: Let Beauty Bloom.' She said, "Sorry if I startled you."

"Hi, no not at all. I'm Ellie." We shook hands.

"Maggie. Small world, I work only a few blocks away."

"I'm sorry for the short notice-" I was going to continue, but she cut my words short.

"Let's wait until we are at a table. It's cooler today, how about a table outside? Less wandering ears."

I forgot we were here to discuss illegalities, it wasn't my usual coop de gras. "Of course." We grabbed our iced coffees and found a lone table tucked in the corner of the patio.

Maggie said, "So, how do you know Lucy and Mike?"

"My husband is in real estate, he's the social one. Has quite the Rolodex."

"My husband is the opposite. It works though since I'm the one talking with people all day. But you didn't meet me here to talk about husbands."

"Is it true you know about the artifacts?"

"I've more than heard about them, I've seen them. Or I should say, *some* of them."

"Where was this?"

"Before I get into this, I need some reassurances. I don't often tattle, if you want to call it that."

"Ok, what do you have in mind?"

She quipped, "What's your goal?"

"My goal? I'm not sure what Mike or Lucy told you, but I'm a researcher at the museum-"

"I know, they told me. It doesn't quite fit, though." She seemed smart, direct.

"What do you mean? Those pieces are the livelihood of my research. Three years of effort."

"Still, someone of your stature does not typically dig this deep, especially when the police are involved. Don't take this the wrong way. I'm not saying you shouldn't, it's just unlikely. There's another motivator, and I want to know what it is before continuing to tell you what I know."

I said, "What makes you sure I wouldn't break down a door to find what was stolen? If you're basing this off of a stereotype, you don't know enough about me to make that determination."

"It's amazing what one can glean from a first introduction."

"I'm not sure what to say." I leaned back in my chair, unsure how to match her quick rhetoric.

Maggie said, "Tell me why."

"What if that's private?"

"I don't owe you the information, you see. But I do want to impart what I know."

"And what if you find it unsatisfactory?"

"I'm not judgmental, but I do require truth."

"Truth from a stranger?"

"Those I do business with are hardly strangers."

I stirred the ice in my drink. "I wasn't lying, before. But there is more. I do want those artifacts returned to their rightful owners. They belong back at Chaco Canyon, with the Native American community, or in a museum. Regardless of my job status, I do believe in justice."

"I believe that. But, still. You wouldn't be risking this. At least not yet, not when more qualified professionals are trying to do exactly what you're doing."

"Even though I seem to be doing a better job? I'm here with you, aren't I?"

She smiled. "Alright, I'm listening."

"I also need reassurance." I said.

"Alright."

"The information I'm about to give you can't be linked with my name. I'm already treading lightly at the museum, I can't lose my job."

"I never kiss and tell."

I nodded. "There's a reward."

A look of surprise seemed to pass like a shadow over her eyes but was gone in an instant. "Keep talking."

"That's the brunt of it. A friend could use the money. And I get to return the artifacts, it's two-fold."

"How much?"

"I don't want to disclose that."

She seemed to ponder this new-found information. "You're sure about the reward? And it's monetary."

"Yes. My source is reliable." I thought about Paul. I trusted his information.

"Alright, I believe you." We both had our arms on the table, leaning in close. I didn't realize the intensity of the encounter until I relaxed, passing her test. She righted her glasses, seemingly finished with her questioning.

I asked, "Since I disclosed my information, I have to ask, why come here and help me? What's driving you?"

"That's fair, I suppose. I work next to another business, and we share a back room. At one point, the building owner separated one large complex and made it into two. More money in rent for him. It's not a bad arrangement since rent is less due to the shared back area. Works all around. But my neighbor has a couple of businesses he's running."

"Illegal?"

"I've been sure for some time that his bookstore is just a front, but he seems passionate about books, too, so it's hard to tell. You have to look deep."

"Are you talking about Mel's on Broadway?"

"One in the same."

"I've been there on more than one occasion."

"I'm not surprised, they seem to stock more first editions and rare pieces than most in the city. Which is also a red flag of sorts. I think it's his passion, as much as it is a front. He seems to get a high from acquiring the rarest finds. I'm sure most are illegally obtained but I don't think his ethics filter out the *way* things are acquired, just that he has them. And in our small downtown? No one would expect such an operation."

Our downtown was quaint. There were tall black lamp posts that housed holiday festival banners, flowers in the summer months, and lights in December. There were rows of small local businesses, restaurants, and taverns. It had the air of a friendly town. The museum was close, so tourists could walk Main Street and have time to stop by the museum. For a small town, our Natural History Museum was impressive, toted as one of the best in the region while also bringing in the much-needed tourism.

I said, "You don't agree with his methods, then?"

"As harsh as I may seem, I'm not in the business of scamming people to get ahead in life. I run an honest floral business and it's taken me *years* to build. That being said, I wasn't about to go telling the authorities. I didn't want to risk my business. Mel's workers are careful, I would be suspect."

"How did Lucy and Mike find out, then?"

"They're avid book lovers, and also use my shop to buy flowers anytime they have a party, which is often. They are friends to both Mel and I. I won't speak to their motives or ethics, that's hardly my business. But…"

"They're at Mel's more often than someone needs a book."

"Precisely. They aren't in his inner circle, though, and he isn't the most forthcoming with information unless you are a serious buyer. Lucy and Mike know I see things. They'll often call me up, wondering about a stolen statue or piece of jewelry. Mel has been next to me for years now, he isn't sloppy per se, but he's lowered his barrier when it comes to the back shared space. I've been vetted."

"So, they store illegal items next to your supplies? Just like that?"

"They have safes, of course, areas I cannot access. They've built walls and such. But recently, it appeared that a large shipment came through, and in short notice. They didn't have the space for everything, at least not where they usually store items. I've seen art pieces come through when I've been in the back, and I know where they typically store them."

"The artifacts were simply laying around?"

"Some were for a few nights, yes. I'm assuming some of the artifacts were in their lockboxes and safe but that's only a guess. We lock the front doors, of course, and they have a security system."

"You're sure you saw something, then?"

"I was in the back picking out wire for an arrangement. I saw these two large pots, beautiful. I didn't know their significance, of course. The turquoise is what caught my eye, they were decorated with a bar of fine liquid silver, adorned beautifully. I've never seen anything quite like it, especially in the back. I could tell they were expensive. And *large*."

"What did you do?"

"What did I do? Nothing, like always. I minded my own business, it's not like the stolen pottery was on the news."

"And you told Mike and Lucy when they called."

"I wasn't going to disclose anything, at first. I like them, but again, not worth losing my business if someone decides to have a loose tongue after too many drinks one night. I like being on the good side of Mel."

"Until something changed your mind."

"These men I've never seen before came by the bookstore and saw me in the back. Threatened me. It's not how Mel and I do it, we respect each other. We don't say a lot, but we agree on that, and I was working, not snooping. It's my space, too. I suspect Mel was in over his head, and let it fly. It wasn't a pretty conversation. I didn't like what they had to say. They were thugs. Large men. This shipment seemed different in a lot of ways."

"You still risked your business, then, telling Mike and Lucy and meeting with me. What tipped the scale?"

"I was angry, to be honest. One of their goons came through the store, walking around for an hour. Just *watching* me. I don't scare easily, but that was something else. He was armed. I was too scared to call the police." She leaned in close. "But I'll tell you what, *no one* threatens me in my own space. I also realized how many people were in on this, people were coming and going all day. Less chance that I would be judged the snitch, especially after his goon eyeballed me. I'm not beyond calling the police now, either. I'll hide certain indiscretions, but this is different. And speaking with you seemed a good place to start. Mike called me a few hours after that man left my store. He asked about jewelry and pottery with *turquoise*. I couldn't believe what I had witnessed, after hearing the origin."

"It's possibly the biggest find in Southwestern archeology to date. If they are genuine."

"It's incredible, and I've only seen a small tasting of the larger collection. I never even saw the jewelry."

"Can you tell me anything else that may be helpful?"

"I don't know you, but I think you should be careful. This isn't a rare book from the 1800s. This has caught the attention of some high bidders in low places. People with weapons and deep pockets."

"I've got help."

"It's your life, thought I'd give you the heads up. This isn't a game to these people, it's their livelihood." She took the straw out of her drink and began chewing on the end. "To answer your question, here's what I know. The pottery appeared Thursday morning when I came to work. There were more people in the shop than usual, which happens sometimes so it didn't seem strange. But they seemed rushed. And by Saturday, just yesterday, everything was gone."

"Did you see anyone loading the items?"

"They're smarter than to showcase their business in broad daylight. But…"

"What?"

"I have a Furbo."

"What on earth is a Furbo?"

"It's a camera for dogs. Sometimes I have to leave my sheltie at the shop while I'm making a run if there are too many flowers in the van or whatnot. She doesn't need to be eating 100 daisies for lunch. Anyways, there's a setting for person alerts. The camera turned on when someone walked by, but they're all in black, a blur. Not helpful. It *did,* however, catch a license plate number from the reflection in the window. And that's what I can give you." She handed me a small, meticulously folded piece of lavender colored paper. I unfolded it carefully and nodded, placing it in my back pocket. "I don't like those men, and I don't like their methods. Isn't good for business. I wish I had more information for you, now that I know what I know. But it should be a start."

Chapter 9
Sunday

I phoned Bill. The items were there only *yesterday*. How far could a massive load of stolen artifacts go? We were close, and it was only 10:00 a.m.

Bill arranged for Lulu and Parker to meet at our house. I quickly filled them in about Maggie, the thugs at Mel's, and their threats. We were seated around the kitchen island, the license plate number floating in the middle, a centerpiece too treasured to be touched.

Parker said, "Anyone know a police officer? You can't go checking people's license plates, right?"

"I'm not sure." Lulu was typing away on her laptop. "I think we can get someone, like a private eye, to do a tag trace. If they're willing to help. Our state has that ability restricted to the run of the mill gal."

Parker and I simultaneously said, "Shelby." He left to call.

"Think he will help?" Bill was looking at the license plate number, eyes narrowed.

I said, "He seemed to have an interest in our previous case, I think he's our best option."

Parker rushed back inside, "He can see us today, but let's be quick, he usually doesn't work on Sunday's." The four of us hopped in Bill's Jeep and headed for Shelby's office.

"I was hopin' that wouldn't be the last of ya's. And it seems you've multiplied. Is our guy up to something?"

I said, "Actually, this is unrelated."

"Well alrighty then. Sounds like you need a license plate checked." I handed him the paper. "What is this in regards too?"

"The place I work was robbed, we're trying to find the perpetrators."

"You guys seem to attract trouble. I'm not complaining, keeps the lights on."

"My friend caught this license plate in a reflection, from her Furbo."

"It's not the first. Dogs are out there savin' the day and gettin' treats to boot. Give me a moment."

He left us in the front waiting area as his heavy walk hit the hardwood floors and disappeared.

Lulu said, "I can't believe you have an in with a private detective. He acts like family. Didn't even raise an eye."

"Trust me, I'd rather not."

Bill said, "What are you guys planning to do with the name he pulls up? You're not ready for the police. Can't go knocking on someone's door asking if they're criminals."

Parker said, "I figured we'd decide once the name came up. I'm honestly not sure. Maybe we'll recognize them."

"You guys are figuring a lot of this out as you go."

I said, "We're not used to espionage, thank you very much."

Shelby returned. "Alright, seems the license plate pulled up a Barbara Heath. Name mean anything?"

"Nothing from the top of my head." I said, "Anything else?"

"I dug a little deeper. I pulled up the latest registration. Here's the address it's tied too, it's not too far. A disclaimer, though, about tag traces. A. the plate might be stolen. B. they might be using a friend's car, it happens all the time. They tell their friend they have a doctor's appointment and next thing ya know…. And C. it could be a fake plate. Doesn't seem like it with all I pulled, but if they're good, you never know. Here is the make and model." He handed over the information.

We thanked Shelby and convened outside, sitting on patio chairs left empty by the closed European market next door.

Parker said, "You're right, Bill. I'm not sure what to do with the information now that we have it."

Lulu said, "Why don't we drive by? That's not illegal. Just take a little peek."

Bill said, "This seems like a slippery slope. But if we're only driving by, alright."

"Thanks, dad." He shot Lulu a look.

≈

The house was only 15 minutes from Shelby's place.

As we drove, Lulu asked, "Are we still meeting up for book club this Wednesday?"

"Amelia made it sound like Sunny wasn't up for *that* again." I said, "and I don't blame them. Not with the boys home."

"We can do it at my place," Lulu said. "I have more liquor than you can shake a stick at."

Bill said, "Do you guys even read books or is it a guise for weekly parties now that you're in your thirties?"

"A little of both," she winked.

"Alright. Here we are, 3280 West Oak place. I'll park across the street."

Parker said, "This feels kinda dirty."

I said, "Remember, they were the ones who stole the artifacts."

"Or maybe their plates were stolen and now we're creeping on regular folk for no reason."

Bill said, "Looks a little richer than your average folk. What kind of car does it say it is?"

"A Toyota Tacoma. Silver."

"Nothing of the sort. Looks like they're home too. Or someone is." There was a red Camaro parked in the driveway.

"Well, I guess we'll hold on to this information," I said. "Won't hurt to have."

Lulu said, "There is a garage."

"We can't just wait here until they open it."

She thought a moment, "I think I could."

Bill said, "Alright, playtime is over." He pulled out of the spot. I don't know what I was expecting, but it wasn't this. A large suburban house on a common block. Nothing out of the ordinary, no people.

～

At home, Bill and I sat at the table, eating lunch. I said, "I don't want them to get away from us, you know? It was at Mel's bookstore yesterday. One day sitting idle could cost us."

"Ok, let's think about it. The artifacts were stolen Thursday morning. It sounds like Mel's wasn't expecting them, though. Which is interesting. You would think with stolen goods of that caliber that would be planned *much* in advance. Or you'd wait to steal it. Iron out the details."

"It's very interesting. Something didn't go as planned. Not like we can find out what that was, though."

"They were there until Saturday, presumably until a new place was found with more security. Maybe they want it close."

"You'd think they would want to move anything illegal far away from the place they stole it."

"Not necessarily. It still needs to be appraised, right? No one is going to buy it until it is. Or that's the assumption, at least."

"You're thinking they're keeping it close until they verify legitimacy?"

"No reason to risk a far move until they know exactly where they want to take it. Each move and mile requires people and people talk. Where is the one place you would store something with that type of value?"

"I don't know, somewhere I could keep an eye on it, somewhere I knew and trusted. But we don't know the people, we can't judge what they trust."

"True, but I'd say we're getting somewhere."

Chapter 10
Oak Street

Monday morning felt bleak. The rain was falling in torrential streams, making it seem hours earlier than it should, the coffee not strong enough to keep up. Lulu pulled into the driveway. Even she looked sullen in her black trench coat and boots, magazine over her head to save the hassle of her morning curl job.

She walked in without knocking. "El, something has been weighing on my mind."

"Good morning to you, too."

"The whole shebang. I was on the phone with Amelia last night, Sunny has been *especially* on edge. A real *treat*. I don't know if we're doing right by her, keeping her in the dark. I feel like shit about it."

"I know, I feel the same. But it's complicated. We have to tell ourselves we're doing this for her."

Lulu said, "Parker wants to wait until he has more information on Sunny, but I'm not sure I agree anymore, and I'm not sure that information is ever coming."

I popped a Tylenol. "What are you thinking?"

"We're allowed to have our own thoughts about this. We don't have to agree with him."

"Ok, but I still think we should speak to Parker about this."

"I know, I'm not in the business of going behind someone's back. Especially Parker."

"I think you ought to know something." I topped Lulu's thermos off. "Before we get into this with him."

"Ok, I'm listening."

"He's in love with Amelia."

Lulu thought a moment. "That kind of changes things, doesn't it?"

"It does and it doesn't. You don't seem surprised."

"It's crossed my mind, but they've never seemed inappropriate, you know."

"No, and he's respectful of her space. But it's why he wants to wait to tell her. He's afraid that with the information Sunny has on him…"

"She'll think him a pariah. That Sunny will spin a wild tale."

"Something like that."

"What a situation."

"Did she say anything about the vandalism to the house? Anything from the police?"

"Dead ends left and right." Lulu chugged her thick, black coffee.

I said, "Since you're a little early-"

"You wanna drive by the house on Oak again?"

"Read my mind."

The rain continued to pour heavily. We ran to her car, the smell of wet hair and humidity lingering in the car as Led Zeppelin played loudly from the speakers.

"Do you think this is crazy? I feel like a stalker." I said loudly over the music as I turned it down.

"If it gets us two hundred G's, I don't know how much I care." She started fixing her eyeliner in the mirror, fingers moving quickly as if a construct of muscle memory. "We'll just do a quick swing by."

The driveway was perfectly the same, but the rain forced a haunted vibrato on the house. I shivered.

"Why does it seem so eerie?" I said.

"Is my eyeliner scaring you?"

"That must be it, not the menacing feel from the house we're stalking. Our near-criminal activities. Must be the makeup."

"Oh, *shit* El, the garage is opening."

"Here we go."

We watched as the garage lifted, revealing a silver Tacoma, as Shelby's handwritten note described.

Lulu gasped, "Shit. *Shit.* What do we do? It's *them.*"

"I don't know, take a picture?" I fumbled to grab my phone out of the leather briefcase sitting at my feet. Lulu suddenly threw her hand across the seat, hitting my arm. I yelled, "Ow, *what?*" I lifted my head. My mouth opened in shock. I couldn't believe what I was witnessing. "It can't be him. No chance."

"The rain is so heavy, El, but I think it *is.*" I started to fidget with her windshield wipers. "El they're on the highest setting for crying out loud." She swatted my hand away and paused. "Why is he sitting there? Did he see us?"

"Maybe he's meditating before going into a workplace full of *stalkers.*"

"That can't be Hugh."

"Sure looks like him. He hardly fits in the driver's seat. How many people do you know that large? I can feel his glare from here."

"But the plates were out to a Barbara Heath?"

"Ohhhh."

"What?"

"Lu, that's his *wife.* Hugh's second wife. They've both been married before. She didn't take his name."

"Are you sure?"

"100%. I don't know about the last name, but her name is Barbara. And he's sure as shit driving that truck right now."

She said, "Do you think he can see us? Does he know what I drive?" His truck pulled from the garage and stopped at the end of the driveway as Lulu ducked.

"*Lu.*" I followed suit, her small car making us converge in an awkward position. "What on earth?"

"If that's her truck…"

"He might not even know."

"Or he drove it that night to Mel's. Or they're in on it together."

"Why are we whispering?"

"I feel like he can hear us through the metal." She was yell whispering, her leg propped over the stick shift and her heal an inch from my eye.

"Has he left?"

"Sorry El, but I left my x-ray vision at home."

I peeked above the dash. "He's gone. To work. *Our* work."

"What do we do?"

"We have to go in and act normal. He's our boss, maybe we wont see much of him today."

"I've never felt more 30 than at this exact moment. I think I'm stuck in this position forever." I pushed her leg back to where it belonged. We sat for a minute, the rain pelting harder against the windshield, the loud noise making me fidget. "Do you think he saw us?"

"I don't think so. And with the rain?"

Lulu said, "Am I going to have to go into witness protection?"

"I don't think it works that way." I took a deep breath. "Alright let's do this. We can't be late. Pedal to the metal."

We parked in our usual spot, sticking to routine. "How have I never noticed what he drives until now?" Lulu said. "Could have been helpful, I don't know, say, *yesterday.*"

"I couldn't tell you what *anyone* drives who works here. This entire situation is reminding me how unobservant I am."

"Here we are." Lulu took a deep breath and turned off the wipers, our trepidation stark.

We ran through the lingering rain, the puddles making our ankles feel dirty and used for too early in the day. When we got to our respective offices, I jumped as Hugh entered with his assistant and a man I had never seen before.

"Ellie, I want you to meet Greg. He's been hired by the museum heads to help me with the investigation."

"Nice to meet you." His hand was meek, and he seemed small next to Hugh. As anyone would, I suppose.

"He's going to be digging around. Don't make his life harder." He stared at me for an uncomfortable second. "We're going to be reviewing each floor, documentation, dates. Starting with the archivists. We'll hit you tomorrow. Have your files available." And with that, they walked out. Our office had a middle area with a large conference table directly in the center, usually littered with photographs and words scattered about numerous project documentation. My office was to the right of the table upon entering, and Gaby had a small desk outside my door. There were two other full-time researchers with offices around the perimeter, and interns housed in desks scattered about the open space. It was small but decorated such that it felt open and warm. When Hugh exited, the area seemed to open wider, his stature and harsh demeanor absorbing any extra space available.

Lulu entered shortly after Hugh left. She said, "Well, guess I'm without an office today."

"They're not letting you work?"

"They don't want me tampering with potential evidence." She mimicked quotations and rolled her eyes.

"Are they busy?"

"They pulled archived boxes from the beginning of the year, on digs not part of this robbery. I'm guessing it'll be awhile. Hugh seems annoyed with his little helper, though. Makes me wonder if our discovery this morning is true. *If Hugh is in on the robbery, he certainly wouldn't be excited about an internal investigation.*"

"Is Hugh staying with them?"

"I don't know his *lunch* plans El, I scattered the moment they entered. Saw his big ass foot pass my office door jam and said *nope*. Not today. I already know more than I should by the name of one large silver Toyota Tacoma."

"If they're going to be awhile…"

"You're plotting."

"Hugh's office is on the third floor, across the mezzanine."

"Oh no. He probably has cameras in there. You want to snoop?" Her stiletto started tapping to the beat of my increasing heart rate.

"He's not allowed to have cameras remember? After that security guard got in trouble. They pulled all surveillance until further notice. And he's with his assistant."

"Yeah, all *known* surveillance."

"I think it's worth a shot."

Lulu sat, staring at me, foot dancing. "Alright, let's walk by, see what it looks like. We don't have to go in. Just a glance."

We casually exited my office and headed to the elevator. "Should we take the stairs?"

"Good point." Lulu's high heels made an exaggerated echo throughout the corridor as we made our way to the third floor.

I said, "So much for stealth."

"If you're referring to the heals, fashion is pain, El."

The stairwell smelled like fresh paint and soil and was making my headache worse. When we finally arrived, the hall was surprisingly vacant. "This is creepy," I said.

"I don't know about this. First, his house. Now his office? How lucky can two people be? We're bound to be discovered. We're just about *asking* for it."

"If anyone sees us, we'll just say we're looking for Hugh and we have a question about the dig." We opened the door that housed his office as well as the other administrators. It was a large area, fit with glass walls overlooking the lower floors. A large pterodactyl hung inches from the small waiting area, its eyes black and glossy. They seemed to know what we were up to, judging. We approached his door and Lulu turned the knob.

She said, "It's locked."

I walked to his assistant's desk and started riffling through the drawers. "When does an assistant not have an extra key to the boss's office?"

"Assuming he didn't take it with him."

"I don't know why he would, he's with Hugh." We began looking through his belongings, trying to keep everything in its original place.

Lulu said, "I don't think it's here. I don't like this."

"Hold on." I slid out the wooden part of the desk holding the keyboard, feeling its underside. "People are rarely *that* creative." I smiled. "Might as well be under his welcome mat." I held out a small brass key, tape flapping across its base. We walked to his door and slid the key inside. It opened.

Lulu said, "This could get us fired. *Arrested.*"

"From the sound of it, I'm not getting my grant. Not that I want to go out in a blazing ring of fire, but I'm jobless either way."

"Let's get this over with."

Walking inside, his office was surprisingly cluttered. I had only been inside a handful of times, and it looked different than I remembered. It reeked of chaos, lost time.

Lulu said, "This reads strange. What are we looking for, exactly? It's not like he would keep plans for mass destruction lying around."

"Guess we won't know until we see it." At first, we were careful, touching little. We didn't attempt his computer knowing it would be protected, and we didn't want the screen lit if he came back. Five minutes in, we had folders open and Lulu was standing on a guest chair looking behind a fern.

She said, "El I don't see anything. We can't stay here much longer. I'm going to puke from nerves. Think he would notice if I hurled in his fern?"

As we began cleaning up, placing items back into the clutter from where they came, the phone rang. Lulu didn't miss a beat and ran over.

I whispered, "What are you doing?"

"Oh, I know phones. Back when I was an admin assistant in college, these things would bug out constantly. Learned a few tricks. It looks like the same brand, not a lot of upgrading, it appears." The ringing continued, then halted as it switched to voicemail and Lu pressed a sequence on the keypad. The voicemail turned to speaker. She turned it down to the lowest setting and we crouched over the plastic piece of technology. Beasts waiting for their next meal.

"This is loud, someone could hear."

"Shh."

Click. "This is Hugh Benson, Director of Research and Development at the Dove Park Natural History Museum of Art and Sciences. You have reached a confidential voicemail. I will return calls within normal business hours, Monday through Friday. Have a wonderful day." Lulu made a puking gesture with her finger in her mouth.

"Hugh, it's Rick. We have secured a new place for the research supplies. Everything has been officially moved as of last night, the larger supplies were hauled over Saturday evening. Call me back, but we're on track for Thursday."

Lulu whispered. "*Boring.* Let's get out of here."

We stood to leave but halted at the sound of the main office door clicking shut. We rushed to the far wall, out of view from Hugh's windows.

"*Shit.*" Lulu wiped the sweat off of her forehead. "Should we sit and act like we're waiting for him?"

As my mind raced for an answer, his office door hesitantly opened. There was nowhere to hide. Time stopped before we could think to move, our bodies frozen in the cluttered space of his office.

A man's voice said, "Ellie?"

"Paul?"

"What are you guys doing here? Against Hugh's wall?"

I sighed in relief, Lulu looked verbally stunned. "Have you seen Hugh?"

"He's on his way back up, I'd suggest getting out of here, as soon as possible. If you're doing what I presume."

"What are *you* doing here?" Lulu questioned as we ambled out.

"I have an actual business-related question if you must know. I'm not *sneaking* about like some amateur sleuth."

We skirted into the main lobby of the admin office, locking the door. I ran to place the key back in its spot as Hugh and his two henchmen waltzed in. His assistant's keyboard slammed down as they looked up in surprise.

Hugh stepped back, "What are you ladies doing?"

"We were looking for you," I said.

"I was in Lulu's office, as I said not but thirty minutes ago." He looked at his watch. His face fell. Suspicion.

Paul chimed in, "I'm sorry, that must have been me. I saw them in the hall and said you wanted to see them in your office."

"Why would you say that?"

"I thought you wanted to speak with them. Apologies."

He let out a gruff sound from the back of his throat. "Yes, I spoke with them this morning. Nothing more ladies, back to the office. Mrs. Banks, you can utilize your office for the next hour. We'll be back shortly after our meeting. You'll need to vacate upon our return. But don't let that be an excuse not to work, take your laptop with you." Hugh hated calling Lulu by her first name. Years ago, we overheard him say that it was a name for children, not working professionals.

"Absolutely, thank you," Lulu said as we walked out of the room. Once inside the elevator, we collapsed against the glass siding.

"Oh my gosh, Lulu."

"That was too close for comfort. I don't think I can work. I'm *spent.*"

"You didn't vomit, I take it as a win."

"A good day for the fern."

"Well, it sounds like you only have to sit around for an hour." I said.

"I'm not going in there, feels tainted. Their grubby hands have been all over my things. I'm sitting with you until lunch."

We made our way back to my office. Lulu said, "Is it strange that I want to lock your door? I feel like I want to run inside a hole."

"Probably didn't help that you had four cups of coffee this morning."

"Well, that was a waste of time. Not the coffee, the office. Coffee is *never* a waste of time."

"Maybe it wasn't."

"I don't know what we expected. It's like with Sunny and those men, we know they're up to something shady, we can't prove it. Another dead end."

At the mention of Sunny, something clicked. I thought a moment. "Lulu…"

She sat up straight. "Tell me you remembered something."

"Wait. Let me piece this together." I reached into my desk and produced copies of the notes from Shelby. I opened it, fanning out the information. "Here it is, look." I spun the folder and held my finger on the names of the men accompanying Sunny.

She said, "Sunny exited with a man by the name of Antonio, and a man by the name of Rick, who presented with a high voice…are you saying this is the same Rick we just heard on Hugh's voicemail?"

I said, "It is a common name…perhaps not."

"Oh shit. *Shit.* He *does* have a higher voice than normal. Tell me what you and Parker heard outside of Sunny's office."

"The man that met with Sunny, he was Antonio. He got off the phone with a Rick saying he secured a location for the goods. Said they would get the haul the next day, which was *Thursday.* But that their original plan fell through, and it would be the following Thursday until they could take the items to the main location. Seems they were in a bit of a tough spot finding a new place."

"El, everything you've told me parallels with what Rick said on the voicemail. They found a new spot. That's why Mel's Bookstore didn't expect such a large haul, it was a band-aid until they found something else. No wonder items were laying around, they had no choice. And didn't Maggie say the items were removed on Saturday?"

"Yes, Lulu, she did. This can't be a coincidence. You know what this means…"

She said, "That Hugh is in on the theft, with *Sunny*."

"That's how the robbery was so seamless, and how they knew where the cameras were. Hugh was able to manipulate everything."

"What else did you overhear Antonio say?"

"They talked about the Mirabelle being the main location."

"The hotel down south?"

"Yes, but it's not available until Thursday. Sunny said they were going to drive down on Wednesday night with the haul."

Lulu said, "This means the artifacts are close until they move them Wednesday. That means we have two days until they are potentially out of reach."

"Unless something has changed. Lu, we discovered that not only is my boss in on the art theft but that Amelia's *husband* is in on it too. If we're correct, this is massive." I flipped through the manilla envelope from Shelby. "It does explain some of Sunny's behavior though. From what Shelby said, Antonio, Rick, and Sunny had a concealed meeting with a group of wealthy individuals at the Sky Lounge. There were bodyguards and money. That must have been artifact related."

"I wish it were anyone but Sunny. Hugh, I mean that's honestly no surprise there. But Amelia's husband?"

"I know. Do we tell the police?" I felt like my breath could hardly catch up with our fast-paced discovery.

"I still don't think we have enough. We don't know where the artifacts are, and we've been breaking and entering. All the information we have is privileged, private. No one will be able to verify its legitimacy. They'll take one listen to Rick's name and laugh us out of the office, what a connection. A simple, common name."

"So, what do we do?"

Lulu bit her lip. "I think we should convince Amelia to hold book night Wednesday. I know I said we'd do it at my place, but if we can get her to do it-"

"You think the artifacts are at the house?"

"I'm not sure about that, but *something* ought to be. It sounds like Sunny is up high in this, there would be evidence lodged somewhere. And if not, we don't lose anything. If we get a chance to snoop, we take it."

"You know, Bill and I were talking. He said it would be somewhere they trust, somewhere close. They have a lot of land and he just got that security system."

"And where in Dove Park can you store things clandestinely?"

"Certainly not at the central storage."

"Exactly. Security cameras dot a lot of those places, they'd want it private. And they don't live that far from Mel's, what, a ten-minute drive?"

"I see your point, but don't forget about the vandals. Let's not get carried away and risk our safety having it at Amelia's. And the boy's safety. They're home now."

"I'll have the boys over that night. Gabe has been wanting to see them anyways. Rex can play ball with them until I get home, shove an Xbox controller in their hands, and next thing you'll know it's two in the morning. We'll be safe. So far, they haven't done anything risking our safety, it's all to send a message."

"Alright, let's try it. But if Amelia isn't ok with this, we need a plan B."

"Deal."

Chapter 11
Under the Willow

Standing outside Amelia's house that following Wednesday I was struck by how much had changed in a few short weeks. The stained-glass window was currently being replaced by a much smaller, less extravagant piece. Sunny didn't care what replaced his gift, so Amelia picked a local artist to craft a new stained window. The scaffolding was still leaning against the side of the house as I pulled in. I felt less of a shiver staring at the stone walls and more of a feeling of revival, something new in the midst but not yet complete.

Hannah walked up, "What are you looking at?"

"The window. I like it, even though it's not finished yet."

"Seems happier somehow, doesn't it?"

I nodded. "How is everything?" I felt like I hadn't spoken to Hannah in ages, though only a week had passed. Our newfound information seemed to alter the pacing of time. We arrived early and sat under the large weeping willow in front of the house, near a brown bridge that arched over a meandering stream. The juxtaposition between the serene yard and our reasoning for holding book club at Amelia's was stark.

"It's going." She said. "Work is tense, but that seems a constant, you know?"

"I feel that. I always wondered what it would be like, working in a hospital, with children. It must be hard to come home sometimes. Heavy."

"It is. And sometimes you're so close to helping someone, and they slip past your fingers. You can only do so much, I suppose."

Georgia startled us by throwing a rock in our direction. She said, "Are we camping?"

Hannah replied, "Under this tree, it would be more like glamping."

Georgia plopped to my right. "It's beautiful out, I could soak this up all summer." The temperature had allowed for a warm night, a rare glimpse into what Fall would bring, the memories of winter long forgotten. It was only six and the crickets were chirping, setting the tone for summer. "I'm glad we're still having book night at Mel's. What convinced Sunny?"

Hannah said, "Amelia said they had a pretty big fight, I don't think he wants us here, to be honest. But it's not like she asks for a lot."

"He seems different than when we first met them together, right? Or was I blinded by the mirage of first-time lovers?" Georgia lifted her hair off of her neck, fanning the sweat beads starting to accumulate.

"No, I think something shifted. Maybe his job, maybe a mid-life crisis."

I said, "I think Amelia is feeling that a little, too."

"I've kind of been re-thinking my career choice," Hannah said.

"I thought you loved being an occupational therapist?"

She sighed. "Sometimes the stress is hard, and the confidentiality. Not being able to talk about it."

I sifted my hands through the thick grass. "You can always talk to us, even if it's limited in what you can say. What would you want to do if you switched jobs?"

"I feel too old to go back to school, so I'm not sure. My undergrad is in criminal justice. That leaves options."

"You're never too old to go back to school."

Georgia dragged her large purse over. "This is a heavy conversation without libations." She pulled a bottle of wine out of her purse.

Hannah said, "Oh, here." She handed Georgia her keychain that had a collapsible corkscrew attached.

"You're a magical person sometimes."

I wanted severely to tell both Georgia and Hannah about our discovery, about everything. It seemed unfair to shield them, to have something dividing us. I wondered if they felt it, a shift, something indescribable but present. A shadow in the room.

Georgia took a swig, "Do you think wine companies sponsor organizations? Like book clubs?" Hannah laughed. "Braid my hair, will you? It's too warm."

Hannah said, "You can never have your hair down for five seconds regardless of the season." Hannah swung her legs around Georgia's back and started running her fingers through the strands. She continued, "I thought about being a lawyer, once upon a time."

"You'd make a good lawyer." I said, "You always know what to say, and speak so eloquently." I took a swig.

Georgia said, "That makes one of us."

Hannah said, "With four kids I'm surprised you're able to get out of the house at all. You amaze me sometimes Miss Georgia."

"You know, I think I've mastered what I've been searching for. A balance between life and work. Going part-time at the hospital was the best decision I ever made, and I'm still able to keep up. It's tough, the medical field is always changing. I feel like once you leave for even a year, they think you use trephining techniques, rocks, and chisels."

I said, "If Bill and I ever decide to have kids, I'd want to do the same. Find a part-time job I really like."

Hannah asked, "Have you started trying? Or it's just a thought."

"Not exactly, we're not using a calendar if that's what you mean. I turn 30 next year, so I do feel a bit like Mother Nature is sending gentle reminders."

Hannah said, "I can't wait to be an auntie to another little one. We haven't had a baby in the group for some time. What, Harley must turn four this year?"

Georgia smiled, "Four turning fifteen."

"I want to take her for ice cream, her and her sister. It'll be a girl's day."

"They'd love that."

I looked at the time, the reality of the situation present. Wherever Sunny and his men decided to store the artifacts, they would be gone tonight. Sunny would be making the trip down south, to the Mirabelle, based on the information we gleaned from his chat with Antonio. Once it arrived down south, our chances were slim for retrieval. Parker, Bill, Lulu, and I decided that Amelia and Sunny's house was the only location that made sense, and the only place we could approach safely. Anywhere else would be guarded and unknown. We were welcome here, invited. At least by Amelia. Bill decided to stay close and went to Spirits in case we needed him.

I looked at our peaceful moment. It seemed flawless, the eye of the storm held over our small group under the tree, waiting to pass and showcase its turmoil. We sat in comfortable silence, Georgia slowly peeling the label off of the wine bottle while Hannah carefully twisted strands of her hair together in an intricate weave. I laid on my back, peering at the sky through the willow's tender branches. A cool breeze kissed my cheeks.

Amelia poked her head out of the front door. "I thought I heard some beauties on the lawn." Georgia summoned her as Parker walked up the drive. The look on his face broke the spell, the reality of the night clear. And for the first time, I saw it. The anxiety of the night switched for that of adoration. Parker hadn't realized we were sitting under the willow as he watched Amelia. She stopped at her flower garden on her way to us, picking at the browned leaves, feeling for moisture, her white dress dotted with small yellow circles fluttered with the breeze. Parker had the everlasting expression of love across his features, and as she stood to walk to the willow, he forced a smile, realizing his group was waiting for him just feet to his right. His spell was broken, too.

Lulu would be late. We decided she had a better opportunity to look around with no one pondering her whereabouts. I was glad to be on the front lawn, able to see if anyone walked through the door. It remained quiet outside of our small book club.

Amelia and Parker met us on the ground, a circle forming without thought. Amelia's dress splayed as she gently sat next to Georgia, who patted her hair in acceptance and threw a kiss to Hannah.

I leaned on my elbow, our book pick, the *Scarlet Letter* sitting to my front. "Lulu will be a little late today."

Amelia said, "She was so nice to have the boys over for the night."

Georgia said, "Did you miss them terribly?"

"I did. It was starting to feel like a part of me was missing. Like I was forgetting something."

"It feels nice at first, the summer camps and short vacations, then the next thing you know, you're looking up pictures when they were a baby. By the way Amelia, why can't *we* get invited to stay in Napa Valley with your sister?"

"You'd never sober up enough to make it back." Hannah laughed as she pulled grass between her fingers.

"Ha-ha."

"It's going to get dark fairly late tonight," Amelia said, "why don't we do book club outside?"

I said, "Sounds refreshing."

Amelia said, "Give me a minute, let me grab some things." Parker stood to help her up, his hand naturally falling to the curve of her back. I texted Lulu to let her know that we were under the willow. She'd have to park up the street and out of earshot from the group.

I asked, "Is Sunny around tonight? Or is he hiding from us?"

Georgia said, "We are pretty menacing. Those who read *books*. The house is a monstrosity, he doesn't have to go far to avoid us. I feel no ill will taking over his lawn at the moment."

Hannah asked, "I haven't seen him tonight, I'm surprised he's not ambling around, throwing insults."

"I thought you were team Sunny," Georgia folded the wine's label into a tidy square.

Hannah paused a moment. "I'm team whatever Amelia decides. My thoughts on Sunny are hardly what matters at the moment."

131

As if on cue, Sunny pulled up in their red SUV, slowing to peer at us.

Georgia said, "The man of the hour." She had no idea how true that was.

Hannah rose to make a call, her Birkenstocks thrown to the side of the tree, her casual manner seeming stiff. Sunny had a way of transforming a room.

Parker and Amelia exited the house with their housekeeper, Marge, holding a table, folding chairs and a basket of food.

Georgia said, "A tablecloth. Amelia, you do amaze."

She said, "Just because we're outside doesn't mean we're suddenly *barbaric*." Marge set the cloth over the table and clipped it along its sides, all of us chatting. My mind kept pulling me from the feel goodness of the moment to the possibility of the artifacts only feet away. I was suddenly angry at Sunny, for ruining this moment, for bringing us along his ride. We didn't ask for this, Amelia certainly didn't.

Hannah walked back, looking around.

Amelia said, "Everything alright Hannah?"

"Just work stuff." She seemed to shake it off. "I'm really glad we decided to have book club here. It is just what I needed."

Amelia smiled and handed her a plate with bread. "Well, good for you, I've made your favorite."

"Is this Soda Bread?" Hannah took a bite and closed her eyes.

"When I'm stressed, I bake." Amelia laid out four other sweet treats.

"I'm glad you're from Ireland. Hand me that marmalade." Hannah lathered on a good helping and pulled out a chair as we joined her.

"And, bread pudding for Parker." She handed him a plate, but he looked morose. He hadn't said much today. I would be concerned if I didn't understand his trepidation. Amelia's future seemed to hang in the balance, her unknowingness to the situation making it bleak. Somewhere deep inside, we knew hiding this information might be the wrong choice. We hoped it was the better wrong choice.

"You really are the best baker," Hannah said.

"You only say that to keep me bringing them around."

"I'm serious, I won't be able to talk about the book. My mouth is going to be otherwise occupied."

Georgia started laughing, "That's what she said-"

Amelia cut her off, "Georgia, so unladylike." Even Amelia had a smirk as Georgia almost fell out of her chair laughing, head thrown back.

I said, "I do love you guys."

"I won't tell Bill." Georgia winked.

Hannah said, "I hate to sound morose, but what if there is another letter tonight? Another message over a sheet?"

It was silent. The wind moved through the tree's tendrils slowly, reverberating a small, rattling sound.

Georgia said, "Then we address it. The person in question has already been given until the gala, so I don't believe we're in danger. Why risk something violent when the task has been given and the time frame not yet expired?"

Amelia said, "I agree. And I believe I've done nothing to warrant this type of attention, or any of us, for that matter. I say we continue enjoying our night. It's what Lulu said to convince me to house it here tonight. Why let them win yet again? We're not criminals."

Georgia said, "And maybe we'll catch someone in the act. How many weeks can go by without someone seeing something? Anyways, let's talk books. Enough of this depressing chatter."

I said, "Had anyone read the *Scarlet Letter* before this week?"

"I was supposed to for school," Hannah wiped the crumbs from her lips, "but never finished. I don't remember why."

I said, "Same here. It always felt like if a book were forced, it wouldn't be a good read. A pity, though. I liked this one."

"Did you know it was written in 1850?"

"Not at all."

Amelia said, "Should we start without Lulu? I'd hate to miss all of her silly jabs about the protagonist."

I looked around the front yard. We said she would be thirty minutes late, and it was already forty minutes after six. I checked my phone, there was a message. I stood up, "Let me give her a quick call, you guys eat away."

Georgia said, "Don't have to tell me twice."

I walked out of earshot from the group. It read:

> *"I parked up the hill and I'm thru the front door,*
> *Marge saw. Said I needed bathroom. I'm on the second*
> *floor."*

I texted back:

> *"anything? Let me know if you need help…Don't*
> *get caught."*

I walked back to the group.

Amelia said, "Is she close?"

"She'll be a couple of minutes I think."

Georgia said, "I'm in no rush, let's wait for a little."

My phone dinged again, I looked down.

> *"I need Parker. Second floor."*

I looked at Parker, who seemed lost in a daze. I forwarded him the text. I said, "Hey Parker, Lulu thinks you're ignoring her texts, she told you she'd be late earlier and you didn't respond."

He snapped out of his trance and looked down. He said, "While we wait for Lulu, I'm going to use the little boy's room."

And suddenly the machine cogs were reeling. I sat back down, antsy, wondering what was happening in the house. Unexpectedly, a blue truck pulled into their large driveway, and Antonio stepped out, followed by Rick. My heart stopped. I fumbled for my phone as I texted Lulu about their arrival. Their presence could only mean one thing.

I said, "Guess the wine hit me quick, I'll be right back. Need anything from inside while we wait, Amelia?"

"Yeah if you could grab the pile of napkins on the side table by the entrance, I forgot them."

I nodded and walked quickly as I could without looking suspicious. The willow was at the bottom of a small hill. Looking back, I could no longer see the tree as foliage blocked the way. I peered from behind a large oak and witnessed Antonio handing Rick a sizable plastic storage container.

My phone made a ding as I fumbled to turn it to vibrate.

It was Lulu. It said:

Coming back down. Meet us in the kitchen.

I replied:

On way. The men are in the driveway.

I debated whether it mattered that Antonio and Rick see me. The front door was next to where they parked, but there were side doors. I thought I'd better not risk it. I made my way up the stairs and tried the side door. It was locked, but Marge was inside. She let me in.

"Thank you, Marge."

"No worries." She smiled, then went directly back to the guest bedroom downstairs. She didn't seem to care one way or the other what door I threw myself through. I was a common enough presence.

I was the first to arrive in the kitchen and I poured a glass of water. I wanted to stay sober. Lulu and Parker finally waltzed in. She said, "I had Parker show me the hidden closet next to Sunny's office."

"Was Sunny inside?"

"He was. Still is, I think."

"What did he say?"

"Not a lot, unfortunately."

"Did you look around?"

"That's the good part. Once I realized Sunny was keeping himself occupied, I waited for Parker, and he led me to the third floor."

"What's up there?"

"It's smaller, a few extra rooms. And the entrance to the attic."

"You checked their *attic?*"

"There was nothing there. Old boxes and the likes. Nothing like what we are looking for."

"You're killing me."

"So, then we thought, not a lot of time. We made good progress, we'll head back to book club. Then he remembered."

Parker said, "There is another secret door."

"Where?"

"In the kitchen."

I turned towards Parker. He opened two long teal cabinets flush and identical with the other cabinetry in the kitchen. Shelving appeared, holding boxes of typical pantry goods, pasta and beans. Nothing out of the ordinary. He placed his hand high on the top shelf. *Click*. He pulled the left pantry shelving towards himself, and another room appeared. Inside, I glimpsed a row of boxes.

Suddenly, the front door to the home opened. The main entryway tagged on to the living room, and the kitchen was a few steps forward to the left. We were invisible at the moment. Parker quickly shut the door and reached for glasses of wine.

Amelia said, "Lulu! I didn't see you come up."

"I thought I'd come straight to where the goods are."

Georgia said, "Are you three hiding out? It's beautiful under the tree. Come join us. We're ready to talk adultery and red letters. But I needed more treats, Amelia was holding out on her sugar cookies." She reached over by the oven and grabbed four, placing them in her pocket.

Amelia said, "Georgia! Have a napkin."

"They're not *you're* pockets." Georgia left, sprinkles falling as she walked. Amelia stayed back with us. I wasn't sure how much longer we could stall. We did what we could, for now. But what was behind those pantry doors?

Chapter 12
Pluck up a Spirit

Amelia spun a strand of hair around her finger as she read. "'She could no longer borrow from the future to ease her present grief,'" We continued to chat under the willow as my mind wandered elsewhere.

Hannah said, "I think we all do a little bit of that."

"Borrowing from your future is only setting yourself up for future failure," Georgia said.

Lulu replied, "Unless the only way to survive in the now is doing so. Sometimes people need to get past the stage they are in."

"Fair point," Hannah said.

Amelia said, "This one rings true for me, 'unless people are more than commonly disagreeable, it is my foolish habit to contract a kindness for them.'"

Lulu said, "That *is* you. You are kind to most, but I don't think to a fault. Kindness is a gift, I think. And you wear it splendidly."

She said, "I hope it's not my red letter."

Parker said, "I hate to break up the party, but I left my cell inside. I'll be right back." He stood. I couldn't find a suitable reason to follow. I held my cell phone close as Lulu glanced my direction. There was nothing else to be done. Him leaving felt like a band-aid pulled off the fine hair of the arms. This was the second time he left the table, I wasn't the only one to notice.

The minutes dragged as we delved into the world of the *Scarlet Letter*. After a pause in the conversation, there came a distant noise, a wail. It crept closer, louder. The five of us looked up, shocked, as police sirens pulled into the circular driveway.

Amelia jumped to standing, "What is going on?" She started to run up the hill as Lulu caught up with her.

Lulu said, "You don't know why they're here, Amelia, slow down. This could be dangerous." She gently touched her shoulder.

Amelia seemed angry. "My house has been nothing but a crime scene for the past few weeks. I have to see what is going on." Her slight outburst seemed to stun Lulu and she backed off, letting her run to the house. We followed behind.

Lulu said, "If this isn't related to the theft, we might be able to sneak in. This could be an ample distraction."

"You're insane, the *police* are here, and you want to break and enter?"

"We've been allowed entry, we're not taking a pin to a lock for crying out loud. We don't have time to ague."

"Let's see what is going on."

At the top of the driveway, we found Sunny outside of the main doorway and three police officers standing at his front. Amelia flanked his side and said, "Honey what is this?"

His voice sounded friendly, confused. "Someone called the police and said we were storing illegal artifacts."

She said, "Wait, us? Thieves? What artifacts?" She turned to Sunny, "this has nothing to do with the recent vandalism?"

The police officer standing closest replied, "I have heard about your recent intrusions, ma'am. But unfortunately, this is unrelated. We've had a call into the station about recently stolen artifacts from the museum. There is reason to believe they may be stored here."

"I'm not sure why you'd have that idea." She turned to Sunny.

"Sounds like someone is after us. All of the vandalism has happened on a Wednesday, I'm not surprised this occurred when it did." He glanced our direction.

We were standing about fifty feet away and were still able to hear the conversation. Lulu leaned in, "El, he's *buying time.*"

"Should we say something?"

"We don't have anything concrete. And we'd have to do this in front of Amelia, how humiliating for her. She'd wonder why we knew and never told her, and Parker never opened the kitchen door enough to see inside. What if the artifacts aren't here?"

"I feel like all we do is hide information, Lu. Antonio and Rick are here, the odds that the artifacts are here..." We continued to whisper as Hannah and Georgia walked up.

Hannah said, "What is this?"

"Someone called in a tip that stolen artifacts are being kept at their house." I said. "He hasn't let the police inside. I don't know if they have a warrant."

Hannah nodded, walking back to the willow. Georgia said she had to get back home to the kids and to keep her posted. She blew a kiss to Amelia.

Lulu said, "I know we have information, but is it ours to unleash? Are we hiding anything?"

"You're sounding like Parker. And yes, we have information that would be quite helpful, no doubt."

"Nothing wrong with being like Parker. What, we tell the police our story with no proof? They've already been tipped off. We can't say we heard a conversation outside Sunny's office without his knowledge. What if they think we're in on the vandalism? The shoe fits. We're here every Wednesday. The vandalism includes *book quotes*."

I sighed. "Fine, let's see what happens. I'm glad they're here, it makes me feel better about keeping our information private."

Sunny continued to speak with the police in a roundabout manner. Lulu said, "Where is Parker anyways?"

"Good question."

As if on cue, Parker appeared on the deck, walking down the stairs and around the garden to join us.

"Did you call this in?"

"*I* didn't, no. We don't know enough yet. I heard the sirens and quickly shut the hidden door in the kitchen. I didn't know what to do, but I sure wasn't about to be stuck *inside*."

"Did you see anything?"

"There were boxes inside, crates. All locked. I couldn't get in, but I tried. I'd bet my life savings turquoise is splashed inside. Why else have such heavily locked boxes behind a concealed door?"

Lulu looked around, "Where are Antonio and Rick? I wish we could step inside…only for a moment."

"No luck there." I pointed to the front as the police entered the home, Sunny with his hands in his pockets, looking at ease.

"I wanna *slap* him. His *arrogance*." Lulu was gritting her teeth.

"This may be the end of the tale."

Parker said, "What happens if they find the artifacts?"

I said, "I'd be kind of relieved for Amelia. She'd know the secret, and it wouldn't be us destroying her life. The proof would be splayed for all to see."

"It's not us destroying her life," Lulu said, "that's Sunny. Just because we have information doesn't make us at fault."

"If we're hiding it, it does." I said.

"The police are here, that's something."

We were silent as we watched the last police officer follow Amelia inside. The closing of the door felt like we were locked outside of a vacuum, nothing in, nothing out. We were enveloped in quiet.

I asked, "What on earth do we do now?"

Parker said, "We wait. Where's Hannah?"

We glanced back as she finished a phone call and walked back to our group. She said, "Any news?"

I said, "They all went inside. Sunny let them in, he seemed the poster child of innocence."

"I have to go, give Amelia my love if you see her." Hannah walked briskly back to the willow.

"If we continue to stand here, we are going to start looking suspicious." I gazed at my surroundings for an answer that wouldn't come.

Lulu said, "We can't leave. How will they know about the secret door?"

Parker said, "Let's go to Spirits and meet up with Bill. We'll only be a few minutes away. We can come back after the dust has settled. How will it look to Amelia if we mention the door? The police? Odds are they can't move anything with the authorities here anyways."

"Alight." Lulu said. "We're just so *close*." A police officer exited the home and rifled through his squad car. Walking back to the house he noted our presence and stood to watch.

"So are the police. We're assuming only we know the details of this robbery. They are professionals, let's give them some credit." I texted Bill to let him know our plans. As I hit send, the ground let out a low rumble, the feeling of an acute earthquake shaking beneath our feet. The willow began swaying in unnatural angles, as the stream bubbled over.

Lulu said, "What the *hell*?" The rumbling stopped suddenly, revealing a large gaping hole in the side of the house. It started to widen, as piles of stone rubble glittered in the sun. We heard Amelia let out a scream from inside. A red and yellow reflection caught my eye, and I realized it was stained glass. The study window was obliterated, once again.

We ran to the cavern on the side of their house. We could see specks of onlookers from within, across from the rubble, the dust wafting in swirls of fog and limiting our vision. It smelled like old stone and moisture as Parker coughed.

Lulu yelled, "Is everyone alright?" There came no answer, yet shouts were heard from inside. Parker ran to the front door, fear stretching across his brow. We followed.

The scene inside was that of chaos, the police officers calling for backup, additional sirens squealing in the distance.

Lulu and I stood in the entryway as Parker ran to find Amelia. I said, "Don't go in the kitchen, Lu. I know what you're thinking."

"I wouldn't." The reality of the situation came barreling down, our cat and mouse game suddenly no longer a game. "I think we're dealing with more than we initially thought."

"I'm wondering if this is related to the vandalism and the book quotes or the artifacts alone."

"I doubt they are unrelated. It's too odd to have two separate crimes occurring in tandem."

"It may be time to tell the police."

"I think you might be right."

We watched, as if peering through a hazy screen. A television show with static. Additional police officers arrived, the present parties attempting to describe what happened. Amelia walked from the chaos with Parker, looking physically unharmed.

"Amelia, are you alright? What happened?" The three of us hugged.

"Shaken. I don't think anyone is hurt. We were standing in the hall and the study door was shut. It looks like an explosive was set off against the study, and it's hard to say if it was from outside or in."

An office approached. "Can I get a statement ma'am?" Amelia squeezed Lulu's shoulder as she left to the living room, offering water to the men.

"Do we say something?" Lulu said.

"I think so. I need some air first. Someone could have died."

We sat outside on the stone rim running the perimeter of the driveway. The sun felt renewing. Parker approached, glancing at the driveway. "They're gone."

"Who?" I asked.

"The truck, it's gone. I'd bet my life that explosion was a decoy."

Lulu placed her hands on top of her head, linking her fingers. "They did this."

I said, "Sunny, it had to have been Sunny."

As we looked towards the smaller driveway, we knew we would find an empty pantry if we chose to look. He said, "In the chaos, I failed to watch them. We could have followed. Did anyone get their plates?"

Our silence was the answer.

Another police car pulled up, making five total. Sunny shouted from the top of the stairs, "Dirk! Where have you been old man?"

"With years comes wisdom, you'd be wise yourself not to forget it." They shook hands and embraced, laughing. Sunny said, "I think we've given your squad all we can for now. Someone is targeting us, and I don't like what I'm seeing."

Dirk hiked his pants and gazed around the property. "I'll tell my men it's time to move along. You're victims, here, that's clear. You're not thieves, I can attest to that. Years of study." They laughed.

Sunny moved his head, with apt attention, towards the three of us standing only feet away. My blood ran cold as they walked away. The front door slammed shut behind him, and we were once again left without answers, more questions than we could fathom. We stood in silence, taking in the moment, absorbing all of its implications.

I said, "That's the same police officer that came to the museum with Hugh, after the robbery."

Lulu nodded. "I'd recognize him anywhere. Looks like we just hit a dead end."

Parker said, "Let's get out of here."

We silently followed, heading to Spirits.

⁓

Bill stood from the bar as we headed for the same table Parker and I met at only weeks ago, when I learned about his history and Sunny's infidelity.

We recanted the story to Bill as he remained quiet, nodding, taking it in. Once we were finished, he said, "You didn't say anything to Amelia or the police, then?"

I said, "We were thinking about it. We wanted to speak with Parker first, make sure our stories lined up. Then Dirk showed up."

Parker said, "I was hoping we would. An explosion is taking it too far."

"At some point," Lulu said, "this may be more than we can handle. And we have to consider that, even with everything going on between Parker and Amelia."

He looked at me and said, "You told her about my feelings for Amelia."

"I didn't, at first. But it's hard to explain your determination while ignoring that part of the story."

"What, my life is an open book now?" He stood and went to the bar. The tension between everyone seemed to hit an apex.

"Shit." I rubbed my temple.

Lulu said, "I'm sorry, I didn't know."

"It's not your fault. How can he expect me to be on his side, and now you, without being fully transparent?"

Bill said, "I think he's scared."

"Scared of what?" I asked.

"That Amelia will find out. That he won't be the one to tell her. I'm sure he's waited years for such a moment, can you imagine being robbed of such an opportunity? And not only that, if revealed at the wrong time it could change the way she views it, the way the future unfolds."

Lulu said, "This is more than just a crush. There is criminal activity hanging in the balance. Our careers and our livelihood."

Bill said, "All I know is that before I asked Ellie to marry me, I would have been devastated had someone ruined the surprise. Or even before that, when I said I loved her."

"That's so sweet." I reached across and placed my hand on his.

"And this is more weighted, she is married. This isn't the time for such information. His integrity is up for question if anything gets out."

Lulu said, "We're not going to tell anyone, why would we do that? That's the last thing on my mind right now."

"This situation is complicated. A slip of the tongue during a conversation, who knows?" Bill sipped his beer. "The more people who know, the riskier the information is."

I said, "I should apologize." As I walked to the bar I was circumvented by a bartender, a plastic tray in his hands.

"For you, ma'am." He handed me the tray and walked away. I assumed it was Bill's tab, but a handwritten note on the bottom caught my eye. The writing looked rushed, barely legible. It read:

"Pluck up a spirit, and do not be all the time sighing and murmuring!"

Underneath that message, it read:

Tell your friend, the one not present, that we are watching. This is more than a warning.

"Parker…" I approached the bar.

"I just- give me a moment. It's humiliating knowing that everyone knows about Amelia. It's not the greatest feeling knowing that your secret is being told to those around you."

"I'm so sorry Parker. I didn't mean ill intent, I hope you know that no one else is aware. I'll never tell another soul, you have my word."

"I know. I guess I feel embarrassed. I shouldn't have stormed off."

"I didn't consider that you would feel that way, this is new territory. I was hoping it would give Lulu better insight, but it was wrong of me."

"Thank you for listening, I'm not angry. I don't know what to do. I never thought myself to be the type of man who would fall in love with a married woman. When I was younger, my plans were all but the reverse. It's hard to wake up living such a different life."

"I know. It's been a hard year with Kelly leaving."

"In a way, it's relieving to be done. She walked out on me, the rest was laid out plainly, my decisions taken from me."

"Would it have been the same had she stayed?"

"In the end, I believe so. It would have taken a lot longer though. It broke my heart." He fiddled with his hands. "I know I haven't spoken much about it."

"You don't have to, you know. It's your life, your information. If you don't feel comfortable you don't need to."

"I told Amelia as it unfolded. At the time, I never once thought of her as anything but a friend. I hope if she ever finds out that I love her, she knows that. I was faithful to Kelly until the end."

"Amelia knows who you are Parker."

"Will she still believe that when she finds out I had her husband followed? That I knew he was cheating and never told her? Partially out of selfish gain?"

"You know it's more complicated than that. If she feels the same as you one day, those details will all but fall away. Sunny isn't a regular man, he's breaking the law. That changes things. And you were respectful of Sunny until he blackmailed and cheated. Your reasons are valid."

"I don't know if I'll ever feel ready to tell her after everything that has happened. I just hope she chooses to forgive me if it comes to it."

"You'll know when it's time."

He sighed. "We better get back."

I almost forgot about the note. "Before we do, look at what the bartender handed to me."

He read, then shut his eyes. It was the gift that kept giving and the notes that kept coming, regardless of location.

Back at the table, we were silent as they read the receipt. Bill said, "I'm guessing a part of this is from your book pick this week?" He threw the note on the table, a look of disgust.

Lulu said, "The top portion, straight from *The Scarlet Letter*."

I said, "They were following us."

Bill said, "Or they overheard your plans. Who was with you when you discussed coming here to meet me?"

"Sunny, a police officer or two, maybe someone else. People were coming and going, unfortunately."

"That still narrows it down considerably, it could be someone who knows Amelia."

"Unless you're right, and we were followed. Could be anyone, waiting outside Amelia's house." Lulu said. "I still don't understand why, if this is Sunny, he would send a message like this using our books, damaging his own home."

Bill said, "I don't know if it is Sunny anymore. And without knowing his motives, we can't answer any of this. Let's look at the facts alone."

"This is the fourth message on a Wednesday that we've received." I grabbed a piece of paper and jotted some notes down. "The first said, 'stop and we won't resort to further action.'"

Parker scuffed his hair, "The second said, 'stop now, we're watching'. Followed by the postcard that said, 'you have until the Orchid Society Gala'. And now, 'tell your friend, the one not yet present, that we are watching. This is more than a warning.'"

I said, "This is the first time there has been violence attached, if you count the explosion as part of the message."

"Unless you count the damage from the bottle, but that hardly seems life-threatening," Parker added. "It's possible the explosion was a decoy. It's *also* possible that it was a decoy as well as part of the message. We can't necessarily separate the two. Especially since the most recent message says 'this is more than a warning'. That implies the explosion, or violence."

Lulu said, "I think that the explosion was Antonio, Rick, or Sunny. A diversion to get the artifacts out of the home. Or someone working with them. The timing was too perfect."

I said, "So the message was written by one of them?"

Bill replied, "It's someone who had access to the book you were reading each week. That points towards someone close, possibly someone who is related, or married, to one of you six."

Lulu said, "Let's not forget the bottom of the note. 'Tell the one who is not yet present?' They must mean either Amelia, Georgia or Hannah, or someone related. What could that mean?"

"The person in question. The person who all of the notes are for. We can count us out, at least."

I tapped the pen on the table. "The notes are indicating that someone knew a bit of information. Perhaps that they should stop investigating?"

Lulu said, "We *do* know something. A lot of somethings."

"Not as much when the first note arrived, though."

Parker said, "I had some information on Sunny, but I don't think there's a way to confirm that was me. Shelby seems legitimate."

We contemplated this. "Then it's directed to Georgia, Amelia or Hannah. And it might not be artifact related."

"Do you think it's Amelia?" Bill asked.

Parker said, "It can't."

Lulu looked empathetic. "It can though."

"She's not vindictive, or a criminal. This is Amelia we are talking about. You think she is investigating crime, poking around where she shouldn't, and allowing threats?"

"It doesn't mean she's any of those things," I said, "It means she has information they don't want her to release, perhaps. Just because someone is threatened, doesn't make them bad. They're just a target."

"Alright, but it says to *stop,* that implies action. Not just knowledge, or information."

Bill said, "Is it possible that she doesn't know she has this information?"

"It's possible."

Lulu said, "Hear me out. We can bring Amelia into this, without discussing Parker's side. We can talk about what we know about the artifacts. Yes, you want the reward, but she doesn't need to know that, either. That can stay separate."

I said, "That's not a bad idea."

Parker said, "It feels risky, bringing her in like this."

"She's not a gentle dove. She can make her own choice if this is too much."

Parker said, "Alright, we tell Amelia."

"And we keep it with the artifacts. Anything involving you is out." I said. "That's your information to share."

Lulu said, "Is it odd to be telling her only the parts we choose? We're leading her destiny. Choosing what she can handle, what she can't."

Bill said, "You don't owe information to people if you're not ready to give it, and if it's not going to hurt someone to wait. Parker is being blackmailed, that's serious, and the money could help her leave. It may not be time to divulge it all."

Lulu said, "I agree."

"I can handle this, but we have to tread lightly," Parker said. "We can't talk about Shelby or our investigation into Sunny before this. That will open up more doors leading to the affair and his reaction."

Lulu said, "So we tell her about overhearing Hugh in the office discussing the artifacts and Rick. Isn't she going to wonder how we know Sunny is friends with Rick? She's going to see past the holes in the story. There are a lot of Ricks in the world."

I said, "We can figure that out, I think. Let's see where the conversation goes."

Parker said, "And what is our goal in telling her this?"

"I think it's finally time she starts seeing past Sunny's front. This could be the first crack. Once we start talking about it, maybe she will remember something. Perhaps she recalls a bit of information she read or overheard. Perhaps this leads to the perpetrator of the notes through conversation. And she deserves to know."

We sat back, drinks in hand. Lulu said, "We tell her tomorrow. The gala is Saturday. If something is going to happen before then, that gives us a few days. The artifacts are no longer at their house, there's no tracking them anymore. Let's take the night and sit on it."

We agreed and left the bar exhausted, unsure what our discussion with Amelia would look like and what would be exposed. In the car I looked at Bill, grateful that he decided to help, and grateful that he didn't think we were insane for trying to find the artifacts. He was part of this now too, and I couldn't be happier to arrive home with him.

Chapter 13
The Hotel Bar Mirabelle

Amelia sat at our dining room table, the rain making the room dark, late, even though the time read 4:30. It was Thursday, two days until the Orchid Gala. Two days for someone to stop, two days until if they didn't, our group of six would be the brunt of those consequences. The writer of the notes left no indication of what was to come, the vagueness leaving our tongues bitter, the room cold.

"Alright, what is it you have to tell me? You guys are making me nervous."

It felt like an intervention. Bill, Lulu, Parker, and I stared at Amelia like we hadn't known her over a decade, like she was harboring some secret to shake the universe.

I started. "Lulu and I overheard a voicemail at work that we weren't supposed to hear. The man's name was Rick. He was talking about bringing by art supplies. It sounded like it was in relation to the artifacts, and the dates matched up."

"The artifacts the police were asking about at our home?"

"Yes. Remember when the museum was robbed? I believe it's the same artifacts."

"Why would someone think the artifacts from your work are at our house?"

"We think the Rick that left the voicemail for Hugh is the same Rick who is friends with Sunny."

"What are you saying? That seems like quite the leap."

Parker interjected, "I also overheard a conversation between Sunny and his friend Antonio."

Amelia said, "Where would you have heard them together?"

"Don't be mad, but Ellie and I happened to walk past them and they didn't see us, so we stayed to hear what they were discussing."

Amelia looked surprised, which didn't bode well for other parts of this conversation. "What did they say?"

"Sunny and Antonio were talking about picking up a load the next morning and taking it to a hotel down south called the Mirabelle. Something didn't work out as planned, and they had to store the artifacts somewhere in Dove Park until then, which is why they'd be at your house. Have you heard of it? The Mirabelle?"

"Doesn't ring a bell. Why does this seem suspicious to you? That sounds like work chatter. I feel like I'm missing something."

I realized we were throwing information at her, chunks of a story full of holes. It wasn't exactly as eloquent as I was hoping.

I said, "After their conversation about picking up a haul of goods, the artifacts were stolen the next day."

"Sounds like a coincidence."

I felt like we were losing traction. "Hugh and Rick were working on a supply drop. Rick and Sunny know one another, and a discussion was heard about a haul of goods. They all happened on the same day. When you place both conversations together, it seems less coincidental. Then the cops showed up, asking about the artifacts…it has to be related."

"Why haven't you said anything until now?"

I said, "It didn't seem like we had enough information, but when the authorities showed at your house, our idea didn't seem so crazy. Our boss has ample access to the artifacts, their whereabouts. Rick and Sunny were talking about money, and Amelia, these artifacts are worth a veritable fortune."

She fidgeted on the kitchen stool. "You know what you're implying, right? That my husband is a thief? And he's working with your boss, who is also a thief?"

Lulu said, "We know this sounds harsh. It's not what we wanted to happen. The information kind of fell in our laps."

Amelia thought a moment. "It still doesn't seem like enough information to go on, but when you pair it with the police presence...did you call them to investigate? Is that why they showed up at the house?"

"No, that wasn't us. I'm not sure what information they have or where it came from."

A rigid hold seemed to come over Amelia. She seemed to be teetering, which side to believe? She asked, "Why are you telling me this?"

Lulu continued, "Because if it were me, I'd want to know. If the person sleeping next to me was tied up in illegal activity, I'd want to know. We're your friends, Amelia, and you deserve to know."

That seemed to be enough. It was as if the scale tipped gently to one side, her dam breaking, unloading months of worry and trepidation. She buried her face in her hands, mascara staining the inside of her palm. Parker looked like he was going to pass out as Lulu stepped off her stool to embrace her.

Amelia said, "You guys are sure?"

I nodded. "With the information presented, it seems undeniable."

"Does that mean the vandalism was geared towards him then, after all?"

Parker said, "I don't know, I wish I did. We were wondering if you had any information on that."

I said, "I feel like he's connected, but I'm not sure how. I don't see why he would damage his own home, though. We're missing a piece of the puzzle."

Amelia said, "He's stubborn. At least he has been, lately. I'm not sure what he is capable of. But I don't know anything else, I'd tell you if I did. What I would give to have a Wednesday night feel normal, untainted by thugs and trespassers."

Bill asked, "What changed with Sunny? It's been a while since we've all been together. Seems like he separated himself from us."

Amelia dotted her finger under her swollen eye. "We were fine for the first 9, 10 years of our marriage. Two kids, a beautiful home. Dinners with friends. You remember, we used to have those barbeques. Then he got a promotion at work, and he slowly stopped coming home at five. He was quick to anger when he would typically compromise. I convinced myself it was the stress at work. How could I complain? I live off of his income."

Parker said, "You're more than living off of his income, you're not his employee. You're his *wife*."

She said, "It does kind of feel like that, now that you say it out loud."

The wind seemed to break the moment, the rain walloping against the shutters marking an end to our reveal. The humidity held a taste in the air, and I took another sip of coffee. I said, "With all of this being said, what would you like to do?"

"You said you think he is storing the artifacts at our house?"

"I think he was, yes. But I believe they have been moved. Antonio and Rick were there with a truck yesterday, they're now gone. According to the information we overheard, some of the artifacts will be sold tonight, at the Mirabelle. We have no idea where they currently are, but they are probably en route down south."

Parker said, "Is Sunny home?"

"He said he is on a work trip until Sunday. That certainly falls in line with your theory."

I said, "Are you alright? This is quite a bit to unload."

"I think if this were three years ago, I'd be stunned, but I'm not. I hope the boys don't notice his odd behavior or find out about any of this." She looked up, wiping her hands on her dress, her face shimmering with tears and the removal of makeup. "So, what do you think should happen now? I'm at a loss. But I believe you. The moment the police stepped up to the door, I knew. Especially when Dirk approached."

It was a difficult position, there was no solution to pose, no action to take hold of.

Parker said, "I don't know, I really don't."

"Why didn't you speak to the police when they were at my house?" Amelia asked. "The artifacts must've been close if they were still storing them there. If you would have informed me, I could have let them search the house."

I said, "He seemed to have a friend in the force, he arrived right before we left. I think his name was Dirk. He said he was going to send his men home. Then the explosion happened, and Antonio and Rick were gone."

"Dirk. He's the captain. They're close."

"We were about to walk up, tell our side. When he approached it seemed like he knew more than he should. He was clearly team Sunny. How do they know one another?"

"They went to college together, I guess they were in the same fraternity. He's visited off and on throughout the years, his daughter is in the same class as Aiden. He was here last week, as well. It was a Tuesday, I remember because my mother was here asking for help with the gala menu."

"I'm glad we stayed quiet then. We were afraid to say anything with his presence." Lulu said, "But now it seems we've lost them for good. We were so *close*. Million-dollar artifacts, feet away."

Amelia said, "I wonder how I never noticed."

"What do you mean?"

"How does one miss a large load of valuables coming through their home? I feel foolish. I should've seen something. And he's been acting so strange. I'm not sure why I never asked him about his odd behavior. There was something about his demeanor that told me to back off, that it wouldn't be a pleasant conversation. In retrospect, that's when you should speak up… when you're uncomfortable. It seemed easier, silence."

I said, "You're the least foolish person I know, Amelia. And he would never do anything while you were there, or awake. This has been thought through. They are thorough."

"There have been a few Wednesdays that he came home early, while we were having book club. The extra garage is far from the den, I'd never know. Who would suspect anything while guests were present? It's not like we're quiet."

"That could be the perfect cover. An alibi, of sorts." I said, "This isn't your fault, you know." I was sensing that she felt lonely in her position, her decisions on display.

"It's going to take time, I think, to come to terms with everything."

Parker said, "I'm so sorry Amelia. We're not completely in the dark, though. We believe the artifacts are at the Mirabelle or will be by tonight. But we don't have a lot of valid information to back that claim. Just a few overheard conversations." Parker wanted desperately, I could imagine, to hold her, comfort her. His restrain was solid, but it were moments like this you could see the love in his eye, his body stiffen at any indication that Sunny had hurt her. I wondered how many times over the past months I had missed these little signs, the struggle of a man unable to love the person he so greatly wanted to cherish.

Amelia said, "Can we call the police with an anonymous tip?"

"I suppose that wouldn't hurt, we've lost our lead. And they've already received anonymous tips on the subject, it wouldn't be overly suspicious." Parker seemed to acknowledge that the reward had fallen out of grasp, finding the home for the artifacts had taken the front seat.

Amelia said, "I'd like to do it if that's alright. It's my house, after all."

I said, "Be our guest."

As Amelia left I said, "She's receptive, if you feel comfortable, I'm sure she'd believe you about the affair, even if Sunny reveals the blackmail. She seems more skeptical of him than expected."

"Perhaps, but it's still a risk. I don't know what Sunny has up his sleeve. She would believe me, at the onset, but days down the road, weeks? Sunny still has his claws in her side. He has my potential criminal ties and records at the ready. And I'd still be presenting her with no options for leaving."

Lulu said, "That's not your responsibility."

"I know it's not, but if I have the means, why not? I'd like to at least leave it as an option. The reward money is still out there."

"She needs to know, Parker. And I don't know if we're going to get anything else on Sunny at this point. I feel that our secret-keeping is coming to a close."

"His blackmail is not to be toyed with, but I understand your point. I do."

Lulu said, "The blackmail is never going to go away. You tell her or you don't."

He said, "I suppose you're right-" He stood to explain the tale, one he never thought would leave his lips, let alone to his close group of friends and the women he loved. The story of his past. As Amelia approached, he said, "I have something to tell you."

She said, "Let's go down there."

I said, "What?"

"The police took my information but didn't seem interested. They wrote down the name of the hotel, but I don't think they'll check it out. And Dirk just about runs the force up here, if he catches wind, he'll shut it down if they are working together like it seems." She sounded excited, a burn in her eyes.

"You mean, drive two hours to the Mirabelle?"

"Yes. I want to see for myself."

"The artifacts aren't going to be laying around, I'm sure they'll be heavily guarded."

"I know that El, I also have his cell location. That has to count for something right? What is he going to do? Maybe I'll finally have some answers. He could be there."

"From the conversation we overheard, they are going to be selling the artifacts tonight. It's already almost 5:00…"

"We can be there by 7:00. I'm not trying to catch them in the act. But something has to be there, don't you think? And I'm sure they're staying there for the night. Or close by. It's a hotel and they are doing business at night."

Lulu said, "Alright, I'm in. But I have to tell the hubby I'm going to be late."

Bill said, "I'll go, but we have to tread lightly. This is not a game, Amelia."

"I don't need to be admonished. I need closure, to see something in person. I'll ask my mom if she can watch the boys tonight."

I said, "We might not like what we see."

Amelia looked serious, "I hope I don't."

And with that, we settled our plans for the night. Bill decided to drive. He said, "We can meet back at my SUV if we are separated in the hotel, or if something goes wrong."

Lulu said, "For Pete's sake you are acting like we're driving through a firing range. It's a hotel full of museum artifacts. I know it's not a joke, but we might not find anything at all. We need to understand that possibility."

Amelia said, "Worse case we end up taking a drive together. I can think of worse things."

~

Amelia, Bill, Lulu, Parker, and I sat comfortably in the SUV, our adrenaline from the choice to act simmering low. I wondered if anyone thought we should turn back. The time in the car was long, enough to sprout doubt, realize the danger present. We were quiet for a time, the scenery buzzing, creating a new vibration to the car's atmosphere.

Lulu said, "At least play something upbeat, honesty Bill what *is* this."

"Do you want to drive? On second thought you've had way too much coffee."

"Pssh. That's when I *thrive*. Put on something to get our blood flowing."

"Fine, fine. How about some Stone's."

She smiled, "That'll do just fine, thank you."

As Mick Jagger screeched about tumbling dice, I said, "I wish we had some of your cake, Amelia. I'm starving. We never ate dinner."

"I'd *demolish* her chocolate cake." Lulu said, "Everyone would be embarrassed."

Bill said, "Amelia, why don't you ever sell anything you've baked?"

"Like online?"

"Sure, why not?"

She seemed to be taken aback by that suggestion, glancing out at the scenery. "In another life, maybe. Sunny would never allow it, with the kids. He's said he would never like me to work, as long as they're in school." She shrugged it off.

Bill's map interrupted the conversation, and we turned off the highway, our destination approaching, the situation close.

I asked, "So, what's the plan here?"

Amelia had her cell phone out. "They have a bar inside the hotel."

Bill said, "I'd hate to risk him seeing us so quickly, or Antonio or Rick. They both know what you look like, Amelia."

"They're going to see me, more than likely, one way or the other."

I said, "Track his iPhone. I'm sure they're all together."

She lifted her phone, then turned to me, eyes wide. "He's actually at the Mirabelle. I guess I didn't really know what to expect until we got here."

"How close can your phone track?"

"Close."

Bill said, "You are his wife, if he's registered at the hotel, they may let you up to his room."

I said, "They know Sunny and his team, they are part of the operation, from the sound of it. The moment we start asking questions their radar is going up."

Lulu said, "So, what do we do?"

"Why don't we go to the bar and look around," Bill said, as we parked. "Get a feel of the place. I'll go in first with Ellie and Lulu, we'll let you know when you can join and if the coast is clear."

Amelia nodded, "Good a plan as any."

≈

The hotel was impressive. The exterior didn't lend to much, but inside showcased fountains, an array of sculptures, and plant life reaching a tall ceiling that completed at the roof of the entire twelve story hotel. When looking up, we could see each floor in an open mezzanine style. Hotel door swung open and closed and a glass elevator rose and fell directly to our right. We were unexpectedly on display. The receptionist's desk looked to be made out of marble laced with gold, and the lobby smelled sweet and alluring. We avoided the front desk and followed the signs for the Mirabelle Bar, keeping our heads low and senses sharp.

The bar wasn't better in terms of discreteness. It was circular, with the bar directly in the middle. A large display of liquors and beers lined the bottom of a large pillar that rose towards the ceiling, water flowing off the siding creating a mote around the bartenders. Clear stools surrounded the inner bar, just inches from the deep mote. A small bridge allowed for entry on either side.

Lulu said, "What is this place? Did we just step into The Emerald City?"

"I could use some bravery," Amelia said.

There were no corners of the bar, no space to hide and observe. We found a table further from the main entrance and sat, taking in the awesome spectacle that was the Mirabelle Bar.

Bill said, "If this doesn't scream money, I don't know what does. They're certainly not being modest about their new funds, look at this place. The hotel has *upgraded*."

"If this isn't a huge red flag." I said, "how come no one has heard of this place before?"

Lulu flagged the waiter. "Maybe they want it like this. A secret for only those who deserve to enjoy its amenities."

We ordered drinks and texted Amelia. I said, "I don't see anyone that looks like they bought 50 million dollars' worth of stolen goods."

"I don't make enough to tell you what *that* would look like." Lulu plucked her cherry off of the stem between her fingers and long painted nails, devouring it in a natural, sensual way.

"I think it's safe for them to join." Bill said.

We waited for Parker and Amelia. The bar was only a quarter full, but it didn't look deserted. It had the feel of class, not forced yet something carefully created over time. The booths had high backs, so we felt secluded. Amelia and Parker quickly scooted into the opposite side.

I said, "Did you see anyone?"

"No one I recognized." Amelia said, "and nothing out of the ordinary, but this place screams cautious. You're right, nothing will be on display here."

The waiter arrived. "Is everyone here a member of the Mirabelle?"

"No, we're visiting from out of town." Lulu locked eyes as if hypnotizing him into barking like a chicken. He seemed to blush.

"I see. We do have an event taking place this evening, at 8:00 pm, but it is only for members. The bar will be closing at that time. Until then, have a drink on the Mirabelle for cutting your experience short." He brought over two complimentary bottles of Chateau Pape Clement Red and set them in front of Lulu. He seemed to move on air, the entire spectacle bizarre.

After he floated away, Lulu said, "That's expensive. Well, not for these people, obviously. I bet one bottle runs about 200 bucks."

"Are you serious?" I said.

"No joke."

Parker said, "I think we're in the right place."

We poured the wine. Bill said, "I think we can safely say what the event is tonight. I'm curious how they plan on distributing the artifacts, and if they're really here."

Amelia said, "Is there a way we can sneak in? Stay an extra moment?"

"I'm not sure," I said. "They already know our status and there's a lot of money on the line."

"I wasn't expecting a spectacle," Amelia said, "I envisioned a back-alley deal."

Bill said, "This does change things. Look, all we need is to lay eyes on the artifacts. That's all. We don't need to see anyone or speak with anyone. Once we know what we are looking at, then we can call the police. There's no chance of us getting our hands on them anyways, not with an operation of this caliber."

Amelia said, "Why would we want to take them? I wouldn't know what to do if I had 50 million dollars-worth of museum artifacts in the trunk of my car. I'd probably have a panic attack."

I said, "To take them where they belong." And spend the reward money on you, I thought.

Amelia continued, "Let's leave that up to the authorities. Plus, the precinct this far south shouldn't be manned by Dirk, I think we'd have a chance. If we can get proof."

Parker fidgeted in his seat. "Who has the best chance of getting in tonight? We have about thirty minutes until the event begins. We have to think fast." Everyone looked at Lulu.

She said, "What?"

Chapter 14
Union of Criminals

I said, "You had that waiter groveling at your feet, Lu."

"I'm a married woman!"

"We're not asking you to *elope* with him, just get in his good graces."

Parker said, "I think that's the only way in. See if the waiter will let you hang around. Act uninterested in the event."

"The things I do for you people." Lulu took a swig of wine and crossed the small bridge towards the main bar.

"I still want to find Sunny. I'm sick of his lies." Amelia said, "He told me he was going to be in California this week. He's only two hours away! Why even lie about such a small thing?"

"I guess he's being careful, too," I said as the table fell quiet. We watched as Lulu spoke with the bartender. He poured her a drink and she laughed.

Parker said, "It seems to be working, he hasn't left his station in minutes. He seems enraptured."

"Poor Lulu is going to get him fired." Amelia said. Parker put his hand on her back in a comforting, gentle way.

A man in a full black suit entered the main entrance, speaking to hotel staff members as he made his way to our bartender, who shook his head and began walking back to the tables. We began eavesdropping on the table directly behind where we sat.

"Can I see your club Mirabelle cards and your receipt token for payment to the event tonight?"

A woman with a deep southern accent answered, "Sure thing honey."

"Thank you. I hope you find exactly what you are looking for tonight."

"I'm sure we will, thank you. I'm quite the bundle of excitement."

He made his way to us. Lulu continued to sit at the bar. He said, "I'm sorry, but if you are not members and have not purchased entry, I'm going to have to ask you to leave the booth and go back to your room."

I said, "Thank you for your hospitality, the wine was wonderful."

He smiled and moved towards the other booths, all of the patrons remaining seated. The anticipation was palpable as the time clicked towards 8:00 pm.

"These people are wealthy." Amelia glanced across the bar, eyes squinted as the lights dimmed. "Look, I know that scarf. That's a Hermes Silk. And the man she's with, that looks like a vintage Gucci track jacket."

Bill said, "They ought to be for buying 50 million dollars-worth of artifacts."

She shook her head, "We are beginning to stand out. This is an elite group of people. It's a good thing Lu is wearing her Jimmy Choo's today."

We stood to leave, prepping for the next stage in the evening. The bartender hadn't rounded back to the bar yet, and Lulu continued to sit, trying to camouflage herself against the bar.

We convened outside the room, suddenly noticeable under the endless, bright hotel lobby lights.

I said, "We need to get somewhere else, and quick."

Parker said, "Maybe we should get a room? A place to lay low. This could be a couple of hours…"

We agreed and Parker headed towards the lobby.

I asked Amelia, "Are you doing alright?"

"I don't know. I'm not sure how to act when I finally see him."

"He'll have a lot more explaining to do than you, that's for sure. Is he still in the vicinity?"

"He's close." That made my heart jump. Parker returned.

"Room 2188 and 2189, in case we need to stay the night. More people seem to be coming in, let's be quick about it. There's a stairwell in the far corner. Let's not tempt fate with a glass elevator."

As I turned, I almost ran into a woman in a yellow dress, black sunglasses, and deep red lips. She looked startled and kept moving. For a moment I thought I recognized her gait but thought little else as we hurried to the stairwell.

"I texted Lulu and let her know about the room," I said, "Let's hope we don't see her for a good while."

Bill said, "Looks like two conjoining rooms, Parker and I can stay in one and you ladies in the other if it comes to that. Worst case we call into work tomorrow."

Amelia said, "That sounds alright. I'm not sure I'll want to stick around if I confront Sunny tonight."

"We'll see how the rest of the night goes." Bill seemed to calm even the most anxious soul. I felt better about being here, with him involved.

We began to climb. When we hit the second floor, a door opened from above. We paused as voices began to spiral downward.

A man said, "But if we let them tonight, then that's it. There's no changing the way things will be done."

A gruff voice replied, "We're nobody to them. If we risk saying something, we're fired. What's worse? Getting less of a cut and minding our own business, or up and feeling like we're in a union of criminals? We got no rights."

"Except they can't *do* what they're doing without us."

"That's how it goes. You think Madonna thanks everyone who loads her stuff on stage? Hangs the lights? Sells the nachos? Shit."

"What, you got a thing for Madonna?"

"Ain't that a stupid question." They stopped talking. Mister gruff said, "Did you hear something?"

"These stairways are rickety. Noisy with metal, you know? Back air conditioner units and such." We tiptoed back a flight of stairs as they waited. We were breathless.

"A thanks. You want a thanks. You're getting soft on me." They stopped walking and exited, the heavy door slamming, making us jump.

"They have to be involved." We ran up two flights of stairs and stood on the landing of the fourth floor. "This is about where they exited, I think."

Bill hesitantly pulled open the door. He peered out, then suddenly pulled back inside. "They're outside one of the rooms."

"Did they see you?" Amelia looked pale.

"No, they're facing the door. Didn't seem to care one way or the other. I think it was a utility door. They don't seem very discrete."

"Do you think they're hiding items in there?"

"I doubt it. But who can say?"

Bill pulled the door open slightly and listened through the crack. "Definitely with the event tonight. They didn't say so outright, but enough."

Amelia said, "Anything about Sunny?"

"No, no names. They seem to be the ones responsible for bringing the crates when a new item is put up for auction. A walkie went off, said they wanted crate number 3."

"Is this enough for us to call the police?"

Bill said, "For all we know, they're selling those expensive scarves you were talking about. Nothing until we lay eyes, or there is something undeniable. You've tipped them off and we haven't heard anything about turquoise, pottery, or even the museum. They went inside the room, but my guess is they'll be out shortly."

"What do we do?" Amelia said.

Bill replied, "We can try to get into the supply closet, but it's locked no doubt."

"I have an idea." Amelia pushed open the door and started walking towards the men. Parker reached for her but was too late. The three of us stuck our heads out the door like a Three Stooges act, except this time, Amelia was the show.

I said, "What is she doing? Is she crazy?"

We watched as Amelia approached the two men, talking. After some time, she walked back, glancing behind her as they exited with a box down the elevator.

We tumbled back in the stairway. She said, "I asked when the last piece was going to show, I told them I was a member and didn't want to miss the greatest reveal. I assumed they would end on something enormous, and I was right."

"Why did you ask that, of all things?" I said.

"We'll know when they'll be back in the storage unit, and for the last time."

"What do you have in mind?"

"Staging something. They said they'll be back at 10:00 pm."

"That's in an hour and a half. This is going to be a long night."

We decided to meander back to the hotel room and wait for news from Lulu. If she came back, that would change things. So, we waited.

Chapter 15
Integrity

The hotel room was large, crisp, and beautifully decorated. The newness seeped into each corner of the hotel. Both master bedrooms were embellished with two grand four-poster beds and a reasonably sized kitchen. A living room with a couch and extra television butted up to the shared wall in both rooms. We had the wide doors ajar, creating one large, open space. Bill and Parker were watching television in their room and opened the mini bar, drinking beers.

Amelia said, "How can they be so calm?"

"I think we show our anxiety in very different ways." I said.

"I'm worried about Lulu."

"I know, but she can take care of herself, she's from the big city, she's had practice batting away the crazies."

"Yeah, going to the mall in Dallas maybe. She's currently surrounded by criminals."

As if on cue, the door to our room swung open and Lulu hurriedly closed it behind her.

Amelia jumped up, "Lulu! Are you alright?"

She seemed out of breath. "Oh, I'm more than alright. Got some good info." She peered into the adjoining room, "You guys might want to hear this. Are you *drinking*? For crying out loud that's going to cost a fortune. Make me a coffee, will you?

I'm full of the jitters." She plopped down on the couch next to me.

"Spit it out!" I said.

"Alright. So, you guys leave the bar, and the bartender makes his rounds. He asks everyone to make their way to the back, and the room gets dark. *Creepy* dark. And they wheel out a stage in front of the bar. It's raised high, has these bright lights posted on these poles. Everyone moves from the back wall to these tables with auction paddles. They rearranged the entire bar, the booths disappeared. It looked like an entirely different room."

"They let you sit there the entire time?"

"They were wrapped up in the event. I was still at the bar, drinking, acting like I belonged, but it started to get weird when the stage set up directly in front of where I was sitting. I don't think people saw me at first. I moved to the other end of the bar, but my bartender eventually made his way back. He said I had to leave.

"I asked if I could watch, as a spectator and not a participant. He looked torn. I feel like he was *this* close to letting me stay, but these two large men walked up and said they'd escort me out. They were no joke. Gave him the *eye*."

"Goodness." Amelia shifted.

"That's not all. Our bartender, his name is Luke, by the way. So, Luke says he's taking care of it and they step back but keep glaring. He takes me through the server's entrance, which is to the left of the bar when you walk in. I know it's a circle, so it's confusing, but stay with me. He asked if I wanted to see something interesting, and of course, I'm game. I'm on edge though, you never know what he could be up to. This whole shebang is *wild*." Bill handed Lulu a cup of coffee with one creamer. Even he knew how she took it. She took a long drag, eyes closed. "Obviously, it took us to the kitchen, but we kept moving past it to a staff room. Nothing fancy. But there was another door on the far side of the room. I would have taken it for a coat closet. It didn't look anything special."

"And you followed him."

"I had my radar up, don't worry. Had my mace at the ready. He snagged a bottle of wine and lead me through the door…"

"This is scary, Lu!" Amelia looked horrified.

"And it was a beautiful room. A fish aquarium. Couches. But it was strange, they were all pointing out towards a wall, the entire room seemed so methodical. Then I looked closer. It wasn't a wall, but a *large* one-way mirror that spanned the entire side, concaved to fit the circular room. It was a viewing station."

"That's insane. No one else was in there?"

"Not at first. The way it was configured you couldn't see the objects on stage but rather the participants. They want to see what the people are up to. And there was a door that led out to the main room if needed."

"What did you see when you were inside?" The three of us leaned in close.

"I was able to hear the first item auctioned. They explained the piece, and it fits. But I wasn't able to see anything. It was a small piece of jewelry. I'm 95% sure it's part of the artifact load, but with a piece of jewelry…"

Bill said, "It could be unrelated."

"Exactly. But what would be the odds?"

"How much did it go for?"

"$18,000. They started small. It was *exciting* to watch. In the end, three people threw their hat in the ring. One being mister Gucci track jacket. He has money. He won it by increasing the last bid by $5,000."

"Do you think the items have been appraised?"

"Sure seemed like it. At the onset they mentioned being able to pick up any winning items at the end of the night, or having them securely shipped wherever needed. They had a pretty in-depth process for doing so. They want to make sure they land where they are supposed to. Seems the pieces are ready and appraised after all."

"There's a lot of people who know about this, then. How do they make sure no one talks?"

"Before they brought the first item up for auction, they had waivers. They also had a scanner."

"What kind of scanner?"

"For their fingerprints. Makes me nervous even being here, after that. Before we arrived at the Mirabelle, I thought this was an exchange happening in a hotel room, the back of a hall somewhere."

"What made you come back early? The night is still young."

"A group of five entered the room, dressed to the nines. Three men and two women, and they took one look at us and *man* Luke was out of there fast."

"Did they suspect anything of you?"

"Luke is quick, he said we were working and taking a break."

Parker said, "You certainly don't *look* like you're working."

"I might be ok, dressed in all black. I match the servers. I think they bought it. They were quite distracted, I think. No time for us."

I said, "Anyone recognizable?"

"No Antonio, Sunny or Rick, if that's what you're after. I do wonder where they are in all of this."

Bill said, "If I was in charge, I'd want the least amount of people possible present. Less to witness the auction if the police were involved."

"I'd believe that. They're *careful*. After that I left and came up here, Luke apologized and lead me through another set of doors popping me out in the main hotel area. I ran up the stairs, and here I am."

"That is something," I said, "not enough to call the cops, though."

Bill said, "I agree. And Amelia already left a tip at the main precinct. For all we know, this is a legitimate auction."

Lulu said, "It's possible. But I'll tell you, it *felt* criminal. It seemed like everyone had an eye on the door. It was private enough, but there was an air of caution. I did catch a couple of names, a Charlotte and Jason, they seemed to be together."

"Jason…" Parker thought, "didn't Antonio mention that name when we overheard their conversation?"

The name snapped back the memory, a sudden recoil back to the hidden closet at Amelia's. "You're right, they said something about Jason getting an ear full. I got the impression that he was in charge, or at least the owner of the hotel, maybe."

"With everything you are saying, the artifacts have to be here. And Sunny is here, somewhere." I said.

We took a moment to absorb the implications. We knew we were close, but this information seemed to escalate the situation to me heights.

"Lulu," I said, "we have an idea. We followed two men that worked for the hotel and they appeared to be discussing the artifacts. They led us to a utility closet on the fourth floor."

"Are you saying some of the artifacts are in that closet?"

"It's certainly possible." We proceeded to fill her in with our proposal, the energy in the room palpable.

She said, "Alright, I'm game. When is the last item to be shown?"

Amelia said, "They said eleven. This occasion comes not only with stolen artifacts, but dinner and drinks. The man said it should be done by 11:30. This is a huge undertaking, from the sound of it."

"Well, it certainly seems you guys have been as busy as me."

"Pure chance," Bill said. "You know what? The way you described the room, with the viewing station. This either isn't the first of its kind, or they're starting something up that's serious. Why else have a one-way mirror?"

I replied, "You're right, we need to be careful. There are millions on the line."

"We have a few hours," Lulu said, "what do we do with ourselves?"

Amelia replied, "Stay out of trouble if that suits you." She smiled.

"Ha, I've had enough fun for a month already. Let's lie low. Wait to see if the plan works. It's as good as any."

Bill asked, "Any news on the vandalism with your house, Amelia?"

"Unfortunately, no. Sunny has just about dropped it. It was odd, he didn't seem concerned about the explosion. Of all the things that have happened so far, that is the scariest. He seemed so concerned about a hanging *sheet*."

I said, "You think he had something to do with it, then?"

"I can't take my mind there. The thought of him setting off an explosive in our house with our children back from Napa has me reeling. That better not be the case."

"How are the boys?" We were relaxing as best we could, but the room was tense.

"They're both headed to separate camps Saturday morning, they'll be gone a month. Seems like I just got them back."

Parker said, "I can't wait to have kids one day. Honestly, in a few years, if I'm still single, I'm going to adopt. And if I'm with someone, I'm hoping they'll want to adopt with me."

I said, "You'd be such a good dad."

The coffee kept coming, the ambiance rich with anticipation. We needed to lay an eye on turquoise, something recognizable. Spiderweb turquoise was unique, identifiable. The evidence was piling high in our favor, but we needed proof.

Finally, we made our way to the hallway.

Bill said, "Everyone ready?"

Amelia nodded, "I think this could work."

We climbed the stairs to the fourth floor, no signs of the two men. So far, so good.

The ding of the elevator hitting its mark had my heart jumping. We were convened outside of room 4918, and as if on cue, both men exited with a dolly, talking casually.

"Ted, for the fifth time, it's not thrifty, it's just cheap. You can't keep buying her things from the Dollar Tree."

"Give me a minute to explain." He motioned with his hands wide. "You may change your tone."

The elevator was close, and they made their way to the utility door quickly. As Ted ran a key card over the sensor, I noticed that he also placed a finger on a pad. We didn't see that earlier.

The other man replied, "My *tone* won't change on that one. You're getting paid good tonight, take her to a proper dinner. Red Lobster, know what I mean?"

As the door opened, Ted propped it open with his foot, bringing the dolly around. "Leo, Leo, Leo. I'm the champ of wining and dining."

"I'll believe *that* when I see it."

"You wish I'd take you to dinner." He almost fell over laughing.

This was our chance. Everyone except Bill began walking their direction. When we were only feet from their stance, Parker suddenly fell to the ground.

Amelia yelled as we quickly rounded on his fallen body. As expected, Ted was drawn to the commotion, their conversation cut short. Lulu started checking for breath and a pulse, as I ran up to Ted.

I said, "Can you help us? Our friend fell to the ground, he appears unconscious." Ted continued to hold the door with his toe, his tennis shoes scuffed and worn, yet he was leaning heavily to the side, curious. He righted the ball cap on his head, deciding what to do. He was thin, tall, and had a dark 5 o'clock shadow that wasn't noticeable until I approached close.

Amelia slipped past me as I continued to plead my case, Leo now popping his head out to see about the noise. Ted told Leo to hold the door and walked over.

"Is he breathin'?"

Lulu began patting Parker's cheeks. "I think so, I don't know. Can you tell? Do you have any medical training?"

"Not formally, no." He liked the attention. He leaned close to Parker as Lulu and I stood near, staring at him. On cue, Bill came through the stairway door and also offered his assistance.

Bill locked eyes with Ted and said, "Let's try and lift him, do you have a friend with you? You seem strong."

Ted ran to retrieve Leo. They both returned and helped lift Parker off the ground.

Leo said, "Where are we going? Shouldn't someone call 911?"

Lulu replied, "He has a seizure disorder, we need to get him back to the room. We know what to do. His meds are there." She looked at Leo, "Thank you, I couldn't lift him myself."

Ego lifted, he said, "Anytime, ma'am."

The three of them carried his body to the elevator and the doors closed, enveloping us in silence. Lulu and I ran to Amelia, who had quickly covered the lock with a shower cap from the hotel bathroom. The door was open, and our time was limited.

Amelia pushed open the entrance. The light was on, the inside large. On first appearance, it seemed to hold the cleaning supplies for the floor. Big boxes of Clorox and a grouping of mops stood in the corner, accompanied by a musty smell that settled deep in the nose.

I said, "That has to be it. The last crate." In front of us stood a large metal box with a lock requiring a number sequence for entry.

Lulu said, "Not a lot we can do without the combination…"

"Unless we took it." Amelia seemed ready to fight, hair tasseled, eyes blazing.

"You're insane. That's insane." Lulu touched the metal.

"Why not? They'll never suspect it was us three women. We look innocent enough."

"We're the only ones they *would* question." I said, "They'll say we were the last ones they saw on the floor. Mix that with a dramatic unconscious man and it seems quite the setup."

"We don't have a lot of time, what do you want to do, then?"

Lulu said, "Shit. The dolly is right there."

"We can't take that down the stairs," I said, unsure which side to agree with.

"It's right here. Don't you think it's worth it? Can we get into trouble stealing something that is stolen? What are they going to do call the police?"

I said, "We can't take it on the elevator."

"Why not?" Lulu pushed the dolly over. "This is our chance. After this, we're done. We've made our case."

"And how do we get it open?"

"Let's figure out the details later." Lulu dragged the dolly over and the three of us helped lift it over the thin slice of metal.

I peered down the hallway. It was vacant. "Now's the time." My palms were sweaty and my hold on the metal handle slipped. Lulu grabbed it and began pushing it towards the elevator. As we approached, the elevator lights crawled slowly to the fourth floor, originating from the second floor and where our rooms were located.

Lulu shouted, "They're coming back…turn *around*."

We flipped our direction and realized we'd only make it back to the supply closet. We ran, dolly in hand, as the elevator dinged. We slipped inside just as they exited.

Leo said, "They'll be fine. What're five minutes to save someone's life?"

"That was a *rush*. Maybe I'll be something medical and life saving after all."

"And what, put me as your reference? Greatest thief in the tri-state area?"

"I have integrity, thank you much."

183

"Shoot, you got something. Wouldn't call it tegrity."

As we set the dolly back down in the damp air-filled space and pushed it off its stand, we could hear their footsteps approaching. We ran towards the back corner of the room and lodged ourselves behind a stack of boxes marked TOWELS. I wiped the sweat off of my brow as we settled in, the floor sticking to our shoes as they entered.

"Be quick. We're already gonna be gettin' shit, I'm sure."

"With what we're paid, they'll just hang on a minute."

We heard the squeaking sound of the dolly exiting, followed by sheer and utter darkness, covering us as if throwing the night sky over our vision.

We were alone.

Chapter 16
Silhouette

I gradually lifted my hand to the front of my face and couldn't see the slightest of light. We waited a few moments, then I stood, hands against boxes and the plastic shelving to find my way to the door. It was locked from the inside. "The door won't budge." I pulled hard, eyes squinting even though there was no light to catch. I made my way back to the corner and sat, my arm brushing Lulu's. "I'm not sure why the light went out, either."

"Feels like we're in a vortex." Lulu was breathing heavily. Or perhaps it was my other senses beginning to increase in resonance, my ears and tongue suddenly sharp. She said, "We're trapped."

Amelia said, "It's alright. The guys will know we're somewhere on the floor when we don't show up. We have to wait it out. But *damn* if we weren't close to getting the crate."

"I saw something a little disconcerting," I said. "They scanned their fingers to enter."

"And suddenly my childhood dream has come true of being Jennifer Garner in *Alias*," Lulu remarked. "If only I could take back that wish. Fifteen years too late."

I wasn't claustrophobic, but I began to breathe hard. Lulu's respirations were making me feel heavy like my body was sinking into the muggy ground. "What do we do?"

Lulu said, "Who locks a door from the inside?"

"Probably for this very reason." I said, "They wouldn't add a fingerprint sensor unless this room meant something important. The lights went out because they left, no one should be inside."

"Seems pretty low key for such status, mops and cleaning supplies locked behind a steel door." Amelia startled, "Oh wait, I have my cell phone. I forgot I grabbed it off of the side table." She pulled it out of the black and yellow purse she had swung over her shoulder. The light had an intrusive element to the basic state of the room. "No service." She tried dialing a few numbers with no luck. "What are we in a steel case or something?"

"Could be. Who knows what operation we've found ourselves in?"

She walked to the front and peered at the door's hardware with the flashlight. "Think we can bust it open?"

I joined her. "What would that do to the fingerprint mechanism? Can't be good. Could be an alarm?"

"Looks like we'll need a fingerprint and a key card to exit." She sighed.

Lulu said, "We can't wait for Bill or Parker. There's no way they could safely convince someone to open that door. We'd be made. What would they do to us if they found us?"

I said, "I'd rather not go there right now."

Amelia said, "Unless they found Sunny and asked for help."

He seemed unreal. No cell phone indicator or overheard conversation had led us to think of him as a true presence in the Mirabelle. He was a separate, other creature apart from the drama unfolding on the fourth floor.

I said, "I think we need to get out of here before that becomes the only option available. And from where I am standing, that is probably it."

Amelia flashed her light around the small space. "Then we try and bust the metal doorknob."

We began searching for something heavy. Most of the items were cleaning products, not heavy artillery.

"What about this?" Lulu was holding up a metal level she found on the shelf pressed against the northern wall. There was a stash of tools in an old plastic paint bin.

"Good as anything." Amelia shined her light as Lulu stood back, swinging the level high and bringing it down on the handle. It emitted a sick, sharp blast as it hit the door. The plastic siding of the level shot off and splintered, the doorknob remaining untainted.

"Well, that's one way to do it."

"Let's keep looking," I said.

Amelia continued to sweep the light. "Do you think there's anything else in here worth noting? It's a secure room, why not use it?"

"Nothing that I can see, but let's keep a keen eye." I kicked something made of steel. "How about a metal bucket?" They nodded and under Amelia's white light attempted to smash the doorknob. The noise was debilitating to the ears. You could almost taste the metal as it collided, a tangy flavor that shot up to my eyes.

"Anything?" Lulu was at the back of the room, covering her ears.

"No, I think I may have dented it."

Amelia said, "Eventually someone will hear us, right? Should we start to yell?"

I said, "I don't think we're there yet."

For the following ten minutes, we continued to damage the doorknob with various instruments found throughout the room. Nothing seemed to work.

"I can't believe no one has wondered about the sounds coming from the creepy room on the fourth floor." Lulu threw a bag of hotel soaps against the far wall. "And worse yet, we're missing the auction. After this, the items will be separated. No reward, no full collection. No grant."

Amelia pulled the flashlight up. "What do you mean, reward?"

I silently scolded Lulu in my head, but it was bound to come out eventually. How long could the four of us go without mentioning a key component to why we are here? Other than wanting justice for the artifacts and the Chaco Canyon site, and updating my grant, this money could go a long way. *Especially* if Amelia wanted to leave Sunny. But this didn't seem the time to wander into that arena of conversation.

Lulu looked up, startled at her slip. She was silent. Thinking, she responded, "Didn't we tell you?"

"Tell me what? What do you mean?"

I tried to help Lulu. "I think in all the commotion we forgot to tell you, there is also a reward for finding and returning the artifacts. It's not our main reason for finding them, of course, but something to keep in our back pocket."

Lulu and I locked eyes in the semi-lit room, frozen. Amelia said, "Who is giving a reward? The museum? That seems odd."

"Someone who works with the museum and wants to see them returned."

"I can't believe you forgot to mention that. Do other people outside of our group know about this?"

I said, "I'm not sure. I heard about it from someone at work. I didn't do a lot of follow up, it didn't seem necessary since the artifacts were so out of reach. Until tonight, we never thought we'd get so close."

"Maybe Parker and Bill are working on that right now." Amelia said. We sat back in our original spot, against the boxes in the corner, my senses adjusting to the strange smells. "I can't believe you *both* left your phones."

"Bill has it."

Lulu replied, "I didn't want to bring a purse, and these pants certainly don't fit a large phone. I was not about to have that thing flopping out as we ran. My heels are enough to make *that* difficult enough. But stylish, I have no regrets."

"I can't believe we are stuck in a utility closet. Great day to wear white." Amelia laid her head back against the box. She was wearing white linen pants and a silk blue button top and looked straight out of a magazine. Lulu pulled her heels off and brought her knees in tight, her black pants screaming at the odd angle. I was glad I donned jeans before meeting with Amelia. This had been one long Thursday night.

Lulu asked, "What are you thinking, Mel? Now that Sunny is here at the Mirabelle?"

"I haven't had time to really think it through. We've been going fast since I found out, it's only been a few hours."

"I'm sorry it's ending like this."

"In a way, I think I'm relieved. Which says a lot, I know. And I don't even know what I'm relieved about, exactly."

I said, "I think it's validating the concerns you've been having for the last year."

"I've been having a lot of thoughts lately. And you know what? I've been toying with an idea."

"What's that?" Lulu stretched her legs out long and wiggled her toes.

"I don't know, it's going to be strange saying it aloud. Promise you won't think I've up and joined the circus?"

"I have just about sent us on a treasure hunt," I said, "I don't think I am in the place to judge at the moment."

"I'd love for one day to bake for a living. Maybe out of the house, the kitchen. Nothing big."

Lulu hit her arm, "Amelia, *duh* I've been telling you that for years! That's the sanest thing I've heard in the last 48 hours."

She smiled. "You think?"

I said, "You would be amazing. You are an exceptional baker. Would you want it to be Irish based?"

"I think a lot of my items would be, yes, but a fusion of sorts. And I've learned some tricks from my parents and their restaurant chain. But I'd want it to be intimate, classy."

"What's holding you back? The boys are in school now, and if you were able to hire help you could be home and run the bakery."

"I mentioned it to Sunny, it was more in passing. He said I wouldn't have the time. He brushed it off pretty quickly. He said he doesn't want me to be stressed."

Lulu said, "How does he know what you do with your time? He's never home."

"I see his point, though. How could I do that and have dinner on the table for Aiden and Ryan, and drop them off to soccer and tennis?"

"Welcome to the working mom's dilemma," Lulu said. "Look at Georgia, she has four kids and still works part-time. I have Gabe and work full-time. I might not always have a hot meal at the ready, but we're happy, the three of us. We have a routine, amongst all of the busy lives we're leading, and I wouldn't have it any other way. I'm happy, you know? Especially if I get out of this godforsaken utility closet."

Amelia smiled. "You're both different. You're such go-getters."

"Oh, and you're not?" I said. "You drove hours to find your husband and confront him about lying. That takes a lot of courage. I think you should seriously consider what you want out of life now that the kids are growing."

"I feel selfish, even though I know that sounds crazy to say."

Lulu said, "You're not crazy. Sometimes our world makes women feel like that way, that if they do something other than raising their children or feed their husbands, they should take a good hard look at their morals. It's all insane, of course. Why should the men have all the promotions and career choices? I for one am going to be working until the day I die."

I said, "I don't know if you will ever die, Lulu."

Amelia said, "Too stubborn."

"If I do, I'm going down with a latte and a vanilla scone from Amelia's bakery."

Suddenly, a slight knock came to the door, breaking our tempo. I ran to the noise and pressed my ear against the metal. The door was large and heavy, but I think I heard something. I said, "Anyone there?"

Nothing. Lulu said, "I *swear* I heard something. Is the darkness driving us all mad?"

Amelia said, "We've been in here about thirty minutes, I'm pretty sure we shouldn't be insane. Yet."

Lulu nodded. "Comforting."

Another noise. I said, "It doesn't sound quite like a knock."

"Do you think someone is trying to come in?" Lulu backed away from the door. "Maybe we should assume our positions by the boxes."

"Can't run forever," Amelia said. "I guess we wait."

191

We met Lulu at the back, eyes on the door.

"Doesn't this make you want to run a bakery even more?" Lulu asked.

"Being locked in here with you two?"

"Realizing how short life is. I'm not saying we're dying, but it does remind one of what's important."

The three of us jumped as the fingerprint sensor from our end of the door beeped three times, then turned green, followed by the sound of a lock unhinging. The door slowly opened, highlighting a short, petite silhouette. It didn't appear to be Bill, Parker, Leo, or Ted, but it was hard to distinguish as our eyes adjusted to the blaring light.

A woman's voice said, "You ladies better hurry before they come back."

I knew that voice. As I drew near, I caught the flittering of a yellow dress. The lady from downstairs...I had almost forgotten the Deja vu sensation she evoked, and now it all came together.

"Maggie?"

"There will be time for pleasantries later. Let's get out of here."

As we followed her out of the room and began walking towards the stairwell, the fire alarm began to squeal. It was a hard assault to the ears, high pitched, and coming from multiple alarms along the hallway. Doors began opening along the corridor as patrons were unsure if they should leave, heads turning our way as we hurried past towards our destination. As we ran for the stairwell door, I glanced back and noted a large grouping of men heading towards the utility closet. We were lost in the crowd of people rushing towards the various exits. We appeared safe, for now.

Maggie had us running down to the third floor and exited as people began flooding through, a wave of hands and legs swimming by. She led us to room 3001.

Lulu asked, "Who are you? How do you know one another?"

I said, "She is the person Lucy and Mike connected me with."

"You own the flower shop?"

"I can explain later, we don't have a lot of time."

Lulu said, "Did we set off the alarm?"

"No, that wasn't us. I entered legitimately."

I said, "You're after the reward, aren't you?" That glimmer I saw in her eye when I mentioned the money wasn't lost in translation. I saw the want.

"I am." She said, "trust me, I wasn't trying to screw you over."

"I can't imagine this could go any other way." I was shocked to be seeing her.

"You can say that all you want, but I just rescued you from a closet."

"True. Then what are we doing here? What's with the alarms?"

"There's no fire, we're fine hunkering down."

I turned to Amelia, "Can you call Bill and Parker, let them know we're alright?" She nodded.

Maggie continued, "You can bring them here, it's safe."

"How did you get this far?" I asked, "finding the Mirabelle was a lucky chance on our end."

"It wasn't hard to do, I placed a small baby monitor in the back closet at my work. I had all the information I needed in 24 hours."

Parker and Bill knocked on the door and I let them in, hugging Bill. I told them, "This is Maggie, from the flower shop." His eyes widened at the recognition. "She's explaining how she got here. She rescued us from the utility closet."

Maggie nodded to them. "I'm guessing everyone here knows our conversation from the coffee shop?"

"Enough so, yes."

"Alright. Then you know I have an adjoining back area with Mel's bookstore. I listened in for a couple of hours, and luckily, some arguments ensued."

"What were they arguing about? I'm guessing it's the same men that were harassing you?"

"Yes, the new men that started coming around. They had moved the artifacts that Thursday, you already knew that from our conversation. But they hadn't moved everything. They had kept the jewelry in Mel's safe since they are pricier. We thought they had moved every piece, and there they were, feet away from me. Not like I could've retrieved them, being in his safe. That mattered little." She was pacing, and I was nervous about Amelia. She was in the dark on my prior conversation with Maggie, too. Eventually, she would note the rift between the knowledge she has and that of me, Lulu and Parker. "The men in the shop were arguing about a man named Jason, and how the timing didn't work out. They weren't happy. But I did catch a location, a hotel called the Mirabelle. Lucky it wasn't at a Motel 6, one swipe of my finger and Google directed me where I needed to be."

"Alright, so you learned everything from the back of Mel's. But you don't know who is offering the reward. How were you planning on cashing that out?"

"That was my only hurdle. I tried asking around but couldn't find a lead, which is surprising knowing the people I do, those who have crossed between Mel's and my flower shop throughout the years."

"What was your plan? Especially working solo like this. I can't imagine you'd be able to haul everything back to the city."

"I'm used to working solo, that was hardly an issue." The alarm continued its vicious howl, it's shriek now meaningless as it rolled into background noise. "I planned to scope it out. Coming here wasn't an issue. What I hoped to find, was you."

"And convince me to help you? Or split the earnings?"

"I wasn't sure what I was going to find, but I thought there would be something. I figured you'd need help, there was no way you would waltz into the auction or buy an entry ticket. They are charging $10,000 a token, and that's not including the membership price. And then there you were, three damsels needing rescued from a closet. It was too easy."

"How did you know we were in the closet?"

"I was watching, observing people in the hotel. I got here much earlier than you and was starting to wonder if you were going to show. I finally followed your two utility men to the fourth floor. They were loud. If Jason only knew, they'd be on the chopping block. As I followed them, I managed to catch your little act and realized that the room held something important. Nice touch with the seizure."

"You were assuming we would partner with you if you did find us."

She looked annoyed. "Do you think we have time for this? I saved your ass. Now I deserve some explanation, myself. And don't forget, I helped you with the Furbo."

"I didn't forget. What would you like to know?"

"You were in the utility closet. What happened? Why didn't you get what you came for?"

I explained the last hour and omitted any knowledge of Sunny. "Until you opened the door, we weren't sure what was going to happen. We were close, but it slipped passed our fingers."

Maggie said, "So, that's where they were storing them. But Enough chit chat, let's cut to the chase. The fire alarm sounded because the police were called."

Lulu said, "*What?*"

"It wasn't me, you can trust that. I was headed for the artifacts, I had no business calling the cops. Drawing attention."

"Then who did?" Amelia and Parker walked to the window, looking at the police cars that began lining up.

"That I don't know. Could be anyone, a mole, a backstabber. I hadn't heard mention of any suspicion from my surveillance, but I only got my information through the back room, a sliver of the operation. There are a lot more men and women in on this in other parts of this state. Until I arrived earlier today, I had no idea how large this was. Who knew it would be such an event for museum artifacts?"

"Ok, so what do we do now? Why save us at all?"

"There is still possibility of finding the pieces. But you're right, I can't do it alone we're running out of time."

"What is it that you know?" I asked, "you clearly have information, you knew the cops were called."

"It was luck."

Lulu cut her off. "Wait, wait. How do we know you aren't in on this? You were able to open the utility closet, and that required a fingerprint and a key card."

"That's how I found my information, actually. I saw you ladies enter the room, and the others take your friend up the elevator. I tried the utility door myself and it was locked, and I noticed the scanner. After some time, it was clear you weren't getting out. So, I went to the main floor and hovered around the Mirabelle Bar, to see what I could find. It was bustling, people were excited. The artifacts must have even been grander than they thought. Long story short, I cut someone's finger off." Amelia looked like she was going to pass out. "I'm *kidding* good lord. I started thinking, how on earth could I get someone to let me in? So, I came back up to my room and changed into all black. I looked enough like a server and watched them long enough to see where they went. How they acted."

Amelia said, "Did it work?"

"I needed a reason that I couldn't open the door myself. I wasn't sure every worker in the building had access, but I figured it was worth a shot to try something. Luckily, I had boxes in my van from a flower run yesterday. I grabbed a few and loaded them with some items from my hotel room. I was working fast. I took my boxes and hovered on the fourth floor for a while. No one came by, so I tried the third, then the second floor. Finally, a maid walked by. I asked her if she could help me on the fourth floor."

"And she opened it, like that?"

"She did. She was in a rush, and I don't think she knew what was stored inside. My guess is they haven't told their workers what kind of operation they are running, aside from those that work the event directly. That would be foolish."

Bill said, "Good thinking, actually."

"While we were on the elevator, she told me police officers were on the main level, and to stay away if possible. Fewer people to question. She had seen workers lose their job by saying too much, too little. I told her I was new. She told me that something similar happened back in March and that they utilize the fire alarm as code to hunker down. I'm guessing it's for those involved to hide whatever contraband is on the premise, but I'm not sure."

I said, "They're hiding the artifacts as we speak?"

"I'm certain they were hidden the moment a police car showed on their radar, long down the main road. But I know little else."

Amelia said, "I can't imagine what we could do now with the authorities here."

"Sure, but they may lack warrants," Bill said. "We can steal away to places they only dream of going. I'm sure this isn't the first time they've tried busting into the Mirabelle."

Maggie nodded. "That's why I'm in no rush. The artifacts are already tucked away."

I said, "What do you presume we do?"

"We wait."

Chapter 17
Confrontation

Amelia looked antsy. She took me aside as the others discussed plausible locations for the stolen items.

She said, "I am concerned about the artifacts, but I don't want to waste this opportunity to confront Sunny. I'm afraid if I don't do it now, it'll never happen. He can't talk his way out of being somewhere he shouldn't be. If I speak to him at home, he could lie. He *will* lie."

I had almost forgotten he was a key player in the events tonight. "Let me think about this. We could use this to our advantage if you're comfortable with that."

"As long as he knows I'm here, that's alright with me." She looked tired. It was late, and we were going to have to call into work tomorrow. "How do you know Maggie?"

"Bill knows this couple that has their hand in the art trade. He reached out to them, asking if they had heard anything. They pointed me to Maggie."

"What did she find?"

Little parts of the last few weeks were coming out, and I was glad. As long as Parker was able to hold his story close, that was alright with me. "She led me and Lulu to Hugh, believe it or not."

"Your supervisor?"

"One and the same. He's involved, which isn't surprising. It would have been hard to pull this off without someone from the inside. It was his voicemail that we told you about earlier, the one Lulu and I overheard."

"I guess that makes sense, he was running the dig."

"It also shows the magnitude of the night. Hugh, Sunny…"

Amelia shuttered. "You know what never crossed my mind? I've been so worried about confronting him that I never considered the fact that he might get arrested. Or hurt."

"Their arrival makes everything seem real, doesn't it?"

"What would the boys and I do?"

"I don't think we're there yet. Let's concentrate on finding him first if he's still here."

She pulled out her phone. "Says he is. But it's a big hotel, he could be anywhere."

We walked back to the group. I said, "I think it's time we find Sunny."

Parker said, "I understand wanting to find him, but once we do, the artifacts will be out of reach."

"Why is that?"

"He's high up in this, if they know we're toying around, any chance of getting close is gone. We've already shown our face to more people than I'd like."

Amelia said, "What if I approach Sunny, acting blind to the artifact situation? I don't have to let on to any of that. I might get more information."

Maggie said, "Who is Sunny?"

"Amelia's husband." I explained, "he's one of the investors, it seems. He has ties to Jason and a few other men here. We're not sure his total involvement, and he isn't aware we know anything."

"You're just telling me this *now*?"

"It's complicated."

Bill said, "I think you're right, this is the next step. There's little else we can do if they've hidden the artifacts. We could wait to see what we find from the remnants at the bar, but we'd likely find little."

Amelia said "So, we find Sunny. Where do we start?"

"Seems we have to start the old-fashioned way, feet on the ground," Maggie said. "I don't think asking around will be wise. Can I see what he looks like?"

Amelia pulled up a photo. "Should we break off in teams?"

Bill said, "Maggie, you come with me and Ellie. Parker, Lulu, and Amelia, you guys take the first five floors and the lobby, we'll take the last six. What do you plan on doing when you see him, Amelia?"

"The truth, minus the artifacts. That he's been lying, hiding his life from me. Perhaps I'll pick up more information. It's our last shot."

I tried to read Parker's face, he looked anxious. Even though he wanted to be with Amelia, he didn't want to see her in pain.

I said, "Seems like a good plan. Is everyone ok with it? If we see Sunny, we'll keep it under wraps. We'll text you the location."

Lulu said, "Let's hope he doesn't see us first."

As the two teams of three separated, the air felt toxic, anticipating a clash. We had been close. It was hard to believe the artifacts existed in true form, a phantom that only some remembered, some believed. Our mindset alerted as the night progressed. It was less about the money and more about returning the artifacts to their true owners. No one should steal history from another, especially for such shallow, monetary gain. The tribes deserved the pieces, and we wanted to see justice served.

We arrived on the sixth level. Every floor thus far was a typical square formation, the elevators in the middle, and the stairs on the sides near the ice machines. We took the ice bucket and ambled along. It was suddenly quiet.

I asked Maggie, "Is that good or bad news the alarm has stopped?"

"It means they sent their message."

We continued up the floors. Some patrons were peering out the window at the end of the hotel hallway, wondering about the sudden silence and the flashing siren lights. But nothing odd, out of place. No Sunny.

"I'm beginning to feel foolish," I said. Bill placed his hand on my back and squeezed.

As we rounded the next corner on the 8th floor, a man almost ran into us, quickly making his way to the stairs. I looked back and knew it was Antonio.

"He's one of the men working with Sunny." The hallway seemed hot, the air thin. We followed Antonio at a slow pace, hoping he didn't notice our change in direction. He suddenly stopped, answering his phone. Before he reached the stairwell, he looked back, squinting. He had seen me before at Amelia's, but was I recognizable? Before I could decipher his reaction, he skirted down the stairs and was out of sight.

"I think he may have remembered me."

Maggie said, "Do we follow him?"

"Yes, what's the worst that could happen?" I said the words as Maggie pulled open the door. She let out a short scream as Antonio stood there, face inches from her own.

"Maggie. Something tells me you're not here selling flowers?" His voice was gruff, a razor. He continued to inch closer as Maggie backed away, the four of us in the hallway. Her back was to the door across from the stairwell. If the guest inside were to look out their peephole, they would be in for quite a scene.

Bill stepped towards the two forces. "We mean no harm."

"Who is this? Your henchman? Too scared from our presence that you hired help?" He let out a deep laugh, one that vibrated through the cheap carpeted floors splashed with red and black ink too bright for the occasion. He took a step back. "I had a feeling that wouldn't be the end of you. I told them myself. You were too curious, it would take more to scare you good."

"You have no proof of why I'm here." Maggie spit.

"Two hours south? I don't have time for your lies." He picked up his phone. I looked at Bill, who seemed unsure. "Yeah boss, our little red-headed friend is here." A pause. "Sure thing. I'd love to." He stepped closer to Maggie, but a door opening to our left diverted his attention. Taking this brief respite and turn of his head, she bolted past us and down the hall, towards the stairwell on the other end of the floor. As a reaction, I followed. Herd mentality kicked in as the three of us suddenly found ourselves being chased by a man selling the very artifacts we came to find.

"You think you can run in here? This is our *castle*." He said the last with such bite that my speed increased. Maggie threw open the stairwell door and began running downward, our breath matching the beat of our steps. Antonio was close, but he was slower. His footsteps echoed throughout the hollow space, marking his distance from ours. We continued down the flights, our arms spinning around the hand railing to reach the next landing. It seemed we were gaining traction but as Maggie opened the door on the second floor, his steps closed in, my sides splintering. We turned the corner to run down another leg of the square, and noticed a close group of people but lacked the time to react. We found ourselves running directly into Sunny and Rick, our bodies cracking with the harsh contact, all parties falling to the ground except Antonio who was able to slow himself with his saved distance. I admonished our group for being reckless, realizing that Sunny had found us before we were ready. I looked up to see blood trickling down Bill's nose. He said he was fine, a scratch.

Sunny's eyes grew wide as recognition splashed across his face. "Bill? Ellie? What the *hell* are you doing here?" He stood up, wiping his hands across his pants. His eyes flashed red. Antonio grabbed Maggie to stop her from running. I quickly grabbed my phone and texted Amelia.

Maggie said, "You know *why*. Do you think you can harass me and get away with it? I don't take kindly to threats in my own turf." Antonio continued to hold her arms as she tried to fight free. Sunny looked flabbergasted.

The stairwell we exited moments prior burst open and Amelia, Lulu, and Parker entered our space, the hallway tight with sweat, adrenaline, and confused familiarity.

"*Amelia?* You have some explaining to do. Why are you here?" He lurched towards her and Amelia backed away.

"I think I should ask you the same question. You said you were leaving the state. You're only two hours away? You *lied*. There's no talking your way out of this one."

"My work schedule is none of your business, Amelia. How did you find me here?" His voice was like a tea kettle, shaking with sweat on the stove. His true self began seeping out, the venom dripping to the floor.

"My cell phone. And it *is* my business when you lie. I'm your wife. I deserve honesty."

"If that's the case, where are the children? You don't trust me if you tracked me here like a snake. My work plans changed. That's all. Now, who seems paranoid?"

Parker's arm twitched and I placed my arm on his shoulder. We instinctually backed away, giving the conversation space it merited.

Antonio interrupted. "What would you like me to do with this one?" Maggie squirmed.

"Take her to Jason."

Bill said, "You can't *kidnap* Maggie. Let her go."

Antonio yelled, "For Christ's sakes, you are in our hotel, we decide what happens."

I said, "With the police downstairs? Good luck. You must not be running things as tightly as you thought." Antonio looked like he wanted to grab me but was tied up with Maggie. He bit his lip as he dragged her away. Bill nodded to me as he followed, telling me to stay.

Amelia continued. "Your work plans didn't change. Another lie. What are you doing here, then?"

"Like you understand investments, or care too. You've never been interested in my work. I bring home the money for you to twirl about, having your book clubs and baking your desserts. How dare you ask about my work when I support you?"

Her face seemed to fall for a moment. "Stop deflecting."

"I'm done with this conversation. Go home. This is highly inappropriate, talking like this in a hallway full of people. What's gotten into you?"

"Then let's go back to your room. I'm not leaving until we talk."

His tone decreased a decibel. "Amelia, I'm telling you, we're done here. I am in the middle of something important."

"You know what else is important? Our marriage. You've been at work more than you've been home. And you know what? Answer me this. Is it you leaving the threatening messages? You that blew a hole in our study? I have a feeling you know a lot more than you're letting on."

He seemed speechless, then pointed a finger at her. "We'll talk later. And I'm certainly interested in how you know Maggie. I'm sure she's filled your head with wild tales. She's off her rocker. I don't want you to be with her another moment." He motioned to Rick and they began to walk away. Suddenly, a loud noise erupted from the elevator as another group of men dressed in all black exited, shouting at Sunny. He whipped his head around quickly.

One man stepped forward. "The police are on to our business. The goods are in the truck. We don't have much time and they're searching for our cars at the front. The bar is emptied and our staff are being questioned, and I can't find Jason. We chose to send the truck out, but it's driving aimlessly. We need direction, boss."

Another spoke, "It's just a matter of time until someone talks."

"None of the members know where we were storing the pieces, and no one knows that they are no longer on-site," Rick said. "We have that going for us." He seemed to be trying to calm Sunny before he broke.

Sunny looked from the men to Amelia, Lulu, Parker, stiff as statues. He said, "Take the truck back to the spot. We'll have to go with plan B."

The front man said, "Mel's?"

Sunny seemed to snap. "No, you idiot. Why are you announcing this in a hallway full of people? What's wrong with you?"

The corridor was hectic as other guests began opening their doors at the noise, concerned about the fire alarm, and wondering if there was a connection.

"I don't have time to hear your opinions on this." The large man was approaching Sunny and was a good four inches taller. "Where would you like us to take your items? The clock is ticking and I'm not about to be stuck in the middle of one of your bad decisions." Sunny approached him and whispered for a long moment. They seemed to reach a decision.

Finally, the group exited, leaving the room hot with anticipation. That was enough proof for me, the artifacts were outside in a truck, somewhere in southern Colorado.

Sunny cursed as he picked up his ringing phone. "It's taken care of. It's all in the truck. Yeah." He seemed worried. "I'm not sure who called it in. We'll figure it out, let's take care of this first."

Amelia said, "Don't you walk away from me. As if you can tell me who to hang out with. What's gotten into *you*?"

Sunny gave one last, long dismissive look, then headed down the stairs with Rick, the door slamming an end to the night.

Chapter 18
Fluttering Pages

Amelia seemed to be holding firm, then her reserve fell. She wasn't sad, as I expected, but fuming. "I can't believe him. I can't believe that is the person I married. The father of my children."

"I'm so sorry Amelia," Lulu said.

"I don't even feel sad anymore, all that's left is anger."

Parker said, "What do we do now?"

"I'm not about to chase after him, like some perverse lovesick puppy."

"You don't have to do anything you don't want." I said, "This is your marriage. We support your choice."

"I know. I will need some time to figure everything out when we leave. Let's concentrate on the artifacts. The rest will come when Sunny and I confront each other at home. *If* he comes home. No sense in ruminating about it now. Let's find Bill and Maggie."

We made our way to the lobby. It was well past midnight, but the hotel was crowded and hot. It felt anything but the middle of the night. The police held a strong presence, but we knew the artifacts were gone. Nothing much to find here.

Surprisingly, Maggie ran up to us. I said, "What happened? Where's Antonio?"

"Jason gave Antonio an earful. He said walking through a hotel looking like he was harboring a hostage was the dumbest thing he had ever seen with the police mulling about. He ran off with his tail between his legs."

Bill approached, looking relieved. He embraced me and we filled him in.

He said, "So, we're back to square one. We might have to call this one, guys. If someone wants to approach the police…"

Amelia said, "I can't imagine what we would say."

Parker said, "You know the artifacts were here as well as I do."

"Can you imagine explaining this to the police? We never even saw them." I yawned, the night catching up to me. "Looks like they know as much as us at this point."

Lulu said, "You might be right. We tried our hardest. And just short of being stuck in a closet for the rest of my life, this was a pretty exciting night out for a full-time working mother."

Bill said to me, "You need to take Lulu out more often if she thinks this is an evening full of fun."

I turned to Maggie, "The artifacts are in a truck, they've left. No clue as to where."

She said, "I'm not surprised, we lost time there at the end. We did what we could, and it's not exactly over. They're still out there, and their buyers have left empty-handed. This is going to cause a stir."

"Are you going to keep looking for them?"

"I'm not sure. I can't keep working next to Mel's, not now anyway."

Amelia said, "I want to thank you for getting us out of the utility closet. I appreciate it." Lulu and I expressed similar sentiment. "You're quick on your feet."

Maggie seemed to relax for the first time I had ever witnessed. "I only wish we had something to show for it. Thanks for looking out for me, too."

And with that, she was gone as quickly as she appeared, her red hair disappearing through the doorway like magic. Parker said, "Let's get out of here before we're questioned. I don't have a great poker face and you guys have been places you shouldn't be."

Lulu smiled and locked arms as we walked out of the Mirabelle. "It was a beautiful bar. Kind of took me back to my twenties."

"Do you even remember that far back?" Parker said.

"Oh funny."

Bill sat at the wheel and we made our way slowly back to Dove Park, stopping for food and disseminating the night's events.

I turned to Amelia, "Do you want to stay with Bill and me tonight?"

"Thanks for the offer, but I have to face the facts eventually. And the boys will need me in the morning. I doubt Sunny will be back tonight, but if he is, I want to be there."

As everyone left our house, the sun threatened to peek above the horizon. Lulu and I left Hugh a voicemail calling in the next morning, and I hardly cared if he thought we were both in it together, faking sick. I needed to sleep. This had been a night to remember.

I didn't check my phone until 10:00 in the morning, Bill and I both dead to our surroundings. When I finally rolled over, I had several missed calls. I dialed Lulu first.

"About time." She said.

"Oh right, three hours of sleep is such a luxury."

"I don't know what to do about Amelia."

"What do you mean?"

"Have you talked with her this morning?"

"No, I just saw that you called."

"There's been another message at the house. Amelia asked if we could meet at her place for breakfast, I was just leaving."

"Shoot. Alright, give me a minute and we'll be over."

I woke Bill and we took a quick shower, washing the feel of the Mirabelle off of our body. It seemed wrong to bring that back to Amelia's, we needed a fresh slate for what we were about to encounter. I didn't yet feel tired, that would hit later.

The rain finally relented, the sun appearing crisp and ready for the day, it's rays and happy vibes giving me a headache. As we parked, Bill looked stricken. "I had no idea it did such damage." He motioned towards the rubble where the study once belonged.

"It seems to be cursed." I realized the explosion had only happened two days ago. It felt we lived an entire year between then and today.

"Is the gala still happening tomorrow?" Bill and I walked slowly up the drive, observing the surrounding area, looking for anything out of place. A napkin from our book club Wednesday had blown itself against the willow, tattered and worn.

"As far as I know. And the notes… something or *somebody* needs to stop by then. Tomorrow. We can't for the life of us figure out what they mean by it. It's relentless."

"Let's see what we find this time."

Amelia opened the door. "I'm glad you guys came. I'm sorry, I know we were just together hours ago. You need to sleep."

Her eyes had circles planted under her lids. "*You* need sleep, Amelia. How did last night go?"

"Sunny never showed, as far as I could tell. But the house is large, I guess you never know."

We followed her through the hallway and to the kitchen where Lulu and Parker sat on the barstools against the island. Lulu had a bagel in one hand and a coffee in the other, eyes groggy. She said, "Is it crazy to say that I missed you guys?"

Parker said, "Seems we only find trouble."

"I wouldn't put that on us." I said, "If anything, we're trying to help trouble that was already happening."

Lulu said, "Alright Amelia, spill. What is the latest message? I'm on the edge of your bar stool."

"It'll do better to show you." We followed Amelia down the hall and up to the second floor. Every corner seemed an option for change, another place for a tucked message or perch of a criminal. Arriving at the master suite, Amelia opened the door. We were stunned. Silence.

It had a beautiful feel that was romantic had we not understood its origin, its target. Hundreds of book pages hung delicate from the ceiling, the windows and doors. One page, in particular, drew the eye. It was hanging from the fan's pull chain. Instead of showcasing a handwritten note, the paper had been highlighted and was otherwise untainted. It read:

...it is only in the darkness of the grave that man will find the peace which the wickedness of his fellows, the tumult of his own passions, and, above all, the inevitability of his fate shall eternally deny him in this life.

I said, "Amelia, did you sleep here last night?"

"No, I stayed at Parker's. I called him the moment I entered my room. I was so terrified I sat in my car, waiting. Once I got to his house, I realized it never occurred to me to call Sunny." Her voice fell as the sentence progressed.

Parker said, "This is more personal than the other messages, they either had access to her home, or they broke inside."

"Everything feels so touched. It doesn't feel safe anymore, anywhere." Lulu placed her head on Amelia's shoulder. "There seem to be no markings of forced entry, but there are a lot of windows and I haven't checked them all. I'm incredibly thankful the boys didn't stay here last night."

Bill, Lulu, and I walked slowly under the canopy built by paper and ink. It seemed careful. The wrong word uttered or an erroneous tilt of the chin, and the pages would fall, crumbling. There was a sound omitting from the pages when they rubbed against one another. When compiled with how many were present, it created a symphony of scrapes that was hard to describe.

Lulu said, "These pages, they're from *The Crimes of Love*, aren't they?"

Amelia nodded. "I hadn't opened this week's book yet, for obvious reasons. This isn't my copy, but it looks old. I think it may even be a first edition."

"De-facing a book, a crime in itself," Bill said quietly as we fully absorbed the scene. "Are we safe here?" He read the page again. "Amelia, this almost sounds like a death threat, depending on how you take it."

Amelia said, "The police are on their way. I think we're alright in the meantime, but yes, this seems different than the others. Whatever action they wanted to be stopped, certainly did not. Or at least not in a manner of their liking. But the deadline is tomorrow, so I don't feel completely in harm's way.

Not yet, unless they changed their mind, but there's nothing to indicate that's the case."

Parker said, "I agree with Bill. I think the message is conveying that if someone doesn't stop, they will find their end. Their grave. What needs to be stopped is beyond me."

I shuttered. "They took time with this. The pages are cut, they weren't torn. It is personal. It looks to be the entire book, doesn't it?"

"I believe so," Amelia said, "and the cover, back, and spine are sitting on our end table." It looked like a gutted fish, a book with no insides was an ugly affair. I forced myself to look away. "I'm entirely out of ideas. I'm not as afraid as the first two weeks knowing what Sunny is into. This has to involve him and his criminal antics. I'm clean, that I am sure of. I only hope his involvement doesn't get us killed. They may think we're at fault when it's him, depending on how he conducted business. It's what I'm most afraid of."

"Should we have meddled?" Lulu was still spinning, reading the pages from above, caught in its hypnotic movement. She said to me and Bill quietly, "What if this is because we followed Sunny?"

Parker said, "I thought the same when we were at the bar, but the first few messages were before we started looking into him." Parker shifted and I took him aside as Amelia and Bill re-read the highlighted portion.

"You had Shelby investigating before the first message."

"A few weeks before, yes. But I can't imagine he could have tied that to me. We hadn't met with him yet."

"Do you think Shelby is somehow involved?"

"I really don't. Do you?"

"No, I don't."

"Even if Sunny saw that someone was following him, how would he link that to me? Then come and vandalize his own home? It still wouldn't add up. I don't think it's us."

"You're right, we're trying to piece together something that isn't whole. We need more information." We walked back to Bill and Amelia and I remembered the phrasing from the note left for us at the bar. "If after all this time the note at the bar isn't indicating Amelia, who is it in reference too? It said, 'tell your friend, the one not present, that we are watching'. We assumed it meant you, Amelia, and you weren't aware you had information. It seemed to make sense at the time, but I'm not so sure now."

"I haven't a clue. And I'm certain there's nothing more I know. I feel like something would have sparked a memory or a clue. I don't think it means me, either."

We thought about it a moment, understanding its implication. I asked, "Did you tell Georgia or Hannah about this message?"

"I texted them to meet up, but they're both at work. They want to see us when they're off, though. When the police tinker, I have pictures."

Lulu said, "Do we tell them everything that has happened?"

Bill lightly touched a page and it twirled. "I don't know if that's wise, quite yet."

"I go back and forth," Amelia said. "I think that could complicate matters. And the gala is tomorrow, if they are targeting one of us here, we'll know it soon enough. Why risk more lives by telling them information that could harm them?"

"Aren't you afraid?" I asked.

"What do you mean?"

"None of us here believe the notes are pointed towards us. If something is happening, we aren't the ones to stop it. What if the perpetrator isn't satisfied? What happens then?"

"We keep moving forward. But something tells me we're going to find out soon enough. I've called the police, there's not much else we can do for the moment. They know the notes have mentioned the gala, and I've told my mother. There will be security there anyway, no doubt. We should be alright attending tomorrow. And I *want* to. What if we find something else?"

The ringing of the front door made me jump as the group turned to leave. Exiting the room of the hanging pages was odd, I felt somehow drawn to the scene but also perturbed. It was a sight I would not forget for some time.

Lulu leaned into me, "We're keeping the police on their toes, calling on a Friday. What's next, a note on a Tuesday?"

"Aren't we the wildest."

"What do you have going on today?"

"Bill didn't have any viewings, luckily. We're probably going to sleep."

"You *are* wild. Hugh hasn't called me."

"Me neither. He somehow doesn't seem the type to call his employees back and ask how they're doing."

"He was probably up all night, too." It was Lulu's time to yawn. "There was a part of me that kept thinking I would see him at the hotel, I'd turn my head and wonder if it was the back of his big head. But it never was. I would know his look anywhere."

"I felt the same. Something tells me he's more the man behind the scenes. He doesn't even like talking to his employees, I'm sure an event of that stature would be low on his bucket list."

We said farewell as Lulu, Bill and I walked out of the home. Amelia was going to stay with her mother tonight with the boys, and they were headed to camp the next day so Shannon and Amelia could get ready for the gala.

In the car, I asked Bill, "Do you think it'll be safe tomorrow at the party? That was some sight…"

"Shannon seems careful, meticulous. But then again, this business Hugh and Sunny have going on is large."

"I'm trying to decide if it's worth it to go to the gala, knowing what we know."

"The artifacts are still out there. Perhaps we'll learn something if we go. Half the town goes, I can't imagine anything dangerous happening."

"Perhaps." I felt wary.

"I'll be there with you. The moment either of us feels uncomfortable, we'll leave. We had a lot of fun when we went last year, maybe we need this after a stressful week. I know Amelia does. We can't keep letting this invisible person run our lives, making decisions for us. And from what it seems, we're not the targets."

I smiled. "You have a way with words, Bill."

The gala seemed to hang in the balance, the ending to some unknown force. There was a relief at the knowing the ending was near yet fear towards the mystery of it all. Perhaps we shouldn't be excited for tomorrow.

As we were driving home, Bill had a recollection. "Did Amelia say the hanging pages were from a first edition?"

"She believed so. Why?"

"When was it released?"

"The first publication was in 1799."

"That's old."

"We like the classics."

"Where does someone buy a book like that?"

I realized what he was getting at. "Do you think?"

He turned the car around at the next light and sped back the direction we came, making his way to First Street.

What could hurt with a little questioning?

Chapter 19
Wise River

We pulled into a spot next to Mel's Rare Bookstore. Maggie's flower shop was dark for prime business hours. Potential customers cupped their hands against the windows, pulling the door handle, and knocking on the glass. The sunlight beaming on her store gave it an eerie iridescent quality. A black pearl among the other lit, busy shops.

"I keep thinking Mel will know we're involved with the artifacts the moment we walk in. As if looking in our eyes will somehow tell it all."

Bill turned off the car. "We're run of the mill customers, we'll blend. They should have no more involvement with Hugh anyways, right?"

"Not that I'd suspect. The artifacts didn't seem to fit inside the shop from what Maggie said. I doubt they would risk having them exposed especially after last night."

"Well then, no time like the present."

The sound of wind chimes swirled as we entered, answered by an ancient ding from the corner of the store. It was hard to believe they would have any surveillance from the 21st century, but we knew better.

A short, round man with large black glasses trotted up and asked if we needed anything, introducing himself as Mel.

I said, "I think we'd just like a look around if that's alright."

"Absolutely, take your time. And we have a small coffee cart in the back, couches and such if you find something worth your while." His smile seemed genuine as he disappeared back into the throw of books, a collection of poems by Edgar Allen Poe in his hand. The shop was large for a rare bookstore, and he was using every corner to his advantage. Books were stacked high in each row, many unreachable to even Bill, yet there seemed to be organized chaos intertwined within its folds. The rows were not symmetric, yet it was better, as if you were foraging for books, a true privilege if you found what you came for. A ladder on wheels sat at the end of the larger rows, allowing a sensation of joy to spring up my back.

Bill said, "It has a smell, doesn't it?"

"There's nothing quite like it, the slow decay of books. The way pages turn yellow, thick with touch."

"Well put. Look, behind the glass. A signed first edition of *No Country For Old Men*. $2,000. I didn't know a newer book could go for so much."

"If you get the right edition, you'd be surprised. I bet it's incredible looking for books to add to the collection."

We made our way to the back of the store, curiosity taking hold. There was an old, wooden employee-only door tucked between two overstuffed shelves holding the Edmund White's and Oscar Wilde's. I felt late, knowing what was harbored behind it only days before. We stared at the rickety door, hoping for an answer.

Mel approached, startling us both. "Find anything? I know it can be a little overwhelming."

"I think it's wonderful." I said, "Actually, I have a question."

"Alright, I'm sure I have an answer." He nudged his glasses higher on the arch of his nose.

"I was given a gift recently. A book. It was mailed to me but the package was torn, the sender unreadable. I have a feeling they bought it here, being a first edition and in such superb shape."

"We get a lot of customers, but I can try. What book?"

"*The Crimes of Love* by Marquis de Sade."

"Oh, I know it. 'The good never suspect others of perpetrating wicked deeds which they themselves are incapable of committing.' One of the most tragic short story collections, if I do say so. And one of my favorites. You must be quite the book lover if someone bought you a first edition?"

"Yes, I'm in a classic book club. It was perfect, really, and I'd love to properly thank whoever sent it."

He looked between us both, taking in our appearance, deciding if we were tricking him into information we shouldn't have. He took off his glasses, cleaning the lens, taking his time.

"A classic book club must be exciting. I know it's an awful question, but do you have a favorite?" The question was weighted, the correct answer seeded into his willingness to assist us with our query.

I took my time answering. I quoted, "I would always rather be happy than dignified."

He thought for a moment. "I want to say Jane Austen, but I know that's not right." He had his eyes cocked to the side, digging into the recesses of his mind. "Ah, there it is. *Jane Eyre.*" He nodded to no one in particular. "I used to have a second edition, long ago. The second page was torn, but it was beautiful. Sold it to a mother and daughter. Her husband was in oil." He brought himself back to the moment. "Alright, *The Crimes of Love* you say?"

"Yes. It looked in good condition."

"Looked? As in past tense?"

He was clever. But I could be quick, too. "I opened it at my mother's house, it's still there. I haven't been by again since."

He seemed to believe me. If he only knew the book carcass was sitting on an end table, the insides splayed out like an animal devoured by its prey.

He said, "Let me check my log. Come on now." We followed. He walked around the register and unlocked a sliding door underneath. He pulled out a large book. "I never can completely trust technology with important information. There's nothing that can truly replace a paper and pen." He flipped through his ledger. "Now, when do you believe it was purchased?"

"Anywhere between two weeks ago and Thursday, give or take."

"That margin may work." He flipped a page, scanning with his finger. He smiled. "You may be in luck…it looks like a first edition sold eight days ago." He looked pleased to be part of our treasure hunt. My stomach turned, could this be the person threatening our group?

"Would you be able to tell us who it sold to?"

"I would if I could pronounce it." He turned the book and pointed his finger on the name. "Abhainn Ghlic. Paid in cash, $3,000. Some slight damage, but otherwise in alright condition from the looks of it."

"Thank you for helping us, Mel." I jotted down the name.

"I hope it was helpful, such a strange name. Must be European."

Leaving the dark store, the sun forced a squint as we hurried to the car.

Bill pulled out his phone. "Looks like it means wise river in Gaelic. I was hoping it was a name."

"I'd try for an alias too if I were committing a crime with a purchase. I'm not surprised, they've been smart so far."

"It does tell us that they likely reside close or are here for an extended period."

"And they know about Mel's."

"There could be a connection between the threats and the artifacts, Mel isn't clean by the standards of law."

"I don't think he would have shown us the name had he known there was a connection. Maggie made it sound like he was a small fish in a large pond."

"You're probably right. It is a strange coincidence, though."

"This whole month has been one strange coincidence."

~

The rest of Friday sped quickly by. We were invited to Lulu's for drinks after work to fill Georgia and Hannah in about Amelia's bedroom discovery. As Bill and I pulled up to her house, Gabe was throwing a ball out front with Rex, the picture of a happy, suburban family. It made my heart yearn for something similar.

Parker was sitting on the porch swing chatting with Rex from a distance, the front door open and inviting. Bill ran across the lawn and intercepted the ball as Gabe tackled him to the ground. I joined Parker on the porch.

"How's it going?" I asked.

"It's hard to sleep."

"So, Amelia stayed with you last night?"

"Don't look at me like that." He let out a quiet laugh. "Completely platonic. She wanted the couch, but I gave her the bed. I was up all night knowing she was just feet away. I was ever the gentleman, don't you worry."

"I'm sorry, Parker."

"It's hell, knowing she's suffering. I can't do anything about it. We talked for some time last night, I think she's seriously facing the facts of her marriage. She can't sustain living like this. I tried my best at impartiality, but I'm in this deep."

"You tried to do something about it, though. Not a lot of men would go on a hunt for stolen jewelry and pottery to reap a reward so the love of his life could leave her husband."

"Sounds almost insane when you say it like that. You know the worst part?"

"What's that?"

"My pillow smells like her perfume. It's killing me. Funny, I thought I would take a quick nap today."

"Give it time."

"What if she does leave Sunny…but doesn't share the same sentiment? What if she never loves me back? I don't know how I'd ever move on. I would be crotchety for the rest of my life."

"I'd still be friends with you, regardless of how crotchety you were. And you're strong, you know?"

"It's the unknown. If I knew she loved someone else or never wanted to see me again, then at least I would know what to do."

"I think you're doing exactly what you should, you're being there for her. I know it doesn't seem like a lot, but it is. She's going through the worst time in her life and she needs a friend like you."

"I don't even care if Sunny did take all the money. I think I've been concentrating so hard on finding that reward as something physical to do. A distraction from thinking about Amelia. It's helped, having that goal. If we got the money, a problem would be solved, and I could be a part of it. A part of the solution." The ball careened our direction and Parker caught it, throwing it back. We watched the boys throw the ball, the sunset a bright orange backdrop as Parker swatted away a mosquito. Lulu came out with Hannah, holding coffees.

"You know you're the only one who drinks coffee this late, Lu."

"Decaf for the wimp, don't worry." She winked.

"I hate that I love your concoctions." Lulu and Hannah sat on the bench next to our swing. It was a beautiful night, but something stirred as an undercurrent.

Hannah said, "Have you guys started *The Crimes of Love*?"

I almost spit out my drink. "Not yet, I finally got the book though."

"It's a wild ride." Hannah crossed her legs on the bench, comfortable with her coffee between her palms. I was almost sad to break the innocence of the last message. For once, I didn't even want to open our weekly pick, it seemed tainted. "Especially for 1799."

Parker's demeanor changed as Amelia's car pulled up, Georgia right behind. He excused himself inside.

Hannah asked, "Is he alright? Seems quiet. And he's lost weight…"

"Just tired, I think."

Lulu shouted to Amelia and Georgia, "Come join! Have some fancy coffee Georgia brought back when she went to France."

Georgia ran and squeezed close, waving Amelia over. The three of us sat, swinging gently. Parker came back after several minutes, sitting in a chair next to Bill and far from Amelia. Rex left to drop Gabe off with a friend for the weekend, and we were suddenly covered in silence.

Georgia asked, "I'm afraid to break the mood, asking about the new note. Part of me doesn't want to know, but my curiosity would kill me."

"Is it bad?" Hannah asked, "No one was hurt, right?"

Amelia said, "No, nothing like that luckily. I wish you could have seen it, it was quite the sight. They broke in, even with Sunny's security system. He can't figure out how it happened. Nothing alarmed, and the cameras didn't pick up anything strange. Another odd part of the story to add to the list."

"What was it?" Georgia had her feet planted on the ground, our swinging stopped.

"It was our book this week, *The Crimes of Love*. The pages were hanging from a wire, all along our bedroom ceiling. They had cut each page out, one by one. Carefully."

"I don't like that they broke in," Hannah said.

Georgia asked, "Was there any message, other than the pages?"

"There was a highlighted page, hanging from the fan." I read her the quote I had saved on my phone. Everyone took a minute to think it through. I read it again.

"Grave? Are you sure we are safe? We are quite the target, all of us together like this. *Outside*."

"I can't promise anything one way or the other," Amelia said. "The police were called, of course, but I don't know. The gala is tomorrow." She fidgeted with her long blue skirt resting at her knees.

I said, "Remember the postcard? It said, 'you have until the Orchid Society gala'. We'll find out tomorrow, I suspect. But none of us know what is happening, this might not be the end. What the consequence will be, I'm not sure."

"And if the person has stopped what the perpetrators are asking for?" Lulu said.

"I suppose the messages will stop, too," Amelia said.

We were silent, unsure how to continue with what little information we gleaned from the last few weeks. Georgia and Hannah still didn't know about the artifacts or our midnight rendezvous to the Mirabelle. It was too much to divulge at the moment.

The sun dipped under the mountain's peak, the glow still emitting from the top ridges. I broke the silence. "Bill and I went to Mel's today."

Amelia said, "The rare bookstore?"

"I love Mel's. It has this old booky smell that gets me every time." Lulu said. "Were you getting *Crimes of Love*?"

"We were asking about the edition that was hanging from Amelia's ceiling. It was old enough to warrant a special purchase."

Parker said, "That was smart. A first edition like that, where else could they go on such short notice?"

Bill said, "Ellie spun a good tale. Turns out, a copy was sold eight days ago. A first edition."

"Oh my god." Amelia set her coffee down on the small wicker table. "Did you find out who bought it?"

"I was surprised he let us know as much as he did. But yes, he showed us the ledger. He writes down all of his sales, it seemed legitimate."

"Who was it?" Lulu and Georgia said together.

I took my phone out, trying to pronounce the name. "Abhainn Ghlic."

Lulu said, "A what? Did you just cast a spell?"

Bill said, "It's Gaelic, apparently. Meaning wise river."

"Wise river? What is that supposed to mean?" Amelia said.

"I don't know." Bill answered.

I said, "I'm guessing it's an alias, could be a childhood name, or perhaps they like a river nearby. It could be undecipherable. They might not even be from here."

Hannah said, "What's the closest river to us?"

"There's the South Platt River." Parker said.

We spent a moment, researching. A small breeze picked up, cooling the sweat on my brow and blowing Amelia's skirt to the side.

"It covers almost 450 miles." Lulu turned her phone towards us. "It would be hard to figure any link."

I said, "I don't think it's the Platt. Seems too large, too obvious."

Georgia said, "We could be here all night if we start looking up every river, trying to figure out if it's wise or stupid."

"And it's not as if this person *wants* us to figure it out. This isn't a game, they want to remain anonymous." Bill said. "It's something to keep in our back pocket, just in case."

Hannah asked, "Is everyone here going to the gala tomorrow, even with the threats?"

"My mom would have my head if I missed it. Plus, I'm picking up the ice sculpture in the truck." Amelia didn't seem as worried as I felt she should, given it was her house the threats originated. "Can you imagine the trouble I'd be in if I was even five minutes late?"

"No one wants a melty Caesar," Lulu said. "I'm kind of on her side with that one."

Hannah said, "It might not be a bad idea to stay home…"

"I don't want anyone to feel obligated to go, just because it's my mother. I completely understand given the circumstance."

Parker said, "I already told Shannon I'd help bring the columns for the entryway. Apparently their heavy."

Lulu joked, "Is Parker saving the day with his big ole' muscles?"

"Like always." Parker rubbed his eyes. "Let's back up. I don't think we should discount this alias. This is the first time we've been close to anything identifying."

"Do you have an idea?" I asked.

"Let's think it through some more."

"Alright." I felt he needed this, something objective to cling to. "What comes to mind when you think of a river?"

"I don't know, a farmer?" He said, "the Nile?"

"Doesn't your name mean Farmer, Georgia?" Lulu asked, "you tell us." She nudged her playfully.

She replied, "Here we go with the warrior…"

"*Famous* warrior. My mother knew exactly what she was doing when she named me."

"Because you've shaped out to be both famous and a warrior?"

"I've got time. Plus, I could *be* a warrior. You don't know."

I said, "Wait…that's not a bad thought." I grabbed my phone, typing. A breath caught in my throat as continued to read. "Ohmygosh. *No.*"

Amelia and Georgia said, "*What?*"

I didn't know what to say, or if it was now appropriate in front of everyone.

Lulu said, "For crying out loud, El."

"Wise river, it means Shannon in Gaelic."

Chapter 20
Saturday

The wind seemed frozen with our small, subtle movements. It was still. You could hear the neighbor across the street laughing in his house, television loud.

I said, "It doesn't necessarily mean your mother bought the book, Amelia."

"El, we're *from* Ireland. She knows Gaelic. Who else in Dove Park knows *Gaelic* or would think to use it?" She stood, pacing. She walked to the front of the porch railing and placed her hands on across it, head bowed. "Give me a moment."

Presumably, she was doing what we all were doing. Thinking back. Processing. Did it add up? Could Shannon be the one placing the threatening notes?

Amelia said, "I can't imagine why she would do such a thing. She would tell me if she were upset. She doesn't communicate well, but this is extreme. She's my mother. And it still doesn't explain what she's wanting us to stop doing!" Her tone was louder than I'd ever heard. Parker looked pale, clammy.

Georgia said, "You know what? She was there. At the beginning of our book club. The night the second message was hung. The sheet."

"You're right," Lulu said, "I remember because she didn't say a word to any of us. She was stern. She hugged Amelia like a big, thick tree."

I asked, "Was she there any other Wednesday, Amelia?"

"I don't know. I can't think straight. She's been at my house more often because of the gala. She's been working with Sunny on the financial side, too, and for the summer house they're selling in California. Both operations are racking up quite the price tag." She sighed. "My mother's motives can be hard to figure. I learned that as a kid."

Lulu said, "Amelia, what can we do? Do we say something to Shannon? The gala is *tomorrow*. Do we go?"

"My mother has been working with Sunny. That can't be a coincidence. We've said that there could be a connection. This looks like a pretty big one to me. Two crimes so close to home?"

"The artifacts and the messages...I can't imagine they aren't connected now." Lulu was putting both scenarios together.

Hannah whipped her head towards Lulu. "What artifacts are you talking about, exactly?"

"Oh right." Lulu smacked her head. "I suppose it was going to come out eventually, no reason to keep it from them."

"What are you talking about?" Hannah was alert. "Tell me what you know."

I started. "You know how the museum was robbed that Thursday a few weeks back?"

"Yes, the artifacts."

"You're going to think we're mad."

Georgia said, "Wait, who knows about this?"

"Everyone but you and Hannah. We weren't trying to keep any information, I promise. It started with Parker and me, and well, Lulu forced it out of us. Lovingly, of course. And we told Amelia because of Sunny."

Georgia said, "Sunny is involved? You guys are sounding crazy."

We spent the next half hour discussing everything we knew about the artifacts, Sunny and the Mirabelle. The only portion we left out was Parker's knowledge of Sunny's affair and his love for Amelia. We brought up the reward, since Amelia already knew about it, but didn't explain further into Parker's motivation. It was plausible enough that we would search for the robbed goods to return them to their owners, and for my grant.

"I can't believe you went to the Mirabelle," Hannah said.

"You've heard of it?" Being two hours out, I suspected no one would have.

She paused. "In passing, I think." She sat back and started texting. I wasn't sure if she believed our story or not.

"I'm so glad you guys are alright." Georgia looked terrified. "And you made it out of the closet. I would have *panicked*."

"I'm sorry we didn't tell you sooner."

"I'm not mad at all, I wouldn't have told me either. That isn't the type of information to be throwing around. But I am glad you told me now, especially since it could be tied to the messages and the threats."

Parker said, "Do we truly think Shannon is working with Sunny?"

Amelia sat back down on the bench with a look of defeat. I said, "Amelia, are you alright?"

"My mother and my husband are conniving. I'm not alright. I think I'm going to call it a night." Parker rose and they stepped aside, talking. Everyone was silent.

After some time, he said, "I'm going to take her back with me."

I nodded as the group hugged Amelia. She was holding back emotion, pain present. I hoped she would open up to Parker, he was someone she could trust.

After they left, I asked, "Do you think we were too callous? I feel lucky that I can go home without fear of whats waiting behind the sheets. This has been weeks of stress for her."

Lulu replied, "You're fine, we've said nothing in poor taste. It's the situation itself, it's something she'll need to come to terms with. But this is going to take a while, those are the two people that should be unequivocally trusting and open with her, and they've betrayed that."

We talked for some time on the porch, the evidence piling high that Sunny and Shannon were working together, at least in some capacity.

I said, "We have the who, but not the why."

"Now that we believe the artifacts are related to the notes, perhaps they think someone knows about them? They felt exposed." Bill said. "They wanted someone to stop looking into them, maybe."

Hannah was unusually quiet. She seemed to be wrestling with something. Before I could ask if she was alright, Rex pulled into the drive, looking the picture of innocence, lacking the signs of weighted stress like the group before him.

Lulu rose, "I guess we should call it a night. We all need to sleep. And who knows what we'll find tomorrow."

Rex put his arm around his wife. "Will I be seeing everyone at the gala tomorrow?"

I almost laughed. We had all decided to go. We felt it would be one thing to threaten your wife and daughter, but another to act in violence. We were going to approach the situation safely, given other key players in the scenario. Shannon and Sunny might not hurt Amelia, but who knows if Hugh, Rick, or Antonio would share similar sentiment?

As Bill and I approached the car, I realized how tired I was. "I'm exhausted. Sorry I've pulled you into this."

"I am so happy you did, I would never want you dealing with this alone." He squeezed my shoulder. My emotions felt unsteady.

"I'm glad Amelia has Parker. I don't know what she would do. And you know, he's going to have to tell her soon, with the reward no longer an option he has no reason to hold back about the affair. The longer he waits the worse it will be."

"She has a pretty good group looking after her, I think she'll be alright."

As we pulled into our driveway that night, I hardly remembered unlocking the door, taking off my makeup, washing my face. My head hit the pillow and I was out, falling into a dreamless, fitful sleep.

~

It was finally Saturday. The gala was to begin at 5:00 p.m., so we had the day to lounge and get ready. I called Amelia at noon, knowing she would soon be meeting her mother. We never heard if she decided to attend.

"Hey, El."

"Hey. Are you alright?"

"I was up a lot of the night, trying to piece everything together with Parker. My mom has been at the house a lot more than usual, and with Sunny. It happened gradually so I didn't notice, but this time last year we always met at the restaurant or her office. Not our home. Something changed, and I can't quite place it. It was about the time Sunny started staying away late. I'm certain. I don't know what it all means. And you know what?"

"What's that?"

"I originally asked Marge if she saw anything suspicious, anyone coming or going Thursday when the pages were left in our bedroom. She said she saw nothing odd. This morning, I asked her if my mother had been by that same day, and she said she had let her in. It was about 6:00 p.m., she remembers because Marge was just leaving for the day. We were long gone by then, on our way to the Mirabelle. But there she was, alone in our house. I told Marge I was coming home late that night and to let herself out, she could have easily told my mother."

"Who would have thought the perpetrator would walk right into your home like that?"

"It makes sense, how things kept happening and no one was around the home, and the neighbors didn't see anyone loitering. I'm not sure if Sunny knows about the threats and my mother, though. I'm still unsure of their connection so I don't want to make a false link, but I don't want to discount it, either."

"The evidence does seem to be leaning in that direction. I know it's little consolation, but I'm sorry. What about your father?"

"I doubt he knows anything, honestly. We have a good relationship, but he's always so busy with the restaurant I don't know if he would notice anything strange from my mother, or me. He's been traveling a lot to Ireland too, to visit my grandmother."

"With everything you've discovered, are you going to show at the gala tonight? Will you say anything to Shannon? I support any decision you make."

"I've decided to go. I'm not hiding away from them, I've been scared of confronting both Sunny and my mother in different capacities for years now. What have I gained from it?"

"You're a strong woman, Amelia."

"I don't feel it."

"Have you spoken to Sunny? Is he home?"

"I haven't called him since our confrontation at the Mirabelle. I sent him a message to let him know about the bedroom, and never got anything back, until this morning. I guess he checked the security tapes and saw nothing suspicious. He seems clueless but he wears a lie well. He said he will see me at the gala. Someone picked up his tux, it was gone when I picked up my dress. I don't even want to be inside our home, especially with the boys at camp, it feels haunted with lies."

"I'll be there with you tonight. Everyone will, we have your back."

"Thanks, El. I mean it. I'll see you soon."

Bill looked concerned. "Is she going tonight?"

"She's ready to face her demons."

"How's Hannah? She seemed sad last night."

"I feel bad, I haven't spoken with her much since all of this started. I think part of me was scared she would ask a question I didn't want to answer, something about Sunny, or Hugh. I didn't want to have to lie. I'm glad everyone knows though. Even without touching on Sunny's affair, I feel lighter. The rest of the information is Parker's to expose."

"He might as well tell her tonight, why wait?"

I nodded as Bill left to help Parker with the columns. I wasn't sure telling Amelia tonight was smart, but it had to come out eventually. What would a day buy her? She'll be wrecked tomorrow, no doubt.

I looked out the window. My dress hung on the curtain rod, blowing restlessly with the breeze. The smell of rain bellowed in, accompanied by a cold flash of air. It was time to reveal our fate, would the threatening notes stop? And was Shannon to blame?

Chapter 21
The Gala

Georgia shepherded us into a red minivan. "Alright, everyone in."

Lulu said, "How and why did I agree to show up to the event of the year in a stolen minivan?"

"*Borrowing*. And look, it fits everyone just peachy, *and* we added the other row. Look at us, saving the environment."

Everyone was accounted for, including Rex, Bill, and Georgia's husband, Chase. The husbands had grown close over the years out of sheer necessity and were happily talking about the minivan's specs in the back. Georgia pulled out, and we were on our way.

We finally pulled into the Dove Park event center housed only a mile from the museum. It was an impressive venue for a small town, and every year the Orchid Society Gala was sold out within minutes of registration. It did wonders for our local businesses, and the entire weekend was filled with events throughout our small Main Street area. During the day on Saturday, awards were given to the best Orchids, rare plants, and impressive scenes made by the best horticulturalists in the nation. The gala was an expensive ordeal, and the profits went towards a non-profit organization that helped at-risk youth by teaching them and their families how to garden, grow crops, and cook healthy meals. There were top prizes for the winners, and a prestigious sector of those who have previously won.

The winner's table. This year was a Greek theme. Columns towered high on either side of the front entrance, framing the red carpet. Shannon was the head of the Orchid Society that consisted of ten board members. It was elite to be asked for a chair, there was no application. I couldn't think of anything stuffier in my life, but they seemed to enjoy it. And what a spectacle it was.

Upon entry, there were large Greek statues, platters of grilled meat, moussaka, Courgette balls, and foods I had no idea if they were dessert or dinner. Champagne flutes seemed endless. We grabbed the first glass we could, already on edge by the large display.

Bill whispered to me, "I know the tickets are pricey and Shannon has money from her restaurants, but..."

"This is next level. This has Sunny's money written all over it."

"I can't imagine anything in Dove Park with this degree of cost. Look at the giant fountain." Inside the fountain were three people on platforms, expertly painted to look like statues. They were perfectly perched and unmoving as the water flowed and sprayed around them. The statues were in the main mezzanine at the front entrance, under a large domed ceiling that was decorated with stained glass. It was our favorite part of the event center, and the sun seemed to sparkle over the fountain in an array of busy colors.

"This is more exuberant than all the other years."

Our group made our way into the main space, sitting at our table for ten. I wondered if Sunny planned on joining us, or if he had other plans.

Lulu sat to my right, Bill to my left. Lulu plopped her black purse on the table and said, "I'm trying not to look suspicious, but I keep wondering, who is here? Shannon couldn't have been working alone. She's not one to paint a white sheet and light a firework, and neither is Sunny."

"I wonder the same. Let's try and relax. The reward ceremony is about to start."

Bill squeezed my knee, sensing my anxiety. So far, the event appeared normal. I don't know what I expected, explosions? Fire? It tamed by nerves to see that everything was running as it should, the schedule similar to last year's gala.

The lights dimmed and Shannon approached the stage, looking elegant in a black sequin gown and short pumps. For 84, she didn't look a day over 70 and still ran a mile every day before tending to her charity events and projects, while still overseeing her restaurants. In the last five years, she had let her husband, Amelia's father, do most of the restaurant day to day operations so she could concentrate on the Society. And it showed. She gave her typical speech, excited at the prospect of helping families in need while showcasing the most beautiful flowers in the world. At the end of her address, our appetizers were served, and the final orchid showcases were wheeled onto the stage. During dinner, we would witness the award show and see the winners.

The showcases were beautiful. Large phalaenopsis orchids draped over vases, moss, and homemade scenes. A large upright piano was wheeled onto the stage, covered in colors of speckled orchids. Next, a man in black brought out one of the largest mirrors I have ever seen, fit with flowers draped along the sides. After setting it up, they brought out a harp to accompany it.

"This is incredible." Lulu said. The room was dim, and once all of the final arrangements made their way to the stage, large lights barreled down on the creations, creating one large, impeccable flower garden.

I looked at Hannah who was directly across from me. She was picking at her food and hardly speaking with Amelia, who was to her right, or Georgia to her left. The vacant seat next to Amelia seemed stark, as Parker looked at her across the gap. We hadn't seen Sunny, and I'm sure Amelia was a bundle of nerves for more reasons than one.

My mouth dropped. Walking in, arm in arm with his new wife, was Hugh.

"Lulu, look."

"Oh shit. I don't know why I find it so shocking he is here, everyone in Dove Park attends these things."

"You're right. My mind goes straight to conspiracy. He could be enjoying a night out with his wife."

And following directly behind Hugh, was Antonio and Rick, arm in arm with two women. Lulu said, "My *god* is the entire team here? What is this an artifact reunion?"

I said, "Aren't they afraid to be seen?"

"They have nothing to hide from. They don't know we know anything. And if Shannon is in on Sunny's little operation, who would they need to hide from? It's not like there's a police presence."

"I feel like we're in the belly of the beast." I leaned over and told Bill. I was glad to point them out, I felt safe with Bill next to me.

I startled as Hannah jumped up and said she was heading to the restroom. Parker looked uncomfortable and followed suit.

"Is Hannah alright?" Lulu said.

"I don't know. I need to take a moment and talk with her, I feel like we've been so absorbed in this artifact situation and then with my grant that we've let other things slide."

"It's not like she's sought us out much, either. It's not all on you, don't feel bad."

"And poor Parker. He's seen Amelia a lot these past few days, I think it's wearing on him."

"And his information, it's eating him raw."

I said, "I've got to go to the lady's room before everything starts."

"Ditto."

We passed ten other tables before reaching the restroom. On our way back, we stood under the main arch, observing as the wait staff lingered, waiting to refill a glass of champagne, or put in an order for whiskey. The silent auction was last, and every year I got the feeling that Shannon wanted people to be just the right level of intoxicated before placing their bids.

Lulu hit my arm. "El, isn't that mister tracksuit?"

"Who?"

"You know, Amelia's rich guy. From the Mirabelle. Sans tracksuit."

"Oh my gosh, I think you're right. I'm surprised you recognized him without the gold jacket."

"I appraise people, too, you know." She winked. "Look around. Some of these people look familiar, and not from the Dove Park Library or community park."

"You're right, Lulu. I can't believe it. Look at the far corner table, they were sitting at the Bar Mirabelle when we arrived. The blonde was more than a little tipsy, she just about fell off of her stool."

"These people all can't be flower connoisseurs."

"They're art connoisseurs, that's for sure."

"This reads funny to me. It can't be a coincidence." Lulu said.

"They do have money, and people like to give money to charity and attend these ritzy events."

"It's a two-hour drive, at least."

"People come from all over the States, though. That would be hardly a hardship."

"Let's not discount it, is all I'm saying."

We startled as Hannah approached, placing her hands on our shoulders. "What are you guys doing?"

"You scared me shitless," Lulu said. "Remember how we told you about the Mirabelle last night?"

"How could I forget."

"There's more than one person who was attending the event that is here tonight. Some of them you couldn't miss, like the man near the front with the strange mustache. He was *definitely* there."

Hannah scanned the room nodding. "Interesting."

"What do you think it means?" I asked.

Hannah said, "I haven't a clue." And with that, she walked back to the table.

I turned towards Lulu, "Maybe she thinks we're off our rocker."

"I get the feeling she might not be on board with us tinkering with the artifacts. And Shannon."

"Shhh." I looked around, feeling watched as we walked back to the table. I leaned into Bill. "Do you notice something about the people here tonight?"

"What is it? Is something wrong?"

"It's the people from the Bar Mirabelle."

"That's it. I thought I recognized the man upfront. I assumed it was from Dove Park, it's such a small place, everyone is recognizable. But you're right."

"What do you think it means?"

Bill thought a moment as the salad course appeared. I was so caught up in the other tables, I failed to miss Sunny, sitting

Amanda J. Smith

next to Amelia. They were talking, and it seemed amicable, for now.

Bill blurted, "I think the artifacts are here."

"I was afraid you'd say that."

"None of the event participants were able to get their auctions, from what we witnessed. Last we heard, they were on a truck. I can only assume somewhere close. They'd certainly want it far from the Mirabelle, it was swimming with police officers."

"They'd want to be careful."

"More than likely if the police were there that night, some of them are being watched closely. I'm sure many of them don't have clean slates, either. What's the perfect cover?"

"They're here to pick them up, using the gala as a guise."

"It makes perfect sense. They all have money, why not attend? They couldn't all convene together somewhere else, it would draw too much attention."

"I think you're right. But where?"

"It's not worth it to look for them, not here. Shannon's got this place on lockdown. Look at the entryways." Large men serving as gatekeepers were standing straight at every door, earpieces settled nicely inside their lobes.

"This is certainly the spot. There is no reason to have men like that at an Orchid Gala."

"Unless you're up to no good."

"As far as we know the auction at the Mirabelle concluded. All that was left was to divvy out the goods and receive payment." I leaned over to Lulu and told her our theory. She agreed.

She said, "I can't eat my salad. What if there's an artifact hiding in with the radish?" I gave her a look. "I know, no time for jokes. But what are we going to do with this information?

244

We can't hunt them down, that didn't work so well the first time and the guard over there has at *least* a twelve-pack."

"I honestly don't know. Maybe we see something that would be enough to call the authorities, after all. No more hearsay, no more privileged conversation heard in a hallway."

As the salad plates were taken from the table, another round of orchid showcases were wheeled onto the stage. Every flower was stark white, and the grandest of all was centered around a vase the size of Lulu herself.

She said, "Goodness, is there an entire tuba in there? Is that necessary?"

"Apparently. Or perhaps not, maybe it got last place."

"We'll find out soon enough."

As Lulu finished her thought, Shannon walked out to announce dinner. It was Pastitsio, Fassolatha, and Dolmathakia. It was a beautiful plate. Shannon said, "Well, it's been a magnificent night so far, wouldn't you say?" A round of applause. "We are going to showcase a few other orchid contenders, then will announce the winners shortly." She went on to thank a multitude of people, and when she mentioned Sunny, I almost spit out my champagne. Sunny stood up from our table and took a small bow, smiling as people clapped in recognition.

Lulu said, "Makes me sick."

Amelia was smiling at Sunny and I suddenly felt a wave of guilt for knowing about his affair, the conversation Parker overheard. I always put that information on him, but I knew it as much as he did, and for almost as long. She will be furious, and she should. Even with the blackmail, did we have a good reason to hide it from her? I questioned my choices until the conclusion of dinner. As dessert appeared, the last orchids were taken off stage, and the lights brightened. We looked at each other and wondered, what was next?

Chapter 22
Outed

Shannon said, "As dessert is served, we will announce the winners of the 19th annual Orchid Society Gala. Following the reveal, the silent auction will be held in the room across from the fountains. While the dance floor opens, the auction will be held for one hour. And as usual, the arrangements from tonight's event will also be up for bid. The items will be available for pick up directly following the event. Please, take your time, good luck, and happy bidding!" She waved a farewell as she exited, and surprisingly, made her way over to Amelia and Sunny.

I watched with abject horror as the two people on our group's radar materialized and were speaking with one another. It was like caricatures coming to life in some twisted tale. Shannon's smile was plastered and fake. She all but ignored Amelia and her compliments of the gala and took Sunny aside as they chatted. To be a fly on that orchid.

Lulu took a generous gulp of her drink, "Well that's horrifying."

"You know what I realized? After all this time Sunny still doesn't think we were at the Mirabelle for the artifacts. He thought we were just stalking him."

"He doesn't think we're smart enough for that. And his ego. It's the size of that tuba vase."

"If he ever finds out the reason we were at the Mirabelle, he'll never believe it."

Parker walked over and we discussed the meeting of minds. Bill said, "The artifacts have to be given out after the auction."

I said, "Will it be that overt?"

Hannah finally came back and sat anxiously at the table, picking at her cheesecake. The winners were announced in an ordeal much too long for my standards. The moment the wooden dance floor was rolled out, we dashed to the silent auction across the mezzanine, the three fountain statues taking different positions in an eerie display of change.

I felt a tap on my shoulder. "I take it we're feeling better, ladies?"

Hugh stood before us, his hand around Barbara's shoulder. She was wearing a tight tan blazer and Hugh appeared more dapper than usual with a tint of alcohol emanating from his breath.

"Yes, thank you. Much."

"I take it we'll be seeing you both on Monday then?"

Lulu said, "Absolutely."

"I was going to tell you Friday Ellie, but you didn't come in, so I might as well tear the band-aid off now. Your grant was denied for an extension."

My jaw dropped. "I thought we wouldn't hear for weeks?"

He shrugged. "I don't know what else to say. It wasn't my decision."

"Do I have a job to come to on Monday?"

"Your current grant expires in two weeks. You'll need to finish what you started. We don't need to be left hanging from your half-finished work. The missing artifacts are going to cost us."

I couldn't believe what I was hearing. I could feel the tension in both Bill and Lulu, but we knew better than to risk a worse fate. I walked away, tears burning in my eyes, and said nothing. I could feel his victorious gaze burn into my back.

Lulu said, "Ellie I'm so sorry."

Bill wrapped his arms around me. I said, "It makes sense, he must have blamed the theft on me, perhaps an error in conversation or a mistyped email. I was the scapegoat."

Lulu said, "Now he can go on running the department as he chooses."

"And he can say I was fired. If anyone asks what action was taken in such a great robbery, he can pull up my file."

Bill said, "Your *clean* file."

"Who knows what else he could add? He has all of the control. He all but runs the place."

I excused myself, taking a moment in the bathroom to center. My face looked thinner in the mirror as an anxious face stared back. Who would I be in two weeks?

When I walked out, the group was all together again. It warmed my heart to see everyone in one pile. It made every instance with Hugh seem minuscule, unimportant. There would be other jobs, and with supervisors who weren't so twisted.

Georgia said, "Let's do this." She linked arms with my own and we walked through the silent auction. We didn't expect any artifacts to be sitting out, of course, but were surprised to find nothing interesting, either.

Bill said, "I think we should bid on something."

"These are priced *high*." Georgia was looking over a massage and day spa package.

"If we win something, we can be there when everyone picks up their items."

I said, "Couldn't Amelia say she is hanging around for Sunny and her mother at the end of the gala instead?"

Amelia said, "They'd find a way to usher me out, I'm sure. It's their favorite pastime."

Hannah said, "I agree. Let's pool our money and bid. With Sunny out that leaves nine of us."

Lulu said, "I can't wait to split the massage. Seven minutes a pop."

We walked along the silent auction items. Bill said, "You know what, the auction gives them reason to claim some of the money as legitimate. It wouldn't need explaining."

"Are you saying some of these items aren't real?"

He thought. "I hadn't thought of that, but it's possible. Some of the higher-priced items might be fraudulent. They tell the Mirabelle participants what to bid on, and for how much. The pay is genuine. Who is going to check to see if the charity is real if no one complains? They could have set up bank accounts under different names."

"Let's watch and see what some of them bid on."

Sure enough, there was a helicopter adventure package, set with hotel and flight. The price was set at $10,000. The top bid was signed by mister mustache himself.

Amelia said, "And no one is going to balk at the pricing, either. It's for charity."

Bill said, "We don't want to bid on something that's for an artifact, though. We don't want to draw attention and they'd outbid us."

"How will we know?"

"Let's find something low. Keep an eye out on people from the auction."

We took our time, strolling past the sheets of paper, looking at those who seemed familiar. Thirty minutes had passed, thirty to go.

Georgia said, "There is an item that is physically here, a signed painting of Pike's Peak. It's going for $500. Doubtful that is artifact related and it won't break the bank."

We agreed to bid. Only one other gala guest outbid us, and we scribbled in $650 as the horn blew to sound the end of the auction. Bill was right, one item for a 15-day vacation to Australia went for $65,000. I wondered which one of my artifacts sold for that much.

Guests started to fan out for more drinks, dancing and gossip. Shannon approached the stage one last time to announce the auction winners and request for immediate payment. If payment could not be secured, the next person on the list would win.

"And one final thank you to our donors, our guests, and the staff here tonight at the 19th annual Orchid Society Gala. Your auction items will be available through the main hallway and directly to the back of the facility in twenty minutes. If a large item was purchased, the room has an available exit for loading. Goodbye, and see you all next year."

Her face was flushed and for once her age seemed to be catching up with her. Perhaps even Shannon herself wasn't impermeable to the stresses of the artifacts. Not surprisingly, we saw Shannon, Hugh, and Sunny make their way through an employee-only door on the main event floor. We hadn't seen Antonio or Rick since the beginning but knew they were close.

Amelia said, "Alright, it's time to claim our painting." We had placed Bill's name on the list, hoping Shannon wouldn't notice the connection.

I asked, "Did you talk with Sunny?"

"Briefly. He sat with me a total of ten minutes. If ever there was a doubt linking my mother and Sunny, that's all but evaporated. I haven't had a chance to speak with her yet, but I'm starting to wonder how I didn't question their connection before."

"Because people don't question family for being together. I don't think you should ever feel bad for not feeling suspicious. That's not who you are. And I don't think that's a bad thing, it's quite a gift."

"I still can't believe he is helping finance an illegal art trade deal, using *your* missing artifacts. With my mother. It makes me so incredibly sad."

"Did Sunny mention your argument at the Mirabelle?"

"He said he was sorry he hadn't been around more and that we could talk tonight. He'll have the time, I suppose, now that the artifacts will be accounted for. He'll finally have time to face me. I'm not sure how to begin, you know? Do we save the marriage? I think it's worth thinking about if he's willing." We continued through the main room and stood by the fountain, the statues had finally made their exit. It seemed empty without their presence. She continued, "And you know, the study still isn't fixed. He hasn't seemed to care. Who doesn't mind a gaping hole in their home?"

Lulu said, "Someone busy with something entirely more important."

To our surprise, Sunny appeared on the other side of the fountain, alone. He motioned Amelia over as we gawked at the interaction. We didn't expect him to show for another hour, at least. If not at all tonight.

I said, "What is he up to?"

Lulu said, "He better play careful."

Parker said, "This is making me ill." A green color shadowed his cheeks.

Finally, Amelia returned, holding something in her right hand.

I said, "What is it?"

"He had a friend bid on one of the pieces of jewelry from France. It is quite beautiful."

"Did you say anything about the artifacts?"

"No, it's not the time." Sunny walked over and helped Amelia place the necklace around her neck, fiddling with her hair, whispering something in her ear as she laughed. Sunny glared spitefully at Parker and surprised us even more by taking him aside.

Lulu said, "Is he trying to make amends? Did he get a necklace for Parker, too? I'm starting to feel left out."

Amelia said, "This is making me nervous. Why on earth would he want to speak with Parker?"

My stomach dropped. Before I could fumble a response, Parker pushed Sunny.

Lulu said, "Oh Shit."

We ran over following Amelia's lead. She said, "What is going on? Cut it out!" The sudden increase in her tone sent a squelching echo throughout the tall and domed ceiling, enveloping the scene in a ghostly shrillness. Neither of them answered.

Sunny said, "It's nothing, dear. We're talking business. Nothing to concern yourself with."

"I believe this *does* concern me. My best friend and husband shoving each other during a public event? An event run by my mother?"

Sunny gave a warning look to Parker. Sunny stepped closer and said, "Don't do anything you'll regret, Parker. You know how this will end. I'm trying to make friendly, here." His chest seemed to puff out in an alpha male demeanor.

Amelia looked startled. "What is going on? Someone explain or I'm walking out."

Sunny and Parker didn't break eye contact, as Amelia continued to beg for answers. It was an uncomfortable interaction to witness. You could feel the stone wall crumble before both Parker and Sunny, their futures hanging in the balance. Would someone talk?

"You don't deserve her. You never did." Parker finally spit.

Amelia said, *"Parker!"*

Sunny said, "I provide for my family. Where's yours? Oh right, gone. Up in *flames*. I'm not surprised your wife walked out."

"My personal life is none of your business."

"And mine is yours?" A few event patrons heard voices rise and started to circle the group. Bill, Rex, and Chase attempted to dissipate the group as they watched closely, ready to step in if needed.

Parker said, "It is when I heard what you did."

"Don't you dare. Not here. You'll be *done*. You know the information I have. I'll tell her in a minute."

By this time, Amelia was in tears but couldn't make good on her threat to leave. She was as transfixed as the rest of us.

"I'm starting to wonder if I care anymore. You can do all you want, I'm putting Amelia first. Not like you would *ever* know what that is like. You're ungrateful."

That was the sentence that broke the dam. Sunny pulled his arm back at an alarmingly quick rate, and threw his fist across Parker's jaw, a snap echoing over Amelia's shouts. Lulu tried to pull her out, but she batted her away.

Parker jumped to his feet ignoring Sunny. He turned to Amelia. "Amelia, I'm sorry I've waited so long to tell you this."

Sunny said, "Don't you think about it."

She said, "Parker, what is it?"

"I caught Sunny on a phone call, with another woman. It was more than a business conversation. Intimate."

Sunny lunged after Parker and he danced away.

Amelia's eyes grew large as she turned towards her husband. Sunny was unsure what to do, noting the spectators. He seemed stunned, his blackmail safety net all but demolished. Antonio noted the scene and ran over as he stopped pursuing Parker.

Sunny said, "Everything Parker is saying is a lie, honey. You don't know who you have as a friend. The things he's done in his past."

"What do you mean you heard him on the phone? Where?"

Parker said, "I went by his office to work on one of my investments. He didn't hear me enter. It was plain as day what was happening, Amelia. He had slept with someone else, just the night before."

Sunny began yelling at Parker. Security staff entered and ushered us to a smaller room and out of the main entryway. I followed Parker close, the others in the doorway.

She asked Sunny, "Is this true?"

"Of course not. You know me better than that. Or I thought you did." He spit.

"When was this?"

Parker said, "Over two months ago."

"*What?*" Tears streamed down her face as she realized the betrayal from both of the men in her life, one from withholding information, the other his vows.

"It's complicated, Amelia. I'm so sorry." Parker and Sunny both were pleading their case, and suddenly she looked done with them both.

She wiped the remaining tears on her face and replaced them with a stern look of disapproval. "I'm disgusted with both of you." There was venom in her words. "And you. My husband. You're my support system, and you failed me. You failed our children, being here tonight, doing what you're doing. Cheating. I'm done with both of you."

Chapter 23
Not Always Wise

The room was hot as Amelia walked out. Georgia said she and Chase would see if she wanted a drive back to the house.

Sunny looked perplexed and still didn't seem to understand her phrasing, her knowledge about the artifacts. He finally turned to Parker, "You will never speak to me, Amelia, or my children again. As long as I live. And if you think I'm below releasing the information I have on you, you're mistaken."

He stormed out as Parker yelled, "I don't think *anything* is below you. She's right, you're disgusting." Parker was at the end of his rope. I ran over as Sunny disappeared with Antonio, the security team following.

Hannah said, "You better get out of here. Before things get worse."

He nodded, clearly too distraught to concentrate on both Amelia walking out and the artifacts simultaneously. It wasn't like the artifacts were going to appear, ripe for the taking. The information was out, and the reward was a distant memory. Wads of cash were never going to take back the events that unfolded, the look in Amelia's eyes when she realized the two most important men in her life had lied. And worse.

Rex said, "I'll make sure he gets home."

The room was suddenly vacant. Only Bill, Hannah, Rex, and Lulu stood beside me.

Hannah said, "We need to get back there and pick up our item while we still have a chance." We followed and made our way back. There were more than thirty auction items, the back area filled and chaotic. Someone was shouting out auction items, while others helped load the heavier pieces. It was taking a while and our painting was visible, leaning against the orchid piano display. We were raw after seeing Sunny hit Parker and being here with another potential confrontation seemed somehow impossible.

I was surprised to see Antonio and Rick helping load the items. Everyone on deck, it appeared. When it came to the piano display, it took four people and a dolly to load it into the truck, the orchids swinging madly, strings letting out deep hums. Nothing seemed out of place, though. Sunny was gone, presumably trying to reach Amelia, or hideaway, embarrassed by his demonstration. I wondered if Shannon knew and if Amelia had a chance to speak with her. Perhaps that was a conversation for another time.

Hannah remained stoic, calculating. Her eyes were darting from one item to the next, watching as payments were handed over or conducted electronically. Mister mustache walked over to the person in charge of payment, someone I didn't recognize. She was tall, with straight black hair, and seemed to sprout intensity with every movement. He handed her a briefcase, opening it to show rows of bills. The woman checked to see if the money was legitimate, nodded an approval then handed the briefcase to Antonio.

Bill gasped and leaned towards Hannah and me. He said, "I've been wondering where the artifacts are."

Hannah nodded, "I can't figure it, either. Payment is occurring though, which is odd. Where's the transfer? Did it already happen? It's possible they already picked up the artifacts and waited until now to send the money. But I doubt both parties would be comfortable with an uneven swap like that. It doesn't make sense."

Bill said. "Look closer. They're in the displays. Look how large they are, the vase, the piano. They not only have space but can handle themselves weight wise. You can tell looking at some of the items they're lifting, the weight is off. Things are too heavy. It's happening right under our noses."

"My god you're right," Hannah said, waiting a moment and nodding. She turned her head to the side and said in a low tone, "We have confirmation. I repeat, the transfer has been made."

I said, "What?"

"You're going to want to back up." Hannah unceremoniously pushed our group to the back as we met her action with questions. We hadn't yet retrieved the painting but could sense her severity and stopped asking. We were as far back as the small room allowed, and before I could ask Bill what was happening, the entryway door flew open letting in a group of armed officers, shouting for everyone present to put their hands in the air and drop to the ground. Hannah pulled out a badge and, shockingly, approached Antonio, throwing handcuffs around his wrists. Rick started to run out of the loading door and was ambushed by three more agents. It looked like he was reaching for a gun and was thrown to the ground.

"What the *hell?*" Lulu shouted. Our bodies were pressed hard against the wall, hands raised, frozen in place. The room was nothing but loud shouts, screams, and flailing bodies. We watched as Hannah, somehow, had the authority to take these men down and began barking orders to three more agents entering the room.

Bill said, "I don't think she's an occupational therapist."

"If so, I need to re-read the job description," Lulu yelled. Hannah handed Antonio over to a colleague as he shouted profanities and swung his leg at her shin. The officer threatened Antonio with a stun gun.

Hannah ran over. "I'll explain later, but you guys are free to go. I'd hurry." She said something in the microphone tucked inside her ear and was gone. People had run out the open door to the loading area, and a tricky game of tag was now underway. A gun shot rang and we ran back the direction we came, not waiting on the grand finale. Bill, Lulu, and I stopped at the fountain, out of breath, and overwhelmed with adrenaline. We had no car for a quick escape and rideshare was 45 minutes out.

I said, "Where do we go?" I was suddenly glad that Amelia left with Chase and Georgia, and Parker went home with Rex.

We heard another gunshot resound throughout the space and splinter up through the tall glass ceiling. Bill said, "We need to get out of here."

The three of us ran to the main door and were met with agents blocking the path, but they let us pass with Hannah's permission. We were almost home free when I saw Hugh running to catch up. He told the agents he was with our group. He approached acting casual, nonchalant, matching my stride. We heard his wife shouting his name as she was stopped by the group of officers. He didn't flinch or turn his head her direction, leaving her confused and barred inside.

"Hugh, what are you doing?" I looked back. The police didn't suspect anything.

"Leaving. Thank you very much." He smirked. He was about to make a run for it as Bill and I shouted to the police, telling them he was in on the theft. Hugh looked genuinely astonished that someone would defy him, especially a subordinate, and started to run. The agents caught up quickly, but he was large, and it took finagling to place the cuffs.

He shouted, "You'll pay for this, Ellie!" The officers pushed his head under the car door and his threats stopped with the slamming of the door. We were engulfed in silence, the stars bright in the night sky as we stood in an emptying parking lot, chaos only yards away.

Lulu said, "What do we do now?"

Before I could answer, bright headlights swung in our direction. It looked like a black, unmarked police SUV.

A man said, "Are you Ellie?"

We approached with caution and the driver said, "Hannah said you might need a ride."

Lulu said, "Just in time."

Bill looked wary, "Wait. We should be more careful with everything going on."

The man said, "Sorry, Hannah said you might be afraid to jump into a random person's car." He laughed. "She said to tell you that angry people are not always wise."

I smiled and said to Bill, "We're good."

"You're sure?"

"That's a quote from *Pride and Prejudice*, we use it more often than I'd like to admit."

"You guys have managed to transform books into a secret language."

We tucked ourselves into the back of the SUV, giving him our address.

The man asked, "So, how do you guys know Hannah?"

Lulu whispered, "I'm not sure we do know Hannah after tonight."

I answered, "We met in college, actually. We were both getting our Ph.D.'s."

"Smart ladies. You're a lucky group, she seems real careful with who she decides to befriend. I've asked her for drinks on more than one occasion, but she's in love with the job. Can't blame her, she's excellent." Our conversation stopped as he answered a call.

Lulu said, "My mind hasn't caught up to the fact that our friend is a secret agent, Sunny punched Parker, the artifacts were mere inches from us and we're now in the back of a police car."

"And poor Amelia," I said.

"She's going to find out we knew, too."

"If she doesn't know, I'm going to tell her tomorrow. It was a shitty thing to do."

Bill said, "Just because the outcome was bad for Amelia, doesn't mean you made the wrong choices along the way. You were stuck, trying to protect two close friends. Don't discount the difficult situation you were put in."

Lulu said, "I'm glad Sunny didn't punch you too, Bill. You're a keeper."

"I wonder if they got Sunny tonight, too." I said, "and Shannon…Amelia is going to need us after all of this."

"I never considered that Sunny would be arrested. He always seemed so impermeable."

Bill said, "We'll know tomorrow."

The rest of the ride was silent. We suddenly found ourselves outside our home, Rex waiting in the drive for Lulu. We hugged, promising to meet up tomorrow and speak with Amelia. And Parker. He had been through an ordeal, too.

After showering off the remnants of the gala, something dawned on me. "In all the chaos, I forgot about the threatening notes at Amelia's. Tonight was the night. No more bottles, sheets, postcards, signed bar tabs, or hanging pages. I hope."

"Huh. You know, me too. Not a lot of time to ask questions."

"If it was Amelia's mother sending the messages, or someone involved with the artifacts, it should stop."

"I'm too exhausted to think one more minute. Tomorrow is going to be heavy. Let's get some rest, we'll divulge into *that* world tomorrow."

He held me tight as we slept for the next ten hours straight.

Chapter 24
Hannah's Tale

Bill and I pulled into Amelia and Sunny's driveway the next afternoon. I said, "You know, I'm starting to feel like we're never home. Why do we pay a mortgage again?"

"It would look pretty suspicious if a realtor didn't have his own residence. I'm only saying."

The hole in the side of the house was hard to miss, the rubble thrown across the lawn. The willow seemed to frown at debris that tumbled down at its base. It looked like no attention had been made to the display, a stark difference to when the bottle first made its way through the stained-glass window only weeks before.

It appeared that the others were already here, except Hannah and Parker. The front door was open, and we found ourselves inside a busy front hallway. I wasn't sure if Amelia was going to be welcoming, given the situation, but she had texted the group early in the morning. I was anxious to speak with her and alleviate the unknown.

There were people I didn't recognize in the main foyer. I turned to Georgia who followed us in, "What is this?"

"Amelia told me she couldn't stand to wait for Sunny to get his act together before fixing the house. She hired contractors this morning and managed to find a firm that was willing to come out ASAP. She knows about Hannah, too."

"The study does look a mess."

"Seems she has a new lease on life."

Amelia was welcoming and waved us into our familiar book club den. Lulu waltzed in with Marge to deliver a tray of coffees.

Lulu asked, "Amelia, I hate to barge in and ask questions, but I have to know. One, are you alright, and two, where's Sunny?"

"I actually feel free, it's something I wasn't quite expecting. And on the Sunny front, he was one of those arrested last night. I confirmed it this morning." We weren't sure whether to be sad for Amelia or glad for ourselves. "And you know what else? He didn't call me. I wasn't his one phone call."

Lulu placed her hand on Amelia's shoulder. "I'm sorry."

"It makes it easier, though. I know where I stand, there's nothing there to save."

Georgia said, "Where is Shannon?"

"I haven't heard from her. I went by my parent's house this morning, ready to finally confront her, but she never came home last night. My dad is a wreck, he seemed oblivious. I don't think she was arrested, though. I called Dirk to see if he could look into it, and her name wasn't registered."

"I hope she's alright," Lulu said.

"She knows a lot of people, she'll turn up. I do worry, though, with her age. We never got a proper goodbye yesterday, or much of any conversation. Even after everything she did, it feels wrong. Odd, not knowing where she is."

We heard the doorbell and footsteps approaching. Hannah stood at the doorway, an apologetic look on her face.

Amelia finally said, "Hannah, sit down! For goodness sakes. You're still our Hannah no matter what you do for a living."

She smiled and sat next to Georgia. "I'm sure you guys have some questions…"

I said, "Whatever happened, it was pretty incredible."

"I've been working undercover for five years now, on different jobs here and there. When I got wind of a large operation involving the art trade, I couldn't say no. My boss almost had a heart attack when I told him I was friends with Sunny's wife. It was too perfect to pass up."

Lulu said, "I was wondering if you became friends with us for the job."

Hannah grinned, "I'm not that skilled in the art of socializing for that to be the case, unfortunately." We laughed.

I said, "Tell us about it."

"Well, there's a lot to say. In short, I've been working this for over a year. I'm a special agent and have been for some time. This isn't the first art trade they've done, only the largest. I had to think carefully about taking this case, as it would break my cover, my face would be in Amelia and Sunny's house every week. No coming back from that. As far as the case itself, we knew that Antonio was a key leader, and he was often with Sunny and Rick. Sunny wasn't a confirmed player until recently, but we knew. *I* knew the moment I started working the case, we just didn't have anything objective. We had some bank account transactions for large sums of money, but we couldn't link it to anything illegal. He was behind the scenes and controlling the money, so it was hard to catch him in any type of physical activity. Turns out a lot of the money was to secure the space at the Mirabelle, long term, as well as pay for the staff and upkeep of the event. They planned on having more like it, of course. How could they pass up such an opportunity?"

I said, "Did you think it was suspicious that Sunny went out with Antonio and Rick on Tuesdays?"

Amelia shot me a look, it must be strange for her to realize how little she knew about her husband. Uncomfortable that it was us, her closest friends.

Hannah said, "That was easily one of the most frustrating bits. We could never peg why they were out late, always a different location. None of our people could get close enough to figure it out, and we've been trying for months. Rick finally confirmed it last night."

"What was it?" Lulu said.

"They were vetting the guests. Interviewing for potential art buyers. They had to be careful, draft documents to be signed. They brought in lawyers, the whole gambit. If one person made a slip, the whole operation would be done with."

I said, "Did you know my artifacts were going to go missing?"

"It wasn't until a few weeks after the artifacts were uncovered at the dig site that we caught wind. They were running a tight ship. We thought they might try something, but we didn't expect it to be before the appraisal. We dropped the ball. When your office was robbed, Ellie, it became more complicated. New players entered the scene and suddenly too many people had their hands in the pot. Hugh didn't appear to be part of the story until recently. Sunny had a meeting with him just a few months ago. They needed someone on the inside, otherwise, it would never have happened the way it did. He was ripe for the taking, his first divorce cost him plenty and his ethics seemed slim. He was an easy get."

I said, "Did you know we were aware of anything? How odd that you were working this case, and then we come out of the blue, knowing what we did."

"I didn't know that until recently, either. I was at the Mirabelle. That's when I started to watch you guys, but I had heard things and started to wonder, before."

"You were there Thursday night?"

"I had disguised myself. Once I saw you there, I was speechless. I assumed you were there because of Sunny, but the pieces weren't adding up. I never thought in a million years you'd be hunting the artifacts on your own."

Lulu said, "I had no idea you were there, this is insane."

"Once I realized your involvement, although I wasn't sure of your motives, I used your knowledge to help the case. Especially last night. Bill threw me the best nugget of all when he realized the artifacts were being stored in the orchid displays."

Lulu said, "Perhaps you should become a detective too, Bill."

"The amount of stress these last few days have been, I think I'll stick to selling houses."

"How is it that all of the artifact buyers got into the gala? It was sold out months ago." I asked.

"She was way over capacity." Hannah said, "looks like she threw some extra tables into the mix, added people last second. Good thing there wasn't a fire." She looked at me, "alright, I have a question. How did you find out Sunny was a potential suspect? He was careful. That was an impressive find."

I wasn't sure if I should delve into the Parker situation yet. But it would be out soon, perhaps not his love, but the story behind it. "Parker became suspicious on his own. He had visited Sunny for an investment deal and walked in on him speaking on the phone to a woman he had slept with the night prior. Sorry, Amelia, I know you don't want to relive this."

"No, please. I want to hear it."

"Let me know if you want me to stop. I also have to say…this may not paint me in the best light, and I'm terribly sorry." Amelia nodded for me to continue, her lips pursed. "There are also parts of this story that might be better heard from him. Part of the story you don't yet know, Amelia. Unless you spoke to him after last night?"

"After I left, he called a few times, but I never picked up."

"When Parker went to Sunny's office and realized what he was hearing, he freaked out. He wanted to tell you immediately, of course."

Amelia shifted in her seat. "Why didn't he? I can't figure it out. I've been going over the past weeks in my head, and I'm stunned. I've seen him more times than I can count. He had every opportunity."

"I'll get to that. Sunny eventually noticed him listening in. He became furious. He told Parker that if he told you…"

I hadn't realized it, but Parker was standing in the doorway of the den. We were so focused on the re-telling of the night's events that no one saw him approach. He said, "I would like to continue if that's alright."

Amelia stiffened. "I don't want you here, Parker."

"Let me tell the rest, and I'll leave. I promise. You never have to hear from me again."

Lulu said, "It's worth a listen."

Amelia looked at Lulu. "Alright, go on."

Parker said, "Sunny said he was going to blackmail me if I told you about the conversation I overheard. I told him it was my story against his, and I would tell you regardless."

She said, "Blackmail you? What on earth has he got on you?"

Parker continued to explain the arson, the potential criminal ties. "He was terrifying, Amelia. And the record doesn't paint me in the best light."

When he finished, it looked like her resolve had crumbled some. But there was deep hurt there, too, and it would take a lot more than a simple conversation to heal that wound. She said, "You didn't think I would believe you?"

"I know, it sounds an awful thing to think of your best friend like that. But Amelia, he's your husband. He has connections and you loved him. I'm your friend, yes, but would you want me to step foot near your children again if he sprouted some disbelief about my dangerous past?"

"It's hard to say how I would feel, I was never given the chance."

That stung. I said, "I knew too, Amelia. I'm not going to hide my involvement. If you're mad at Parker, be mad at me as well."

Amelia said, "You were comfortable telling Ellie, and not me? You're my closest friend." She had tears in her eyes, feeling the betrayal deeply. "But I do understand, a little more now. I'm sorry you were blackmailed."

I turned to her, "Parker didn't tell me, exactly. His friend, Paul approached saying he thought Parker was in over his head."

"Why would Parker be in over his head?"

Parker said, "I started looking into Sunny after he blackmailed me. He wasn't right in the head, Amelia. My friend Paul researched more on his background, and then I got a detective. It's how we knew Sunny was having meetings on Tuesday nights."

"I was there, too," I said.

"You had my husband *followed?*"

"I did. I was concerned about you." He looked so in love. The true heartache he felt was palpable, he wore it on his sleeve, yet he didn't say the words. "And that's when I found out about Antonio and Rick. The rest is history, and you know about the Mirabelle. Everything there is true, except that we were also looking for the reward."

"Is that why you were looking for the pieces?"

"That, to help Ellie with her grant and to return them to Chaco Canyon. I planned to get the reward and give you the money."

She sat back, taking it in. I wasn't sure if she believed him, it was such an outlandish thing to say. "Why would you do that? We live comfortably here. I don't understand."

"I didn't want to tell you Sunny cheated without you having a way to leave him. And you could keep the kids in school. The money would pay for that, and more. Perhaps a house to live in. I know you signed a prenup. I was scared for you and couldn't say anything because of the blackmail. It was the only thing I could think of to do."

"Parker, I can handle myself. And you're right, it looks like I'll be in that predicament shortly. Our marriage is all but done." The stern expression on her face was replaced with something more. Perhaps their friendship could be saved.

Georgia, Chase, and Hannah seemed shocked at the newfound information, on top of everything else that had transpired. For a room full of people, it was eerily quiet.

Amelia continued, "This is much more complicated than I expected. I'm not mad, Parker. I'm disappointed. I'm grateful you thought of me in that way, to attempt something so ridiculous for my family. But I don't need money, I'd rather have the truth. Trust."

Lulu said, "I'm not one to lie either, Amelia. If you are going to be mad at Parker and Ellie, put my name high on the list. Paul told me about Parker's involvement as well, and he's the one that told us about the reward. It wasn't Parker who told me, but I knew about the cheating. I knew about the artifacts and his possible involvement."

I said, "That was my doing. Without me, you would have never known."

Hannah chimed in, "And I knew about Sunny's involvement, of course. It was hard, coming here the past few months, knowing that he was involved in illegal activity."

Amelia said, "It feels odd, being the last one in a group to know about your own husband."

Lulu and I both apologize. What else could be said? Amelia continued to stare ahead, too much information to process in such a short amount of time. She didn't say much else.

Parker said, "Since we're being honest, I should tell you about Paul." Lulu and I had wondered at their connection more than once. "He's my step-brother."

"You have a step-brother?" Amelia seemed perplexed.

"After my father left, my mother eventually remarried. I was out of the house by that time, so we didn't grow up together. But we became close. He lived with me for a while during a rough period when he was on the force. I helped him get clean. He feels he owes me, which is ridiculous. That's what family does."

I said, "And that's why he is so protective over you. I can't believe we never knew you had another brother."

"He likes to keep his work life separate from family, he's ashamed of his past. I like to honor those feelings. He's a very private guy. But today, nothing is off of the table."

I said, "You know what? We never found out who was releasing the reward."

Parker said, "I spoke to Paul last night, about everything. I ended up staying with him and he opened up about the case. He felt comfortable now that the artifacts are in custody along with the key players. The person who posted the reward was Wynonna, and she had every intention of returning the items to their rightful owners."

The name rang a bell, but I couldn't place it. "Does she work at the museum?"

Lulu said, "No, that's Hugh's *first* wife."

"How on earth does she have $200,000 to give away as a reward?"

"Sounds like she knew Hugh was involved in the art trade and was using the money from the divorce to try and take him down." Parker said, "It wasn't a pretty separation. And others were looking for the artifacts as well. Not sure how far they got."

Lulu said, "Well I'll be damned."

Bill said, "Not to overwhelm an already complicated situation, but do we know anything about the threatening notes? Since the gala has concluded, has anyone heard or seen anything? Were we correct in assuming it was Shannon who at least played a part?"

Hannah said, "Oh my gosh, I'm so sorry. I should have said something last night." She put her hands across her face. "In all of the action, it completely left my mind. The notes were for me."

Amelia said, "Did someone from Sunny's team know that you were working for Special Forces?"

"I hate to confirm this."

"What is it, Hannah?"

"The vandalism and messages were from Shannon, after all. They were her idea, although she had help. They were meant for me, but she wasn't sure which of us six it was at first, which is why everything seemed so vague. She was too afraid to approach anyone or be too specific, for fear she'd have to explain herself or someone would start talking. That's why she used book quotes. She knew we'd think the messages were directed at Sunny, so she made it unquestioningly pointed towards one of us to drive the point home, to show us she was watching. What better way than to use our books as a tool? I assumed from the beginning that the threats were for me, but I wasn't sure who from Sunny's team was leaving them. At that point it hardly mattered, I knew they wanted me to stop investigating, whoever it was that left them. We were too far in to stop, of course. But don't worry, we had extra detail watching your house, Amelia. I would never let a threat like that continue without making sure you guys were safe."

"I didn't notice."

"You wouldn't, my guys are good."

Amelia said, "You're sure it was my mother?"

"Unfortunately. I'm sorry, I wish it were someone else. It was only an assumption, until last night. Rick was offered a deal for information, and he gave us exactly what we needed."

Amelia replied, "I knew it was true that night at Lulu's, but I didn't want to believe it. My mother never asked about our book club or when we met, until a month or so ago. I thought she was trying to connect with me." Her eyes filled with tears as she patted them gently away. "I genuinely thought she cared."

"The note from the bar." Lulu said, "tell the one not yet present. We thought they meant Amelia."

Hannah said, "She had narrowed it down at that point."

"Why would they suspect it was any of us six, to begin with?" I asked.

"Amelia, forgive me, but I went into Sunny's office on more than one occasion. Once was during our book night, a couple of weeks before the bottle flew through the study window."

"You were doing your job, I can't blame you for that."

"Sunny had sophisticated technology, more than I expected for a computer in his study. Next level stuff. I downloaded a few files, and it alerted him. I messed up. He knew book night had happened that night and told Shannon. She put two and two together. I don't think Sunny figured it out until later, he would have never let Shannon damage his home like that. They were close, but only as far as the artifacts were concerned. Their personalities often clashed. I was able to witness a meeting they had together. I don't think either knew who was fully running the show."

Amelia asked, "Who was my mother in all of this? How does something like this happen?"

"I'm not sure how it all began, to be honest. Antonio and Rick had worked with Sunny before, on money laundering, then they were suddenly trading pieces of art. It sounds like Antonio heard about the artifacts, and it snowballed from there. They needed someone with community connections, someone with art ties and money. Shannon checked all of the boxes. It seems like they tied her in pretty early, Sunny dropping hints over the first weeks of the operation. Seems she bit pretty quick. And Rick knew Jason, from the Mirabelle. If I hadn't called the police that night at the hotel, it could have ended there. Things seemed to be going smoothly."

I said, "That was you?"

"I wasn't ready to blow my cover, but I knew the event had to stop. I never saw an artifact that night, so didn't feel comfortable sending my men in on a whim. Other deals have happened there, drugs, different pieces of art. That wasn't the first time they had used that space for such an ordeal. I wasn't ready to assume that's what it was, we just didn't have the information. We had a full team there, but we couldn't get anyone inside the bar. They handpicked the guests, there was no token to be bought by a random civilian. We even tried posing as staff with no luck. It was an impressive show for the illegal art trade."

A thought suddenly occurred to me. "Was it you who called the cops that Wednesday night, while we were under the willow? The night we read the *Scarlet Letter*?"

"That was an interesting scenario. I was attempting to follow Sunny yet remain under my guise. Again, we didn't have enough to go on, and nothing that would justify a warrant. When I left to make a call, I was telling my team to stand down. I felt I could get in after we ended the club for the night. They were antsy with the arrival of Rick and Antonio and thought they were going to leave with the artifacts right under my nose. I felt differently."

"They called the cops anyway?"

"And look what happened. They didn't have a warrant but hoped to get inside. It was Rick who set the minor explosion as a decoy. They didn't plan for it, but the police startled them. They were able to load the artifacts while we ran to the study. I sometimes wonder... if my team hadn't called in the team of officers, I could have found them that night. And it seems Shannon found out about the explosion shortly after and piggybacked off of it. That's why the note was quickly written and sent to you at the bar. That's also the night I noted Dirk's involvement, which made the situation even more sticky. This scenario would have ended much differently had things gone my way."

Amelia said, "Unless I saw you in the house, looking around."

"I'm sorry Amelia. I didn't want to be sneaking around your house, it felt wrong. A violation. A dichotomy between my work responsibilities and my trust with you."

Georgia said, "I still can't believe all of this was happening right under my nose."

"I hope you don't feel we left you out," Lulu said.

She smiled, "I'm only grateful you didn't, after last night."

Amelia asked, "So, Dirk was in on it too?"

"He was," Hannah said, "but didn't control the whole Dove Park department. I think he talked a big game, had people thinking he was someone he wasn't. We brought him in last night."

Parker said, "I've said my peace. Amelia, I can't tell you how sorry I am. You are family to me. If I knew this was how it would end, I never would have kept this information from you. I can't imagine never speaking to you again." And with that, he walked out, giving her space.

I said, "Amelia, is there anything I can do?"

"I think I need some time to process. I understand why you did what you did, but it's hard being the target of such a decision. I just need some time."

Bill, Lulu, and I stood and walked out, knowing there was nothing else to be said.

"I've thought about this conversation a million times." I said, "I thought I would feel lighter after."

"Me too," Lulu said, "but instead I feel like a hundred tons of cement have been dumped on top of me. Things will never quite be the same, will they?"

Bill said, "Sometimes that's alright. Change doesn't always have to be bad. Give it time."

Chapter 25
Dead Center

It was Monday. Lulu picked me up and we made our way to the office, stopping for double shots of espresso. I said, "See if they have a coke, too." Lulu leaned back in the driver's seat and pulled out a diet coke, handing it to me. "Where on earth did this come from? What is your car the portal to Narnia?"

"You always want a coke after coffee when you're stressed. This counts as a little stress, I think."

I popped it open as we parked, noting Hugh's empty parking spot. "Alright, let's do this." We weren't expecting much, perhaps a memo from HR, or nothing at all. Hugh had only been arrested two days ago. But when we walked into our main hall, people started to stand outside their offices and applaud. "How does everyone know about our involvement? What is going on?"

At the end of the hall and near our dueling office doors, was Paul. "Ladies, it seems a congratulation is in order."

"Hannah is the one who closed the case, we just happened to be there."

"No, not about the artifacts. People caught wind that you turned Hugh into the authorities as he was running away from the gala. Everyone knows he was in on the heist." He winked.

I looked at Lulu. She patted Paul on the back as he fidgeted, slowly squirming away from her touch. She said, "Paul, you're alright."

"I know you know about Parker. It's fine. I'd rather no one know my business, but if I were to tell anyone…"

We smiled and chatted, as much as Paul chats, as we entered my office. I looked up. Seated at my desk was the president of museum operations. Hugh's boss.

I said, "I think we have to break up our little party. Lu, I'll talk to you at lunch. Thanks again, Paul."

The president stood and shook my hand. "Ellie, it seems we have some catching up to do. If you're not too busy."

"Absolutely. Sir, I'm not sure where to start."

"Call me Razi. It seems Hugh has been busy. I have to say, after Saturday night I've hardly left the office. That wasn't the only unethical business he has achieved while employed here, I'm sure you're not surprised."

"I wish I was."

"It seems you sent your grant request through Hugh?"

"Yes, he said he needed to approve it, then send it forward. I know it was denied, he told me Saturday before his arrest."

"That's just it, he never sent it in for review. It seems he wanted to use you as the scapegoat if anyone came asking about the artifacts. It's been clear since the beginning that someone internal was involved. You were his backup plan if things turned south. A fired employee looks like he's done his due diligence."

I felt sick. "Thank you for telling me. Regardless, my last day is in two weeks. That's when my current grant expires."

"Not on my watch. It's hard to get past the grant situation, I'll give you that. Your team would cost quite a bit if coming directly from museum funds. But…"

"But?"

"I'd like to offer you a promotion. Hugh's job, if you're interested. You'd be running all of the research in this wing, the archeologists, and the appraisers. You don't have to answer me today but think about it. We'd love to have you."

"I'm speechless. Sir, I would love the position. I don't need to think twice."

"I was hoping you'd say that." His smile was warm. "Over the next few weeks, we'll hash out the details and I'll have HR contact you. You'd be on permanent payroll. And the authorities were able to retrieve every missing artifact, you can help us gather our bearings and figure all of *that* out."

It was music to my ears. I couldn't wait until lunch to tell Lulu and burst through her office, telling her the good news. It was the silver lining throughout weeks of anticipation and worry. Even if Amelia didn't speak to us right away, there were no more secrets, no more lies. We could somehow move forward with the truth.

～

The weeks flew by. Lulu and I didn't want to push Amelia into speaking with us. We decided to let her reach out on her own, hoping she thought we were worth it, but understanding if she didn't. Sometimes, time was the only cure.

Wednesday nights felt wrong, an empty void. Lulu and I still met with Parker each week, but it felt inappropriate to invite Georgia and Hannah, leaving Amelia out again. We felt the rift between them as well, even though it was unintentional. Wednesday nights were our day to catch up, otherwise, we were busy working, with family or involved with special forces. Well, one of us at least.

It was the fourth week since the gala, another Wednesday lunch with Lulu and Paul. He had slowly started to join us but continued to enjoy his isolation from time to time. Both Lulu and I had finally spoken to Amelia over the phone but hadn't seen her since that afternoon a month ago. She called us both last week to let us know that Shannon turned up in Ireland, staying with a cousin. The relief in her voice was unmistakable, yet overlaid with other, more complicated emotions.

Amelia's absence was a larger void in my life than the lack of Wednesday nights, and I was struggling. I'd think of something that I wanted to tell her, too afraid to text in case she ignored me, or thought it callous. I was afraid of where the slow drift was leading but couldn't think of a way out of the storm.

Breaking my revere, Parker walked into Floyd's during our lunch and sat next to Paul. He hadn't seen or spoken to Amelia in four weeks. He looked excited, more cheerful than he had in days. Parker said, "You guys are still free tonight, right? You too, Paul. I want you to see this. And bring Bill and Rex."

I said, "Bring them where? Aren't we meeting at my place tonight?"

"Change of plans. Here's the address. Be there at seven."

Lulu said, "Are you ambushing us?"

He thought about it a moment, "Kind of. Promise you'll show?"

"Of course."

He dashed out of the coffee shop, a skip in his step. I said, "That was weird."

"He's been up to something," Paul said.

Lulu brought up a map and switched to satellite view, "Looks like a building, not too far from here. I think it might be attached to another business. Hard to tell."

"Aren't you a sleuth." Paul smiled at his remark.

"Ok not everyone was a detective in a prior life. I *appraise*."

~~~

It was finally time to leave for the mystery location. When Bill and I pulled into a parking spot in front of the empty building, we looked at each other questioningly, re-checking the address. I gasped as another car pull up.

"What is it?"

I said, "It's Amelia." I scanned the lot and noticed a black minivan. "And I bet that is Georgia. It looks like he brought us all here. What is he up to?"

We walked up to the door and tried the handle. It didn't budge and the windows were dark. Looking around, we realized the others were in their cars. Amelia and Hannah approached, followed by the rest. We loitered outside, not saying much, the forced closeness reeking of familiarity yet we felt anything but.

Amelia said, "You guys know what this is about?" She shifted, unsure how to approach after all these weeks.

Georgia said, "Not a clue."

I was stunned that Amelia would decide to come, perhaps even she couldn't decline such a strange offer. I wondered if she knew we would be here, maybe that would have changed her mind.

Finally, Parker approached. Everyone from book club was present along with the husbands and Paul. We were quiet as we watched him place the key in the lock. He said, "Before we go in, I want you to keep an open mind." He was looking at Amelia as he said it. He took a deep breath and pulled open the door.

It was a decently sized business space, yet it was anything but empty. There were small white lights strung along the top rafters, the walls painted in matching pastels. Stainless steel kitchen appliances were stacked in neat rows along open shelves above a cash register to the right, a kitchen peeking through behind. Chic small tables were set out for patrons of the store, and the most surprising of all, on the wall directly to our left, was a mural. In the middle, it said, "Amelia's Bakery."

I looked back to Amelia, who entered last. Her head seemed to be spinning, confusion quickly replaced by the realization of what she was witnessing.

She said, "Parker, what is this?"

He walked behind the counter, picking up a piece of cloth. He walked over to Amelia and handed it to her. She unfolded the square. It was an apron, her name across the front in professional, bold, pink letters. The mural and logo were behind it.

"I've spent the last few weeks in utter turmoil." Parker said, "the weight of what happened during those weeks wouldn't let up. Partially because I never told you the full story, that day in your den, following the gala. I'm not here offering you this shop as a way to bribe you back into my life. I'm here to tell you that I unequivocally love you, and I have for over a year. Seeing you in pain destroyed me, and I wanted so badly to make it stop. I hunted artifacts, sought a reward, and lied. I did it because I thought that in the end, it was what was best for you. But now I know that you are the only one who knows what's best. The only one who can make that choice."

She had tears in her eyes as she said, "Parker…"

He continued, "Once Sunny was arrested and the investigation started, I was able to sell my investment. I made a profit and was sitting on a large sum of money, depressed. It occurred to me, this money didn't feel right staying in my hands. You have a gift, Amelia, and I hope one day you can open this shop and show the world. With or without me."

There wasn't a dry eye in the bakery as we had stepped back, allowing them space. We all stared at Amelia.

She took a moment, looking over the apron, touching the strings and the painted letters. She said, "I thought that removing you from my life was the answer. I felt that, if someone does something that hurts you, you never let them do it again. And the only way to do that, in my mind, was to never see you again. These past weeks have been horrible, and not because Sunny is in jail and my mother hiding away in Ireland. It's because I missed you terribly, and I didn't know what to do. I picked up the phone a hundred times, only to assume you had moved on after I pushed you away. Parker, I don't want you gone from my life, I want you dead center. I want you with me as I run this bakery. As more than a friend."

Parker's hands were trembling as he took a step towards Amelia and embraced her. They held each other for a long moment, and as he pulled away kissed her ever so gently. He said, "We can take our time. I don't want to overwhelm an already difficult situation."

"For once, I want to make the decision. I want to be with you, starting today."

Lulu let out a small cheer and suddenly everyone was clapping and holding each other close. There was nothing more to say, they had said it all. We all loved one another, in our own way. We wanted to see each other succeed, and be there when we weren't. As we celebrated, the front door opened, and Maggie walked in. The surprises kept coming.

Parker said, "I have to give credit where credit is due. Maggie helped me considerably, she owns these two buildings. Her flower shop is moving in next door, I think it might make a nice partnership." Maggie seemed light and relaxed as she told us about the buildings. No more Mel's, no more threatening men or illegal activity surrounding her. A new start for her as well.

Amelia and I finally embraced as Parker pulled out champagne bottles from behind the counter. Lulu popped them open and Georgia squealed as a cork flew past her head. It quickly was like no time had passed.

Hannah handed me a glass and put her arm around my shoulder. I said, "You better hand this back to Lulu."

"What's wrong?"

"It would be poor taste to drink for two." Bill started to laugh. It took a moment for the sentence to sink in, and when it did, Georgia almost capsized me with her hug.

She said, "Are you serious? You're serious. Maybe I should lay off the squeezes."

"I'm only a few weeks along, we just found out. I think I'll survive your hugs, Georgia."

Hannah said, "I can't wait to be an auntie again. Congratulations."

"She spoils them rotten, fair warning." Amelia was laughing with Bill, the act suddenly contagious.

Parker walked over and placed his arm around Amelia, asking, "So, what do you think?"

"I think it's the best gift anyone has ever given me."

"Are you going to start baking?" Hannah said.

"What, now?"

"Soda bread doesn't bake itself." Lulu punched Hannah in the arm and suddenly they were playing their own game of chase.

Amelia pulled on the apron. "You know what, why not?"

Before we knew it, we were covered in dough and flour was sprinkled across the shop like a baking blizzard had moved in.

I leaned over to Bill and said, "This is turning out to be one hell of a Wednesday night."

Acknowledgments

As always, a big thank you to my parents, Matt and Susan, my husband Brian, and daughter, Evelyn. And to the community of friends and family who read Paper and Ink, edited, and gave suggestions. It truly takes a village to complete a book and get it out to the world, so thank you.

About the Author

Amanda is originally from the beautiful state of New Mexico. She is currently a Medical Social Worker for a hospice and resides with her husband, Brian, and 16-month-old daughter, Evelyn, in Colorado.

Book reviews help independent authors spread their word. If you have a moment, please let other readers know what you think. Thank you again for reading.

For more of Amanda's writings, please visit:
www.octoberamanda.wordpress.com
or
https://www.goodreads.com/amandajsmith